Crazy for Loving

A Robin Miller Mystery

BY JAYE MAIMAN

Bella
BOOKS

2010

Copyright © 1992 by Jaye Maiman

Bella Books, Inc.
P.O. Box 10543
Tallahassee, FL 32302

Printed in the United States of America on acid-free paper

First edition 1992 Naiad Press.
First Bella Books edition 2010

Editor: Christine Cassidy
Cover Design: Judith Fellows

ISBN 10: 1-59493-195-X
ISBN 13: 978-1-59493-195-6

About the Author

Jaye Maiman was born on October 31, and so learned early on that life is a series of tricks and treats. She grew up in Coney Island, Brooklyn, not far from the rumble of the Cyclone and the tantalizing aroma of Nathan's French fries.

Jaye is the author of seven books in the Robin Miller mystery series, including the Lambda Literary Award winner *Crazy for Loving* and nominee *Someone To Watch*.

Dedicated to Sharon Cyd Gresh, for teaching me to laugh and to Vivian Roll, for teaching me that Sisyphus was a jerk. And, as always, to my clan...

Acknowledgments

Back when time began, I used to slink into New York City's gay bookstores. Furtively. Glancing over my shoulder, waiting for the fickle finger of fate to stab me between the shoulder blades. That was long before my parents barreled into A *Different Light* demanding to know why my first book was not in the front window.

Back then, almost all the books I read had the same five letters on their spine. N.A.I.A.D. When I wasn't fantasizing about being the Man from U.N.C.L.E., I was dreaming about being the Gal from N.A.I.A.D.

I'd like to thank Barbara Grier and the entire Naiad team for making my first dream come true.

Bear hugs and sloppy kisses go to my incredible friends who have passed out flyers on P-town beaches, prodded me for more Robin Miller mysteries, and most importantly, reached out and pampered me when the hard times set in. Thanks to the backbone of my life, old friends and new: Pauline, Risa, Elaine, Jill, Annie, Joan, Maureen and Victoria.

Thanks to my parents Ira Ray and Sylvia, for being down-to-earth, funny, loving, accepting, and damn good cooks. I miss you every day.

And finally, to Rhea, for teaching me the meaning of *basheert*.

This book takes place in 1991, a bit of close-in ancient history, when people relied on strange instruments such as pay phones and computers were just beginning to take over our every day lives.

Chapter 1

The air was close and dank. I took a deep breath and stretched my arm out into the darkness. My fingers curled around a crushed beer can, its edges nicking the tip of my thumbnail. I brushed it aside and shimmied forward on my stomach, my lungs burning with the stench of urine and decaying food.

I could hear him breathing, just inches away. I scoured the blackness, searching for the telltale glint of light from his eyes. Nothing. I dug my nails into the dirt and shifted to the left. Suddenly, the crawl space tightened. Panic knotted my chest and my breathing quickened. I knew he must smell my fear.

I dropped my cheek into the foul mud and tried to calm myself. Gradually, my breathing slowed. I needed to get out, smell the cool early morning air, scrape the sludge from my clothes. I started to back up. And then I heard the sound. A distinct scratching just to my left. A rumble deep in his throat. Threatening. I was in his territory and he knew it.

I bit my bottom lip and shot my hand out in front of me. His nails sliced across my forearm, lighting fire along my nerves. I lunged forward, grabbed a limb and held on for dear life as he batted my head.

Seconds later, I was outside the crawl space, holding onto the meanest looking Siamese by the scruff of his neck. I was back at the office in 20 minutes.

Wonder Woman strikes again.

"Not bad, Miller." Tony Serra snatched the mad Siamese from my arms, tossed him into the bathroom and slammed the door. "The laborer is worthy of his hire'...Luke." I knew Tony well enough to read the sarcasm in his Biblical compliment. Sure enough, he turned his irritating Cheshire grin on full beam. "Better put some peroxide on those scratches."

I looked down at my arms. There were tears in my blue cotton shirt and a bloodstain that was steadily spreading. Tony was huddled over his desk. As always, he was wearing a white, heavily starched shirt and navy pinstripe slacks. The suit jacket was slung over his massive, cranberry leather chair.

The man is well over six feet, with broad shoulders, no neck, and a scattering of hair so thin you can read his scalp bumps through it. While he can be called ruggedly good-looking, his appearance always borders on unkempt—like he just completed the one-hundred-yard dash through Grand Central only to find his train was late. Even now, sweat pools formed below his armpits and his pants sagged.

"The Crawford lady's gonna be thrilled you found Alexander," he said, flipping through his rolodex. "Which means a fat check in my pocket and another satisfied customer. Rich customer. My favorite kind. By the way, you're excused." He picked up the phone to punctuate my dismissal.

I considered kicking his flat behind, then stamped out of the office instead.

Tony and I have run this Brooklyn investigative agency for almost two years, and though I've successfully tracked down one murderer, two hit-and-run drivers, countless adulterers, too many runaway teenagers, and the occasional corporate criminal, he still delights in throwing me the Bozo jobs. Like the case of the missing Alexander Ming, a blue-ribbon Siamese who had the good sense to escape from a silver-haired bitch who calls his one-ounce servings of cheap caviar "wages."

I threw open the outer door, muttering under my breath, wondering why I ever decided to get into this business. I sure as hell don't need the job. I'm a successful romance writer. By churning out two books a year for the past seven years, I've earned three feet of shelf space at Doubleday's. Two of them have even earned the dubious honor of being produced as television movies. So why was I chasing after cats and taking orders from a Bible-quoting ex-cop who smells like gorgonzola cheese whenever the temperature tops seventy?

Before I could answer my own question I spun around the corner, colliding with a slightly underweight woman with short Farrah Fawcett hair and rose-scented skin. Her chin trembled as our eyes caught.

The hair on the back of my neck bristled. I was developing a taste for trouble, and I had a feeling I was in for a feast.

"Sorry…" she said, fumbling to secure her purse under one elbow. "I'm looking for Mr. Serra. Is this the right place?"

I took two steps back, glanced over my shoulder and saw Tony slide into his leather chair like a snake settling into a coil. I flashed my dandiest smile and swiftly escorted the woman into my office, a walk-in closet that had been stripped bare and crammed with a metal desk, chair, file cabinet, and trash can. Tony's office, by contrast, was palatial.

"I'm Robin Miller, Mr. Serra's associate. How can I help you?"

"Well…" Her eyes skimmed over my bloody sleeve and muddy jeans, then darted in the direction of Tony's office. A piercing cat howl emanated from behind the walls.

I stepped around her and closed the door. "Mr. Serra is

involved with a priority client right now, but I'd be happy to present your case to him. Why don't you have a seat." I pointed to the slightly faded red director's seat wedged into a corner near my desk.

"I really came to see Mr. Serra," she said uneasily. "A friend of mine recommended him very highly. I believe he used to be a detective with the New York Police Department?"

I nodded and did a quick once-over. The woman was rich. Born rich. She wore an Armani suit I had seen advertised in last week's *New York Times* magazine section. Her makeup was carefully applied, her fingernails manicured and painted a shade of mauve that matched her silk blouse perfectly. Her shoes were probably Italian. Not a single scuff mark. I avoided looking at my Nike sneakers and lifted my eyes to her face. She was probably in her late thirties, just a few years older than me. But she looked tired. And ready to bolt.

"Why don't we start with your name?"

Her ice-blue eyes flickered with fear. "Marion Ross," she said uncertainly.

I smiled. "Like the mother in 'Happy Days?'"

"Not exactly," she replied, stone-faced.

Suddenly my small joke seemed cruel. I leaned forward, a whiff of her heavy rose perfume tickling my nostrils. Given the choice between everyday body odors and cloying sweet perfume, I'd go for the B.O. every time. Unfortunately, the choice usually isn't mine. I stifled a sneeze and somewhat nasally asked, "What can we do for you?"

She lowered her eyes to her lap and began twisting a tissue into a tight braid. On closer look, her fingernails were the type you could buy at Upper East Side beauty salons. One cuticle was brutally gnawed, but the nails themselves were perfect ovals.

"I don't know where to begin," she said, her right foot breaking into a frantic tap. "My husband…David…he's in some kind of trouble. But I don't know what it is. Lately, he's been so jumpy. Last week, he disappeared for two days. No explanation.

Nothing."

She stared at the trash can with an intensity usually reserved for Rembrandts or Van Goghs. I figured she didn't want to make eye contact, so I swung around the desk, leaned close to her, and asked, "You want us to follow him?"

Her eyes were bloodshot. Up close, you could tell that plastic surgery had attempted to smooth the crow's feet around her eyes. But it had been a waste of money. Worry was etching even deeper lines into her skin. Parallel furrows marked the space between her eyebrows. It was like gazing at a plowed field from thirty thousand feet.

All at once, her eyes filled with tears. "I want you to find out what's wrong. Please."

I've never been able to resist a woman pleading for my help. This time was no different. I took out my notebook. "Why don't we start at the beginning?"

Thirty minutes later, I didn't know much more about my new client or her husband. Marion was curiously evasive about describing David's behavior over the past few weeks. The only straight answers I got pertained to David's age, his physical description, the make of his car, and his occupation. The more I heard, the more intrigued I became.

David Ross taught elementary school in a crime-plagued district in Brooklyn. When I casually commented on the discrepancy in social status that apparently existed between my socialite client and her husband, her eyes flashed. "Love doesn't recognize such distinctions," she snapped indignantly.

I didn't buy the Hallmark sentiment. I figured either the sex was great, or Marion had a thick rebellious streak. Maybe both. I was just about to pump her for more information when my door opened.

Tony looked at my client and did a double-take. "Marion Ross...what an unexpected pleasure." He pumped her hand like a politician. "I'm sure you don't remember me. I did some work for your father a few years ago."

Marion stood up and the two of them made some small talk. If I didn't step in soon, Tony would have Marion's case and I'd be out chasing after some rich lady's Pekinese. "I didn't know you two knew each other," I interjected.

"We don't. Not really," Marion said quickly. "Tony helped my father out a few years ago. We met once. At a cocktail party. Mr. Serra was quite enchanting that evening. We had both just stopped smoking and he was my compeer that night. To be honest, I wouldn't have recognized him." She smiled at Tony. "You've lost so much weight. You look terrific."

Tony beamed at the flattery. Not many people had good things to say about him these days. Especially about his weight loss.

"Well, then, I'm sure Tony will be thrilled that I've agreed to take your case," I added with a dare in my voice.

Tony shot me an irritated look, then turned his charm on Marion. "Robin's pretty new at this business, but she's good. And I give you my personal assurance, I'll be tracking every step of her progress."

"Thank you." She squeezed his hand meaningfully, as if they both understood I was the underling. Then she snapped her purse open, pulled out a prewritten check and handed it to him. "I hope this will serve as a retainer," she said.

His eyes were riveted to the numbers, but mine were glued to her purse. Peeking out from underneath an unopened box of Gray's toffees was the handle of a pistol.

My blood pressure picked up a notch or two. I raised an eyebrow at Marion, who flushed under my gaze. With an agility that I wouldn't have expected from her, she swept her purse strap over her shoulder and linked arms with Tony. "Would you mind escorting me to my car?" she asked too brightly.

"My pleasure. Miller, you wait here. I'd like to discuss your caseload when I get back."

I was still pondering the significance of the pistol when Tony barreled back into my office. "Okay Miller, what's this about? You know all cases go through me." He used that "me Tarzan, you Jane" voice that always makes me want to tear out the seventeen strands of hair he still has left on his head.

"Tony, we've been working together for almost two years. When you took me on, you said you needed a business partner, someone you could train to take over the agency…"

His eyes glazed over. "'Better is the end of a thing than the beginning….and the patient in spirit is better than the proud in spirit.' Ecclesiastes."

"Don't pull that shit on me again. I didn't come to you for Bible lessons."

The glaze cracked and the anger flooded in. "That's right," he shouted. "You came to me when you thought your publisher was going to drop you over that dyke business. I let you work with me as a favor to a friend. As a favor to you."

I knew exactly what Tony was talking about. And I didn't like it one bit.

Two years ago, while looking into the death of my ex-lover, Mary Oswell, I earned the wrath of a San Francisco politician. He decided to pay me back by announcing that Laurel Carter, author of the famous Harbor Romance series, was actually Robin Miller, *Notorious Lesbian.*

The fact is I wasn't notorious at all until the story hit the newspapers and television entertainment shows. The initial publicity resulted in a flurry of curiosity and a spurt of higher sales. But just two months later my books were sticking to the shelves like Crazy Glue. My publisher had an obligation to release my last book, *Love's Lost Flame*, but he made it clear that it was time for me to take a break from Harbor Romance.

To tell the truth, I was sick to death of writing about torn bodices and swarthy men with rippling muscles, but the royalty checks came in mighty handy.

I was financially and emotionally prepared to fall back on my travel writing. But Detective Thomas Ryan—a San Francisco cop who had helped me search for Mary's killer and, in the process, became one of my unlikeliest friends—had other ideas.

"Stop playing 'Fantasy Island,' Miller," he had bellowed long-distance. On my dime, too. "You're a born dick."

Ryan has a way with words.

Two weeks later, Ryan's old friend Tony Serra called me up and made me an offer I was too dumb to refuse. I made a commitment back then to the Serra Investigative Agency, a commitment I decided to keep even after *Love's Lost Flame* unexpectedly jumped to the top of the best-seller list.

I still remember the day my publisher appeared at my doorstep with a dozen roses in his hand and desperation carved into the wrinkles around his mouth. I stood on the stoop of my brownstone plucking the petals off the roses, one by one. Samuel G. Taylor the Third flinched with each pluck as he pleaded with me to forgive his error in judgment and return to the fold. When the last petal landed at our feet, I looked him in the eye and slammed the door. That was almost eighteen months ago.

My life has changed a lot since then. Detective work is in my blood now and has come to mean more to me than my fourteen Harbor Romance titles–for reasons I still don't entirely understand.

I stood up to my full 5'9" and stared into Tony's narrowed eyes. "I want this case, Tony."

His eyes stayed flat, but his mouth curled into a sardonic smile. Something green was tucked in between his front teeth. "It doesn't matter what you want, Miller. Remember that. You're my *apprentice*."

I watched him retreat, the anger swelling in me. "You need me as much as I need you," I shouted at his back. "Don't you forget that. When you promised me a partnership…"

He spun around, his hand slicing the air, cutting off my words. "I was sick then…"

"You still are."

The words popped out of my mouth like a pebble from a slingshot.

Six years ago, Tony walked into a Brooklyn bodega at the wrong time. He had gone in to buy a pack of Marlboros but bought a twenty five caliber bullet in his shoulder instead. The bullet shattered his clavicle. The subsequent operation left him HIV-positive.

Contracting the disease was bad enough, but Tony soon made the mistake of confiding in his partner. The next thing he knew, his partner had transferred to another precinct. A few months later, he was strongly "advised" to take an early retirement. For his sake, of course. He opened SIA almost immediately. Its success was his revenge. And his life.

When Tony hired me in the summer of 1989, he had been recovering from his first bout of pneumonia and driven by fear. The kind of fear that squeezes the intestines and makes you ready to take chances.

Tony likes to say he hired me as a favor to Ryan, but the truth is no one else had been willing to work with him. And he was determined that someone would take over SIA when he died.

Reluctantly, he had settled for me. After almost two years, Tony and I still don't like each other very much, but we need each other—a fact neither of us cares to admit.

Now I watched his face reassemble itself as my words sunk in.

He leaned against the doorjamb. "So what's the story with Marion?" he asked wearily.

"She wants us to investigate her husband. For the last couple of months, he's been acting strange. Running out of the house in the middle of the night. Waking up with sweats..." I glanced down at my notes. "The phone rings and whoever's on the other end hangs up if Marion answers. That type of thing." I omitted mention of her gun on purpose. If Tony knew Marion was toting a handgun, he'd pull me off the case in a flash.

"Sounds like an affair to me. Did you ask her about that?"

"Come on, Tony. Of course I did. She said it wasn't possible." We looked at each other knowingly.

"Right," he said with a tight grin. "It's a shame. She's a nice lady. I'd hate to see her get hurt." He headed out of the office.

"So the case is mine, right?"

He turned to face me. The fluorescent light in the reception area painted his skin yellow. "Sure. You need the experience. But stay focused. If the guy's cheating, find out who she is and get out. I may need your help with the investigation at Torstar Brands." He paused. "By the way, I've got a doctor's appointment later today. Maybe you can deliver Mr. Ming to Crawford for me?"

Just what I needed. Another battle with the demented Siamese. But Tony rarely asked for favors. And I rarely acquiesce. "No problem, Tony."

He brightened unexpectedly. "Have a nice day. Partner." His sarcasm was thinly disguised. Just as he reached his office, he looked back and grinned. "Meee-ow."

Unamused, I slumped into my chair and started to type up my notes. I had the distinct impression that there was more to this case than just another philandering husband. I picked up the photograph Marion had left on the corner of my desk. David Ross stared at me with laughing eyes. A chill swept down my spine as I dropped the photograph into my file drawer.

The next morning, I sat in my car polishing off an Egg McMuffin as David Ross's battered Nissan Sentra pulled up to the corner of Atkins and Washington in the East New York section of Brooklyn—a neighborhood famous for its contribution to New York City's burgeoning crime statistics. I checked the clock on my dashboard. It was five to eight, just as Marion had predicted.

David was pounding on his steering wheel in time to some unheard song. From the looks of it, he was tuned to heavy metal. After an especially dramatic riff, he snapped open his car door and scrambled across the street to P.S. 189, where he worked as an elementary schoolteacher. Looking far younger than forty-one years old, David was wearing stone-washed jeans, a gray striped shirt, and a tie that looked suspiciously like a flounder. A couple of kids, no older than ten, shouted something at him as he approached. I think it had something to do with eating fish. Another youth, wearing a black leather jacket with metal studs spelling out the name "Tito," ran up behind him and spat at his back. David slowed his pace and pushed past them with a studied calm. I noticed he had a slight limp.

I waited until he had climbed the steps before I reached for the latch on my door. The damn lock was stuck again. I owned a 1976 mustard-yellow Plymouth Duster nicknamed Bella. The chassis was shot to hell, but the engine made mechanics cluck their tongues with admiration. Normally, I have an unnatural attachment to Bella. But right then, I wanted to twist her steering column. It took me a good five minutes to get out of the car. By the time I ran up the school steps past the chaos of students, David was long gone.

I stepped inside, overwhelmed by a severe case of déjà vu. There's a particular smell associated with public schools, one that I remembered all too well. Stale and chalky. But the sounds were different. Rap music pounded through the hallway, mingled with the high-pitched shouts of kids who hadn't yet reached puberty. A dull roar, like the sound of an airplane revving for take-off, shook the walls. And over it all, the clang of hundreds of Reeboks and Nike pump sneakers stamping up metal stairs. My nerves were immediately on edge.

Just then a thigh-high demon barreled into my side. "Outta my way!" He maneuvered down the hall like a running back, knocking over a small Hispanic girl wearing a Bart Simpson T-shirt, and careening into another kid who looked like he wanted to run outside. I couldn't blame him. It was like being trapped in a bumper car at Coney Island without a steering wheel.

I started to weave my way down the hall, when a female security guard tapped my shoulder. "Can I help you?" The woman was in her fifties with smooth skin, the color of toasted almonds. Her name tag read Juanita Morales. She was thin and wiry, her eyes alert and ready for trouble. I had a feeling she was rarely disappointed.

"I have an appointment with the school psychologist," I ad-libbed.

All at once, she shouted over my shoulder. "Yo Jermaine! Get your ass back upstairs! Now!" I jumped back involuntarily. "Sorry," she said. "You gotta be mean or the little savages will devour you. You said you have an appointment with Virginia?"

"Virginia?"

"Savarin. The school psychologist." She stared at me hard now.

I squared my shoulders. "Ms. Morales, my son is one of the 'little savages.' So, if you don't mind…" I tried to sound like an indignant parent.

She cocked an eye at me suspiciously. "What's his name?"

"Tito," I said impulsively. "Actually, his real name is Theodore, but his father insists on calling him Tito. We don't live with him anymore, but Tito is his father all the way through. Now, where can I find this Miss Savarin? I'm already late for our appointment."

Once again, my skill at dissembling served me well. She pointed toward the end of the hall. "Second floor. Far corner."

I circled the second and third floors twice before I found David's classroom. He was standing in front, screeching numbers onto a cracked blackboard with a thumb-sized piece of chalk. A shiver shook me. I positioned myself at the edge of the door. There were close to forty kids packed into the room. Several of them were sitting on a window ledge playing cards. One boy was desperately trying to pay attention, despite the fact that the kid next to him was slapping a rolled-up magazine on the back of his chair.

I took a closer look at David Ross. He was slim and muscular, probably an inch or two taller than me. He had bushy black hair, parted in the center and thick eyebrows that almost met above the bridge of his nose. A wiry mustache topped well-shaped lips. All at once, he turned my way. He jutted his square chin at me, his coal-black eyes twinkling like the silver rope chain half buried in his wiry neck hair.

Smiling seductively, he asked, "Are you lost, little girl?"

He reminded me of the boys that hang out in Bay Ridge, their jeans threadbare over strategic bulges as they strut back and forth, rating every woman that passes. The kind of kid that thinks Eau du Armpits and "Yo baby" are all the foreplay any woman ever needs. For some women, David's dark glare and implicit threat might have been a turn-on. It left me in a deep, shuddering freeze. I shook my head and walked down the hall, his laughter running up and down my spine like a cold finger.

I passed his classroom a few more times, careful not to catch his attention again. Considering that I planned to spend the next few days tracking this guy through the congested streets of New York, I wanted to get a solid imprint of his voice, mannerisms, attitude. And there was plenty of attitude. Once, I saw him hurl an eraser at one of the kids on the window sill. Another time, he sat on the corner of the desk, staring at his hands while the students tossed wads of paper at a nearby trash can. He was clearly out of control. And he seemed too tired to care.

I spent the last half-hour before lunch sitting on a stairway window sill that overlooked a burned-out apartment building that doubled as a crack house. I watched one man enter and leave the building sixteen times. Cars pulled up, paused while merchandise and cash were exchanged through heavily tinted windows, then tore off down the block. The envoy, a black man in his early thirties, was built like a boxer. He wore orange sneakers that undoubtedly glowed in the dark. Shortly before noon, he hopped into a silver Mazda RX-7 and roared off. By then, it was time to check on David again.

I started down the hall, just in time to see him cattle-driving his class down to the lunchroom. He spoke briefly to another teacher, then jogged outside. The streets were swarming with construction workers who were demolishing a building on the next block, but David's limp and height made him easy to track. At Washington and Scanton, he stopped at a pay phone. I crouched down between two abandoned cars, my eyes glued to his profile.

He made three phone calls, one after the other.

By the last one, his face was twisted with rage. I had to be at least twenty feet from him, but he was yelling so loud I was able to catch a few words. Something about paying off a cruiser.

The word repeated in my head. Did he mean a police patrol car? At the thought, my calf muscles went into spasm. Why would David Ross need to pay off cops?

He crashed the phone into the cradle and stormed back to the school.

I didn't want to encounter the security guard again so I waited by a side door until someone exited. Then I snuck back upstairs. David was sitting at an undersized student desk in an empty classroom, looking an awful lot like Gulliver bracing himself for another attack of the Lilliputians.

"I'm drowning. That's what I mean," he said suddenly.

At first, I thought he was talking to me. Then I noticed a hand on his shoulder. An attractive woman stepped into view. She had shoulder-length strawberry blonde hair, wide hips and long, delicate arms. The pearl-white shell and forest green skirt clung to her curves like gift wrapping.

A bell pealed out and doors swung open all along the hallway. Within minutes, the classroom was swarming with kids again. My eyes settled on one boy, who was standing in the doorway. He was almost my height, with an angry burn mark across his cheek. His eyes were bloodshot and his knuckles had thick scabs. He took off a black dungaree jacket and bent to lace up his sneakers. From beneath his torn jeans, the edge of a rusted pipe showed. Our eyes caught. For a second, he glared at me with an unnatural fury. Then the anger collapsed, as if he were too tired to carry the emotion. In that instant, I glimpsed a frightened boy who must have given up his childhood a long time ago. I knew the scenario too well. My stomach knotted.

When David came back into view, I backed off. According to Marion, he would be teaching the rest of the afternoon. I figured

14

it was an ideal time for me to take a break and check in with Tony.

Bad move. Tony is always in a foul mood the day after a doctor's appointment.

"What the hell have you been doing all day?" he barked at me.

"I just told you. Keeping tabs on David Ross."

"In a school, for God's sake! The man's working. What do you expect to find there?"

I rolled my eyes. "I'll know when I find it."

"Great. In the meantime, I need you to go down to the DMV and ask Pete to find out who belongs to a tan Mercedes, license QDP-7891. If it's who I think it is, we may have cornered the guy who's trying to make the Atheneum Group go belly up."

"If we had a computer..."

"But we don't Miller. So we do it the old-fashioned way. Talk to Pete."

I was in no mood to spend the rest of the afternoon in the motor vehicle jungle with a Barney Fife look-alike with bad breath, but Tony was in his commando mode. And since Jill Zimmerman, our part-time assistant, was honeymooning in Bermuda, I was the only foot soldier available.

"Miller, you still there?"

I grunted.

"It's the DMV or another all-night stint at Pathmark, trying to eyeball the cash register junkie."

I caved in. Five minutes later, I was in my car and headed toward the DMV. Little did I know then how much that move would cost me.

Chapter 2

"Geeja! Mallomar! I'm home." My two cats scurried to the front door and immediately began to whine. "What do the two of you have to complain about?" The girls weren't having any of my lip. They made a beeline for their bowls and stepped up their cries. I dropped my Land's End briefcase on the couch and followed them into the kitchen. "All right. You'd think I was starving you."

"You do."

I glanced back to my front door through the kitchen cut-away and made a face.

"Dinah, don't you knock any more?"

Dinah is my best friend and my housemate. She lives on the bottom two floors of our Park Slope brownstone, and I occupy the top two.

"Why should I bother? You haven't had anyone up here since the last time Cathy visited. And, if my memory's correct, she probably won't be visiting again, for quite a while."

I rinsed out the cat bowls and pulled out a can of tuna and cheese. "Don't start on that. The relationship had just run its course."

Dinah opened the refrigerator and wrinkled her nose. "Anything you say, Rob. I'm sure the therapist you stopped seeing seven months ago would agree completely." She pulled out a green Tupperware bowl and popped the lid. By the way, I think the science experiment is a success."

"Did you come up here to disparage the joys of single life, or do you have a more sinister purpose?"

"Had a good day, I see. Well, I was just between sessions and thought you should know that Tony's looking for you. Stopped here about twenty minutes ago and said you had better call the office. Stat. Seems someone you were tailing was killed this afternoon."

One loud call and a short drive later, I found myself back where I had started the day. The entrance to the school building was blocked by what seemed a battalion of police. I slipped past the crime scene unit van and glanced at the crowd on the other side of the yellow plastic police tape. The neighborhood was ripe for conflict. You could smell it. Like the scent that heralds a lightning strike.

Just then someone hurled a beer bottle at a patrol car parked next to the morgue wagon. Instantly the air was crackling with the sound of breaking glass and racial epithets. Six or seven cops rushed in that direction, but unexpectedly one of them swiveled toward me, his thumb twitching on the hammer of his thirty eight. I recognized the telltale quiver of a rookie and quickly flashed my identification card. After giving me and my card a snarling once-over, he pointed me in Tony's direction.

My sweet-natured partner was talking animatedly to a stocky man with a gray crewcut and a Gorbachev-style birthmark across his forehead. Lieutenant Sergeant Frederick Rodammer, also known as the Hammer. Classic bigot and one of my personal favorites on the New York police force. Right then Rodammer was knocking another cigarette out of a half-crush pack. I stopped in my tracks and scanned the crowd for another source of information.

Unexpectedly, a baritone voice boomed in my ear. "A beautiful woman. Must be searching for me."

I turned and found myself looking into the Basset-hound brown eyes of Isaac McGinn, a 6'2" detective with thin blond hair, a crooked grin, and a penchant for gourmet food and birdwatching.

"Don't flatter yourself, Zack. I was actually hoping that the cute redhead from the seven-five would show up."

Zack smiled and squeezed my shoulder. "You must mean Audrey. Ah, fate is cruel."

"Give it up. You're the happiest married man I know."

Zack and I met last year while I was investigating a Medicare scam at a local clinic. He's a study in contrasts, from his name down to his dual memberships in the Animal Protection League and the local deer-hunting club. Now he thrust his sharp chin in Tony's direction and said, "The SIA man's busting a gut. I heard him telling the Hammer that you got burned today."

"Burned, my ass. The guy lying in that morgue wagon didn't even know I existed. Tony pulled me off for some goose chase at the DMV."

He stared over my shoulder toward the skirmish near the morgue van. The street lights flickered on. "Figured as much. Doesn't matter though. They already picked up the perp. Black kid. Only twelve years old. A real shame. Looks like he used a twenty-two." He was talking in a distracted shorthand that told me he needed to be elsewhere.

"That's it? Case solved? Sounds a little fast."

Zack frowned and stepped past me. "Sometimes we cops actually do something right."

"What did you do right this time? Walk into the room and find the kid waving a pistol and shouting 'Take me, Officer! I did it, I'm the one.'"

He flashed me a sideways glance to make sure I was kidding. To tell the truth, I'm not sure I was.

"It's a good thing we're friends, Miller," he said, his eyes snapping back across the street. "The custodian—Hyung Kim—saw the kid running from the classroom with the weapon in his hands. That was just around four o'clock. From what the M.E. said, the guy couldn't have been dead more than a half-hour by the time we got there. Satisfied?"

It still sounded too convenient to me. "What's the motive?"

"Things aren't always that neat."

"Finding a black kid with a smoking weapon in his hand sounds pretty damn neat to me. Too neat. Come on, McGinn. Something isn't right here."

"The teacher's wallet was missing, Robin. But just for you, I'll check around. If I find someone's screwing with the facts, I'll let you know."

"Okay, Kimosabie. Now, can you get me inside?"

Without taking his eyes off the crowd, he smiled. "Not a chance in hell. The Hammer would cut off my earlobes and feed them to his pet pig." He glanced at me. "Besides, there's nothing to see. An empty classroom, a bloody desk. That's it. The only thing of note is some sawdust we found mucking up one of the blood stains. You know what I mean, the shit you find on the floor at fruit stands or some of those Korean stores. The kid probably tracked it in on his sneakers. Now, if you don't mind, I'm going to check out the action near the death limo."

I took a deep breath and headed in Tony's direction. He saw me and shook his head disapprovingly. "Good work, Miller. You tail a guy all morning and bail out just in time for him to get killed."

I nodded at Rodammer, who was already gnashing his teeth in my direction.

"You pulled me off, Tony," I said.

"Yeah, I pulled you off." He made it sound like I had

hallucinated our phone conversation. For a moment, I tried to imagine what he'd look like with a cucumber stuck in his left ear.

"You two can discuss this later," Rodammer interrupted. "In the meantime, I have a few questions for Ms. Carter." For some reason, he insisted on using my pen-name. I think he viewed it as a form of high wit. "Before you conveniently disappeared, did you notice anything unusual?"

I immediately thought of David's heated phone calls, the tall kid with the rusted pipe beneath his jeans, the blonde with her hand on David's shoulder. Marion's gun. Then I looked at Rodammer. The guy voted for Reagan. He has a signed eight-by-ten of Bush on his office wall. I shrugged and said, "No. Not that I remember."

Rodammer is a social moron, but he's a smart cop. He knew I was holding out—the pulsing vein in his forehead told me as much. "Maybe it's time for you to get back to what you're good at."

My eyes narrowed with pleasure. "Mmmm. I'd love to, Freddy, but my girlfriend's out of town."

Rodammer turned the color of rare roast beef and stormed away.

"You're a pain in the ass, Miller." Tony scurried after his good friend who, I had often noticed, made a point of never stepping within spitting distance of Tony. After all, you can't be too careful. Doctors may discover that AIDS can be transmitted by sibilant speech.

I scanned the crowd, trying to find Zack again. Instead I found a young cop taking a statement from a dark-haired man with a towel hanging from his back pocket and a ring of keys hooked to his belt. Instincts told me that this was Hyung Kim. I waited for the cop to move away before heading over. "Tough district you work in."

The man removed thick aviator glasses and rubbed leathery palms over his eyes. "You don't know, man."

"You work in this school long?"

He couldn't have been more than thirty, but his face was careworn. "Three years." He looked at the school with distaste. "I hope they fry him."

"You mean the kid you saw? The one with the gun?"

"Damn straight." Kim pulled out a pack of Camels and slapped a cigarette into his palm. "Kid's a troublemaker. Mugged my wife last year." A cloud of smoke blew my way. I stepped back. "Mind?" He waved the cigarette under my nose.

"You sure it's the same kid?"

"No question. I saw him come out of the classroom. Still had the gun in his hand."

I took a closer look at his thick glasses. They magnified the broken blood vessels in his eyes. I scratched the side of my nose and asked casually, "How far away were you?"

He flicked ash at me. "He was running."

"Toward you?"

"No." He began playing with his lighter, switching the flame on and off. "Away."

I was starting to get a bad feeling in the pit of my stomach. "How far away was he?"

He turned a wheel to make the wick higher. Then he looked up. "Not far. He was wearing a black jacket, torn jeans. Had a pipe on him when the cops picked him up."

I remembered the kid with the burn mark on his face, the one standing outside David's classroom. "Did he have a scar, right here?" I drew a finger over my cheek.

Kim smiled bitterly. "That's him, man. I wish I'd caught him. I'd have killed him myself. With my hands." He waved thick-skinned hands in my face.

"What's his name?"

"Name? Thomas Emerson. The kids call him Pooley." A smirk hid at the corner of his mouth. "Did he have problems with Ross?"

He sucked in the cigarette smoke. "Pooley has trouble with everyone. You think he needs a reason to kill somebody?" Bitter

21

amusement lit his eyes. "Pooley doesn't need a reason to kill. Maybe Ross didn't say good morning to him. I hear these kids. They got a beef with someone, could be their best friend, they buck him. That's what they call it. Bucking. It happens all the time around here. Kids ten, twelve years old, walking around with guns tucked into their pants."

I struck my best tough-guy pose. "What kind of gun was he carrying?"

Guns are not my favorite topic. I felt my nose tickle with the distant memory of gunsmoke. I shook it off.

"Cops say it looks like a twenty-two." He pointed to his temple with his index finger, his thumb extended like a trigger. "Right here. Boom!" He watched me for a reaction.

Heat rose to my face. Stay focused, I warned myself. "A twenty-two is pretty small." Small, but deadly. The memory of a slim twenty two caliber handgun snapped into place. The metal gleaming like a gutter under a moonlit rain. My eyes dropped to my hands, my fingers quaking ever so slightly. Suddenly the nightmare broke out of its cell, a killer out for my blood. Again.

I squeezed my eyes shut and for the thousandth time felt the weight of the twenty two in my three-year-old hand, the crack of the hammer. Felt the thunderbolt fling me back against a stack of shoe boxes, my nostrils singed by gunsmoke, my sister wailing my name over and over until finally her voice collapsed into a dull rattle deep in her chest, the closet air filling with the cloying stench of her thick, sweet blood.

"Hey, you okay?"

I opened my eyes and refocused on Kim's hands, the cigarette there now burning down to a stub. I swallowed and asked, "How'd you see a gun that small from a distance?"

My voice was too thin, my shoulders pressing down. I straightened up.

Kim shuffled away from me. His face was flushed, his lips tight with anger. "What are you trying to pull, man? I know what I saw. It was Pooley. Pooley done Ross in. That's it." He speared the cigarette at my knee and stormed away. I watched him for a moment, then took off in the opposite direction. Zack had better take another look at the facts. If Kim was the only witness, then this case was wide open.

As it turned out, the infamous black-rights advocate Reverend Gordon Whaley and I were the only ones who doubted Kim's testimony. As far as the police were concerned, the case was closed. Tony felt the same way. Even the papers bought into the police version. Kim was an upstanding citizen, Pooley a twelve-year-old punk with a short temper, and Whaley just out for more fiery publicity. Still, the case trailed me like the stench that lingers after a three-alarm fire. Black, acrid smoke. The scent refuses to dissipate.

By Sunday morning, I was desperate to leave the case behind. I put on a Louis Armstrong CD full blast and plunged myself into a hot bath. Dipping my ears below the water level, I focused on the air fern hanging from the skylight. The leaves were turning yellow. I closed my eyes and joined Satchmo in a half-hearted rendition of "What a Wonderful World," trying hard to remember what the hell made it so wonderful.

Just as I was about to spin into a depressing litany of the world's ills, starting with too-small bathtubs and ending, no doubt, with Saddam Hussein nuking my very house, Mallomar attacked the faucet. She miscalculated and joined me in the tub. Laughing, I fished out my chubby, blue-eyed calico and let her quiver against me for a moment, gratefully capturing a flash of what Louie was singing about.

I spent the rest of the morning finishing an article on the Canadian Rockies for *The Single Traveller* magazine. Mallomar, fully recovered from her brief dip, had just leaped onto my computer keyboard for the eighth time when the phone rang around noon.

"It's Marion Ross." Her voice was hard and steady, not the sound of a woman whose husband had just been killed two days earlier.

23

"I'm sorry about your husband." I saved the article, waved a spray of cat hair away from my face, and moved into the living room. "Tony thinks…"

"I know what Mr. Serra thinks. I've talked to him. But we don't agree."

"I'm not sure I understand." I stretched out on the couch, lifting Mallomar onto my lap.

"My husband's murder was not random, Ms. Miller. I'm sure of that. I never thought I'd be siding with that awful Reverend Whaley, but this time the man has a point. For some reason, they've decided to railroad some poor child and let David's real murderer off scot-free. I need your help."

Geeja, a black-haired reincarnation of Cleopatra, watched Mallomar knead my lap and let out a jealous hiss. I stretched out an arm to the green-eyed cat and said, "Ms. Ross, I understand your concerns…"

"No, you don't. This was my husband, remember? Now, I want a simple answer from you. Will you continue your investigation?"

If Tony had told Marion that the case was closed, I really didn't have the right to tell her otherwise. No matter how much it grated on my nerves, he was still my boss. And he had made it perfectly clear on Friday that my reservations about Kim's credibility meant diddley-squat.

I shifted the phone to my other ear. "Yes. I'll continue the investigation." I heard her sigh. "One condition, though. You have to come clean with me. No lies. No omissions."

"Absolutely."

"What's the gun in your bag for?"

The phone went dead. "Excuse me?" she asked. Clearly, she was buying time.

"You had a gun in your handbag the other day. So far I haven't mentioned that inconsequential fact to anyone." That was a blatant lie, but I figured it was my best bargaining chip. "You play games with me now, and I'll call the precinct as soon as we hang up."

"I did not kill my husband. If I did, would I be asking you to investigate his death? Come on, Ms. Miller, I am not a stupid woman." She sounded irritated. It was a reaction I was used to provoking.

"On the contrary, calling me could be a very smart move on your part. You find out whether I've told the police about the gun, while professing indignation and concern about the way your husband's death is being handled. No. I have no doubt that you are very smart indeed." I was so intent on trying to match her upper-class affect that I almost missed her answer.

"The gun is for protection. In case you haven't noticed, this isn't a very safe city. Besides, I knew David was in trouble. I wanted to be prepared."

The woman on the phone didn't seem like the same one who had sat in my office and worried a tissue into shreds just two days ago. From her tone, she could be Dirty Harry's new partner. I sat up, ignoring Mallomar's protest and Geeja's unforgiving stare. "Prepared for what?"

"Look, the bottom line is the police know about the gun, so your threat is unnecessary. Are you satisfied?"

I was far from satisfied, but both Marion and the case intrigued me. Besides, I was pretty sure that Hyung Kim was not telling the truth, and I have a very nasty streak when it comes to railroading children—even children who look like they could roast me, slice me up, and serve me for Thanksgiving dinner without losing a night's sleep. We hung up, agreeing to keep our business arrangement confidential.

I tried to get back into the Canadian Rockies, but every time I started to write about Mary Shaeffer—the first white explorer in the Maligne Lake region—I typed Marion's name instead. I figured if my subconscious was working that hard, I had better cave in. Besides, I was mighty curious to see what plans the stoic widow had for the rest of the day.

Chapter 3

Marion's address put her smack in the middle of prime real estate.

Brooklyn Heights is a fashionable neighborhood of narrow, tree-lined streets studded by brownstones, prewar apartment buildings, and drivers desperately looking for parking spots. The most exclusive buildings in the neighborhood border the promenade and directly overlook the Manhattan skyline–including the murky East River and the permanently under-construction Brooklyn Bridge. For the most part, the promenade buildings are populated by investment bankers and old-money families, not schoolteachers and their wives. Marion must come from pretty big bucks if she could afford to live there. And David must have been one hell of a stud.

I double-checked the address, then looked up and smiled. Spying on Marion was going to be one of the easiest jobs I ever had. I slumped onto a park bench and gazed through curtainless, six-foot-wide windows on the first floor. I had a pretty clear view of her dining room, living room, and library.

A chandelier with crystal teardrops and gold filigree leaves hung over a baroque dining room table bearing a silver candelabra. It was too far away to tell for sure, but I would have bet big bucks that the candelabra had leaves as well. Big, curly ones. Or maybe gargoyles with Mick Jagger tongues. It was that kind of room. Hard as I tried, I couldn't picture David Ross sitting at that table. David was one hundred percent Brooklyn. Marion, on the other hand, looked like high society.

She stepped into the dining room to pour brandy or sherry from a decanter on the buffet table. Glancing right over her shoulder, she took a long swig, emptying the glass in one gulp, then she refilled her glass and another one as well. After sipping from both glasses, she straightened her shoulders and returned to the library. I switched benches.

The library was a writer's wet dream. A collection of books, probably unread, lined the walls on gleaming, cherry wood shelves. A ladder with rollers was hooked onto a thin ridge midway up the rear wall. I couldn't see it, but I knew there was a fireplace lurking somewhere in that deep-toned space. Marion held out a glass toward the left corner of the room. For an instant, I thought she might be toasting some ancient portrait of her great-great-great grandfather landing on Plymouth Rock. Next thing I knew, Tennessee Bellflower stepped out of the shadows to accept the drink with a small smile.

I must have emitted a sound because the elderly gentleman sitting near me muttered something under his breath and moved to the next bench. I looked back up at the windows.

T.B., as his associates call him, is one of the city's medical examiners. He's a year or two older than me, thirty-four at the most, but looks fifteen. He has copper-red hair, a nose like Ron Howard back in his Opie days, and eyelashes thick as a paintbrush. I worked with him just eight months ago on a car accident that turned out to be an insurance agent's creative

27

alternative to divorce. What I remembered most about him was his slow, Southern drawl and an unsettling obsession with Al Pacino and all things Italian. His dining room table consists of a matinee poster of *The Godfather* sealed in lucite and mounted on a marble base.

So why was T.B. in Marion's apartment? Medical examiners don't usually hand-deliver autopsy results to the victims' families. Besides, it was Sunday and the results of the autopsy probably wouldn't be in for another day or so.

Were they lovers?

I edged closer to the bushes under Marion's windows. If they were lovers, they were pretty bad at it. T.B. turned his back to Marion and scanned the shelves. Marion took the opportunity to swallow the contents of her glass. When he turned around, he looked uncomfortable. He took a sip, then put the glass down. I watched them move through the rooms until they reached the front door. They shook hands stiffly, then T.B. left.

I was torn between continuing my vigil of Marion's apartment and cornering Tennessee. While I was backing away from the bushes, the decision was made for me.

"Robin!" T.B. shook my hand enthusiastically. "What're you doing here?" A thick, muscular arm wrapped around my arms and dragged me toward Montague Street. "Join me for an espresso and dessert? Maybe a cannelloni?"

I had the feeling he meant the pastry and not the pasta, but I didn't have the heart to correct him. Besides, he seemed genuinely pleased to see me—as well as oblivious to the fact that I had just been spying on him.

"What are you doing in these parts, T.B.? I thought you lived in Little Italy."

"No," he laughed. "I'm in Chelsea these days. I was just visiting with a friend."

"Anyone I know?" I tried to sound jocular.

He slapped my back. "Now, how am I supposed to know who you know? That's your job. Checking up on people. C'mon, there's an open table at that cafe."

We lunged across the street and claimed two chairs. Quickly ordering, T.B. launched into conversation with enthusiasm. I had forgotten how exhausting he could be. We spent the next two hours eating Italian pastries and discussing everything from *The Godfather III* to William Kennedy Smith's arrest. It was the last topic that gave me an opening.

"So are you working on any interesting cases?" I asked. Subtle, Miller, very subtle.

"Not at liberty to discuss them, you know," he said with a wink that told me he couldn't wait to give me all the gory details. Unfortunately, they were the wrong ones. Enraptured by the thrill of his work, he proceeded to give me a blow-by-blow account of how he had helped the cops find a man who had melted his landlord's body in a bathtub filled with sulfuric acid.

Needless to say, I decided to forgo the rest of my Napoleon. Smiling reluctantly, I tried again. This time, I actually hit pay dirt.

"Got this one case," he said, his Southern accent kicking in. "It's a doozy. Man gets shot. Bullet to right temporal lobe. First thing about the case is that I know the man. His wife is one of these big social types. She and her dad show up every P.A.L. benefit, you know, Police Athletic League. Real generous. Well, the pressure's on to get results fast, so I pull a Quincy, staying up all night long. I was so tired I almost sawed through my hand rather than his head." He stopped to laugh. I guess you had to be into autopsies to appreciate the humor. "Anyway, I get inside and guess what?" He stopped again.

Christ. He actually expected me to guess what was in Ross's head. Suddenly, I wanted desperately to be back home.

"You find the bullet," I answered. My tongue felt thick.

"Wrong." He stabbed the air. "That's just it! No bullet. The wound's like thousands I've seen. A ring of abrasion around the hole, skin scraped into the edges. Real typical. I'm already taping, just assuming it's a twenty-two caliber gunshot, but then there's no bullet. And get this. No exit wound. So where's the bullet?"

I shook my head. Was he playing with me? Maybe he and Marion had seen me after all. "How's that possible? Where could the bullet have gone?" I asked.

He leaned back satisfied. I half-expected him to poke me in the ribs and shout "Gotcha!" Instead, he shrugged. "Don't know, Robin." He ordered another espresso, his expression slowly changing. "The thing is, everyone's on my back. This lady is important, and the case is real high-profile. I've been getting calls from everyone from the Mayor down to that hot shot News Four reporter. You know, the guy with the broken nose? Half the city wants me to keep what I know quiet, and the other half wants me on the cover of *New York Magazine*.

"Today, I even made a special trip to the widow's house to try to smooth things over. Imagine how she feels. Her husband's dead, the cops got a suspect in jail, and I can't find the darned bullet. I've only been working here a short time. I don't want people looking at me and saying 'That's him, the one who lost the bullet.'"

"Is that what happened? Did you lose the bullet?"

He looked up at me, his eyebrows curling up in disbelief. "You kidding me?" His voice practically cracked.

I reached over and squeezed his hand. "It's okay, T.B. This is New York City. No one's going to remember one case. Besides, there has to be an explanation."

He covered my hand with his and nodded, his normal exuberance slipping into place. "You bet. That's why I took more slide specimens than usual. Believe me, I won't rest till I figure this one out."

Finally, T.B. and I had something in common.

T.B walked me back to my car. He was warmed up now and was gleefully treating me to the best of America's autopsies for the last century. At some point, I realized I had only one escape route available. I opened the car door, revved Bella's fifteen-year-old, six-cylinder engine, and tore off. I wasn't ready to head home, so I spent another half-hour trying to find a new parking spot. By the time I walked back to the promenade, it was after four o'clock and Marion's lights were out. I cursed T.B. under my breath. Then I had an idea. I searched for a telephone booth. The first two were broken. The third had gum glued to the receiver. I ended up back on Montague Street. After ten rings, I was satisfied that Marion had left the apartment.

I stopped at the car to pick up a few select items, then walked back to the building, a thrill running along my limbs like an ocean breeze. I was about to indulge in my favorite PI activity. No. My second favorite. Breaking and entering was what I liked best. I was getting pretty damned good at it too, thanks to my brother Ronald who had spent the better part of his teen years making a living at illicit visitations. He had a real fondness for gas stations and first-floor apartments in Jewish neighborhoods, which I figured was his way of giving our father the proverbial finger. He cleaned up his act after his best friend was caught and sentenced to seven years. The fact that Dad died around the same time probably helped.

Now Ronald is a locksmith living in Staten Island with a pain-in-the-ass wife, three unappealing kids, and our mother's Florida telephone number in position one on his phone. I'm not even sure what town she lives in.

For years, Ronald and I hardly spoke. My current profession, however, has brought back fond memories for him, and we are beginning to act like brother and sister. The relationship is strange for me, since I've spent twenty eight of my thirty one years without family connections to anyone but my older sister Barbara.

Right then, however, I was not planning to practice my breaking-and-entering skills. For several reasons. The most prominent being that Marion Ross probably had one of those killer alarm systems that transmits an electric spark up the spine of the Chief of Police and every Doberman within a square mile. Instead I settled for favorite PI activity number two: searching the trash.

Managed correctly, trash-blasting (as I refer to it) can be enlightening. Even liberating.

I passed through the gates of Marion's building and nonchalantly tapped down the steps to the garbage foyer, a long, dark concrete tunnel outfitted with six metal trash cans and one blue recycling bin.

I paused to listen for distant footsteps, then prepared myself for the task. First, I whipped out a pair of anti-dishpan-hand gloves, a stick of peppermint gum, and a red bandanna that had cradled a bar of apricot soap for a good four months. I stuck the gum in my mouth, tied the bandanna under my nose to mask any offending odors, then slipped on the gloves like a surgeon.

I was prepared to search through all six cans, but didn't have to. I found Marion's trash, dragged it into a back corner, and turned it upside down. That was the liberating part. You'd understand the thrill if you spent most of your life attracting lovers who ironed underwear and folded them into two-inch triangles arranged by color and pattern.

Next, I began the search. In the past two years, I've solved a number of cases just by sorting through discarded phone bills and credit card statements. Unfortunately, Marion's garbage spoke of a fairly mundane life. First of all, the woman hardly ate. I usually sort through the food remnants first, since the smell occasionally defeats my enthusiasm. But Marion's trash bore two half-eaten apples and one empty tofu container. That's it. The rest was junk mail, a shoe box of OTB stubs dating back to January, an empty Unisol container, a stack of old racing forms, a bottle of surprisingly cheap Pinot Grigio, and a March issue of *For Women Only*, a new magazine featuring Candice Bergen on the cover. She looked pretty hot and the magazine was in good shape, so I tucked it under my arm and started repacking the can.

Just as I was about to toss the last of the garbage back in, I heard someone open a door somewhere above me. I dropped the trash and zipped to the front gate, discarding the bandanna and snapping my gloves off as I trotted back to the car. Candice Bergen was nuzzled under my arm.

I didn't get into the office until ten the next day. When I arrived, I found a note from Tony telling me he had checked in a case that he wanted me to take over. The note was unusual, as was Tony's absence. I checked his desk and found out why. Tony may have dumped Marion's case, but he wanted to stay in her favor. His desk blotter contained the information on David's funeral. I glanced at my watch. I had an hour to make an appearance. My brownstone was on Third Street near Eighth Avenue, just seven blocks away from the office. I locked up shop and jogged home.

I hopped up the front stoop, noticing on the way up that my therapist-slash-housemate had a client seated in the Haitian cotton club chair by the front window. I was pretty sure it was the same guy I had seen circling our block for two hours last Wednesday night. Dinah never talked about her clients, but something about this guy gave me the creeps. I stepped down and took a closer look.

Dinah's matching chair faced the steps and a small frown told me that she had registered my presence. She tried hard not to be distracted as I paused to whirl my index finger next to my temple in the accepted sign language for "wacko." When her frown turned to a grimace, I knew I had better move on.

By the time I dug up a black dress and a pair of nicked black pumps from my cramped closet, I had twenty minutes left—more than enough time to get to the funeral home on Coney Island Avenue. But as soon as I walked outside, I realized I was doomed. In New York, we have this quaint custom called "alternate side of the street parking"—which means that for three or four hours on select days, your car has to find another place to rest its weary wheels. The problem is, since most people just double-park their cars on the "right" side of the street, waiting for the time limit to pass, I was blocked in. So I sat fuming in my car until eleven a.m. ticked past and all the car owners shifted to the other side.

I pulled up to the funeral home just as a stream of sleek

limousines drove away. Checking the time, I realized I had to make a quick choice between parking and dashing inside to see if the services were still in progress, or betting that the services were over and the limos were for Ross. Parking didn't appeal to me, so I shot past the red light and joined the end of the procession. An hour later, we were in Long Island and I was squeezing Bella between a nineteen-ninety Mazda and a Subaru station wagon.

The first person I spotted was Tony, his flat butt laying low under charcoal cotton pants that may have fit him six, seven months ago. He had a pocket King James Bible in his right hand, which didn't seem entirely appropriate since this was a Jewish funeral. I edged my way to the far side of the crowd, looking for Marion and wondering whose shoulder she had chosen to cry on.

I found her standing alone, her hands clutching a navy alligator purse. Snap open. Shut. Snap open. Shut. Her fingers moved so deftly, they could be knitting. She caught my gaze, cocked her head in surprise, then acknowledged me with a nod. Tony followed her eyes and met mine with his usual disapproval. I blew him a kiss. Then all at once the rabbi's deep, solid voice penetrated my consciousness, drawing me inward.

The prayers made my throat tight, bringing back the two deaths with which I still hadn't come to terms. First my father's funeral flooded back, the sight of my too-controlled mother wailing in perfect concert with the rabbi's song. I couldn't understand the Hebrew words. My father had wanted it that way, reminding us always not to act too much like *Jews*. It wasn't until I was fourteen that I fully understood why. When I heard the full story, it came from my Aunt Fagy's lips.

In nineteen forty two, when my father was just thirteen years old and living in Antwerp, Belgium, the Gestapo broke into his home and killed his mother, father, and sister. He fled the house and hid in a sewer for four days, surviving on a single lump of bread and the company of rats. Finally, he emerged and crept into the alley next to his home. A neighbor found him, sheltered him, and raised him as a Catholic. He spent the rest of his life running from the memories, even avoiding other Europeans. Sometimes, he'd retreat to his bedroom closet, sitting inside with a gun clenched in his fist, the door tightly closed. My mother would shoo us away, her eyes cool as ice. It was with his gun that I accidentally killed my sister Carol.

My father and I never spoke again after her death. Twenty-three years of silence.

My fingers started to tingle, warning me away from the one memory that has haunted me all my life. I couldn't let myself revisit Carol's funeral. I pulled myself back into the moment and examined the mourners.

David's relatives were easy to pick out. It was a warm day in late spring, but they were all wearing black wool coats and jackets, as if funerals could only take place in bad weather. The women huddled together, crying loudly, competing for the most heart-wrenching howl. I would have given them all prizes. Tears were already rolling down my face. Someone tapped me on the shoulder and passed me a tissue. I accepted it with a reluctant snivel. "Thanks." I turned to see who I was thanking.

It was T.B., and holding onto his arm was the blonde I had seen comforting David in an empty classroom just hours before he was murdered.

Chapter 4

At the end of the services, we all shuffled by Marion to drop off words of sympathy. It was like tossing pennies into a coin fountain that would never deliver on a single wish. The woman was expressionless, her eyes flat.

I lingered to one side to see if I could get a handle on who was who. A woman wearing a fishnet veil and an outfit that could best be described as Madonna funeral wear clung to Marion, her sobs shaking the two of them. Marion pushed her off like a linebacker and held her at arm's distance. Two men stepped up, hooked arms with the veiled lady and moved her to the side. Then I saw Tony heading my way. I tried to get lost in the crowd.

"Tony, good of you to come." I heard a booming male voice and I turned to look. Tony was shaking the hand of one of the mourners. He was obviously a businessman. A prosperous one. He had foxtail gray hair and bushy eyebrows that arched off his forehead like hotel awnings. They hung over gold-rimmed Ben

Franklin glasses and cheeks that had the golden tones of a salon tan. The only jarring feature was a poorly concealed zit on his square chin. He was wearing a well-tailored blue pinstripe suit and power-yellow tie. He looked like the type that resented any interruption to business. Including funerals.

"I'm really sorry about Marion's loss," Tony said.

The two of them had taken a few steps away from the other mourners. I hovered nearby to listen in.

"To tell the truth, it's probably for the best," Eyebrows answered. "David wasn't good for my daughter." He scanned the crowd as if it were a cocktail party. "No press." He and Tony shared knowing looks. "Funny. A man who has built his career on public relations, image development…" He shook his head, deciding to let the sentence hang. Tony seemed to understand.

"Well, again, let me express my sorrow and wish your daughter well," Tony said.

They shook hands formally. Tony started to turn, then snapped his fingers. "I almost forgot." It was a Columbo move, one that I had seen him make a dozen times before. "Here's my home number, Mr. Haas. Just in case you need my help again and would prefer not going through the office." He leaned in and said, "You know, I could do a background check on anyone Marion dates. To avoid this kind of…"

"Very kind of you." Bushy Eyebrows slapped Tony on the back to forestall his conclusion. They headed away from the grave site toward Tony's car.

I let their conversation sink in. Haas. Marion's father was William J. Haas. Part owner of Haas, Adams and Wilkie, the second largest public relations agency in the country. I remembered seeing something about the firm in the papers recently. I made a mental note to check my newspaper files. Then I checked the line of mourners one last time.

T.B. and his girlfriend had just passed Marion, who was now standing with a handful of David's relatives. I waved and started back to the parking lot. T.B. and the blonde followed me to my car in silence. I was almost embarrassed to admit Bella was mine. I could afford better. Much better. But Bella was, well, just Bella. I leaned against the Mazda with a proprietary air, hoping they'd assume the classic silver sedan was mine. It might have worked, too, if T.B. hadn't pulled out a set of keys and opened the passenger's door.

"Need a lift?" he asked.

I straightened up. "No thanks, T.B." If I wanted to find out more about the blonde, I had better move fast. T.B. opened the door for his friend who, I suddenly noticed, had devastating brown eyes with rich flecks of copper sprinkled throughout the iris. Tiger eyes. "Hi." I reached out my hand. "T.B.'s manners are abysmal. My name's Robin Miller."

She smiled. Oh yes. "Virginia Savarin," she said. The school psychologist at P.S. 189. Interesting. "Well, it's a pleasure to meet you."

T.B. beamed at me over the Mazda's roof. "Back off," he said good-naturedly. Virginia looked puzzled. "She's my sister. And she's married. To a cop. Who carries a big gun."

"Tennessee, what are you going on about?" she asked, her voice like butter melting over a warm mound of grits.

Virginia had a more distinct Southern accent than T.B. I love Southern accents.

"It's a private joke," I explained, my gaze caught on her eyes.

"I can't believe we've bumped into each other two days in a row. When I saw Tony at the funeral home, my curiosity was tweaked. You two doing work for Marion?" T.B. asked.

I tore my eyes away from Virginia. "We did a while ago. You know Tony. He likes to impress clients with his sincerity."

"Right. Hey, look, Ginny and I are heading over to our sister's place for lunch. It's in the Village. She just hired a new chef. The guy's terrific. Uses lots of garlic. Want to join us?"

Tony would be expecting me back in the office. I snuck a look at Virginia, who was now sitting in the car, blowing her nose. She and David must have been close. It was up to me to find out how close.

T.B. misconstrued my glance. He whispered over the top, "We could use the company."

I claimed Bella as mine and agreed to follow them. I had just pulled out and started after them, when the Mazda shuddered to a stop next to a group standing beside a small van. I recognized the veiled lady and her companions. I got out of my car to see if there was a problem just as Virginia exited hers. She and the woman embraced. I walked a little closer to see if I could hear anything. One of the men glanced my way. He was about six-two, with bulging biceps, dark curly hair, and piercing green eyes. He was wearing a midnight blue silk shirt under a hunter green suit that smacked of polyester. The clothes didn't match in fabric or tone.

I had a feeling he didn't care.

The other guy had chestnut hair and was slimmer than me. His hand trembled as it rested on the back of the woman hugging Virginia. Then he flicked his head and turned my way. Something about him was familiar. I dropped my eyes and pretended to check the tires. From what I heard, I gathered the women worked together. They finally separated and I got back into the car, still trying to remember where I had seen the slimmer man before.

It took close to two hours to get into the city, and another forty minutes to find parking spots. By the time we met in front of the restaurant, I was ravenous. For food and information. Experience told me that one was going to be a lot easier to get than the other.

The restaurant was called Our Daily Bread. I almost groaned out loud. Not another vegetarian restaurant. Not that I have anything against vegetables. It's just that lightly sautéed sprouts and broiled tofu don't exactly fill me up like a three-inch slice of lasagna or a thick, juicy burger with two slices of cheddar and a spool of red onion. As it turned out, Our Daily Bread had a menu that must have been conceived in heaven. I was just commenting on that to Virginia when T.B. brought his other sister to the table.

Heaven must have been very busy.

"Robin, this is K.T." He paused, waiting for my reaction. K.T. had short, loose curls the color of autumn and hazel eyes that flashed leaf-green when she smiled. The eyes focused on mine and held.

"A pleasure," I whispered, my voice suddenly thin.

A few, delicate freckles powdered the bridge of her nose. Her lips were full, well-formed, and her body had curves in all the right places. I stood up. She was just an inch or so shorter than me, and her square palm squeezed mine just a second longer than a first meeting warranted. I felt a pulse down under.

"What does K.T. stand for?" I asked, the electricity crackling between our hands. I almost jumped backwards.

She laughed, deep and solid. Like brook water over rocks. "Kentucky. But most of my close friends just call me K.T. or Kate."

It was my turn to laugh. "Wait a second...I think I detect a trend here."

"You should." She squeezed my arm lightly and nudged me into the booth, sliding in next to me with a purpose. "Dad was a truck driver. He named all of us after states he drove through. Except Montana. That's where Dad wanted to live." Her eyes darkened.

"There are more of you?" I had this vision of a magnificent house filled with gorgeous women with Southern drawls. I filed the vision for a later fantasy.

T.B. said, "There's us three, then there's Georgia. She's still down South with our Mom. So's Alabama. Carolina's out West. Montana's here in town." He looked at K.T. "Is that it?"

"That's enough," I said.

"What do you think?" T.B. angled his head toward K.T. I did a double-take. Was T.B. matching me up with his sister?

"Don't you recognize her?" he asked.

I thought for a moment. "She looks a lot like Virginia."

They all chuckled. For a split second, it was like being in a fun house where hundreds of mirrors bounce around the same image with minor distortions.

"So much for fame," K.T. said. "I have a cooking show on PBS. 'The Casual Cook!' Surely, you've heard of it?" Her tone was self-mocking, but her eyes were doing something else. "Every day at four o'clock?" she asked, her voice suddenly husky.

They were undressing me, that's what they were doing.

"Casual cuisine for the individual who loves spice without the price? Brought to you by the Garlic Association of America and Occhipinti Olive Oil?"

I felt myself flush. The woman wanted me. Pure and simple. Suddenly, inexplicably, I wanted out. "Sorry. I love eating, not cooking." I focused on the menu.

In the background I heard some country singer crooning about someone being crazy for wanting someone. I hate country music. It reminds me of prisons and Johnny Cash and redneck sheriffs who despise hippies and New York bagels. "How's the soup?" I asked.

"I've been training the new cook. The gazpacho's great," K.T. said. Her eyes were still fixed on me.

We all ordered the gazpacho. By the end of the meal, my mouth was on fire and so was my brain. I felt a desperate need to get out of there. My reaction to K.T. was irrational. I didn't care. I also didn't care that Virginia looked preoccupied and kept breaking into tears. And I didn't care that T.B. looked like he had swallowed a canary. I dropped a ten on the table, nodded at the whole Bellflower clan, and hightailed it back to Brooklyn and the comfortable disdain of my nasty partner.

Only Tony still wasn't there. Instead there was a new note on my desk: "You have a 4:00 p.m. appointment with a Christine O'Donnell. When you hear the case, you'll know why we have to take it. I'll be in tomorrow." It was already after six, so I figured O'Donnell was long gone. That suited me fine. I needed time to gather myself.

Why had I run from K.T.? I started thinking about Cathy

41

Chapman, a woman I had met in San Francisco two years ago. We had been seeing each other long distance until last New Year's. Six months ago.

On New Year's Eve, we had bundled up and boarded the Staten Island ferry, crossing the river four, five, six times. At one point, she straddled my lap, ignoring the drunks carousing along the rail. Her tongue drew a chill line along my neck, when suddenly her hands reached under my jacket, rubbing firmly between my legs. She'd stop suddenly, wait until my body pumped almost involuntarily against her palm, then start again, faster, harder, her tongue exploring all of my mouth. Suddenly, she undid my pants and her fingers were inside me, my breath coming out in quick loops of smoke.

"Say you want me," she breathed into my ear.

I opened my eyes and found her staring at me, her hand suddenly still. "Say it. I want to hear it. I want everyone to hear it. I *want you*." Her hand moved against me. "Say it, baby," she whispered, close to coming herself. "Say it, and I'll move the world to be with you. Better. I'll move cross country. Just say it loud."

I never came. The next day, we had a throw-the-toaster-across-the-room fight. She's called me a couple of times since. I haven't answered.

I was trying to decide how she would react if I called her now, when someone knocked on the front door. It was O'Donnell. She was a tiny woman. Five feet at most. She had dark circles under dull brown eyes. I wanted badly to tell her to go away, but the need in her face was compelling.

Since Tony had dumped the case on me, I decided to use his office for the interview. I sat down in Tony's squishy leather chair and waited for her to start. She looked puzzled. "Did Mr. Serra tell you about my situation?" She had thin, colorless lips.

I wanted to tell her that I didn't care, that I had too much on my mind already. Instead, I shook my head politely. "I'm afraid not. Why don't you recap?" Her miserable, gray face told me all

I needed to know. Her husband was playing around, and she just had to find out with whom.

She turned her head to the side and chuckled bitterly. "Sure, why not? It's a fun story." She sat back in her chair, her eyes nailing me. I had a sinking feeling that I might have miscalculated.

"I own this business," she started. "It's a food service franchise. Companies rent our snack carts. Pretzels, chips, trail mix, that type of thing. You know what I mean?" I nodded even though I had no idea what she was talking about. "Well, last September, I went to this trade show in Atlantic City. All these food companies trying to pitch their snacks at me."

I have chronic insomnia, but O'Donnell's story was threatening to cure days of sleeplessness. I started to drift, fragments of the funeral racing around the edges of my thoughts.

"So I met this great guy one night." I focused back in on her nasal singsong. So I was right after all. "He was beautiful. Like Tom Selleck. Big shoulders, a thick mustache, and the sweetest breath. He was always sucking these little fruit Certs. You know the ones with the specks in them?" Come on, O'Donnell. I got cats to feed.

Suddenly, she tilted her head back and gave me this look that I couldn't comprehend. It was almost a dare. "You ever dream of finding the right one? Someone who makes you believe all the fairy tales you ever heard? Someone who walks into your life and sees all the wounds you've been hiding, sees them and walks right up and touches them…" She balled a hand up into a fist and shook it at me, her voice cracking. "Touches them and seals them shut. Someone who can make the hurt fade?"

She was waiting for an answer. My face was burning and a sour taste crept into my mouth. Christ. I did know what she was talking about. And it scared the hell out of me.

"Yes. I know the dream." I didn't need this. First thing tomorrow, O'Donnell's case is going back on Tony's desk.

She nodded. "Mike did that. He made me feel safe. So I went back to his room. A suite with a king-sized bed. And we stayed there for four days. Four days. We ordered room service every morning. Champagne. Eggs and caviar." Her eyes closed and she started to sway. "I wake up the fifth morning and I find a black box and a rose on the pillow next to me. I figure Mike's already in the shower. So I open the box…"

And find a wedding band, I thought. Now, the guy's cheating on her and she wants us to prove it. Big surprise.

"There's a note inside," she continued. "Simple. 'Welcome to the world of AIDS. Love, Mike.'" My skin went cold. "That's it?"

"That's it. The bastard fucked me, like it was a game." Her eyes were throwing sparks. "Now I'm HIV-positive, and I've got a death sentence hanging over me. But before I go, I want to find that prick and spit in his face. I want to find him and make him look at me and see what he's done. Serra said you'd help me."

"You bet your ass I will."

Chapter 5

Monday nights, I take a 7:30 p.m. course in Tae-kwon-do at the Women's Awareness Center on Ninth Street. The O'Donnell interview got me to class ten minutes late. To make matters worse, we had a guest instructor—the slit-mouthed Master Rhee. With braces on his teeth, the guy could have been in James Bond films, playing Jaws's lost brother. Right then, with the flickering fluorescent lights overhead, he was the spitting image of Lurch, the Addams Family butler. In either case, he looked ready to devour me. I bowed unwillingly and faded to the back of the class, my concentration blown beyond repair. Rhee knew it. I could feel his sensors homing in on me.

With O'Donnell's story bouncing around my head and the Ross case nagging at me, the last place I wanted to be was in this windowless box with pea-green paint cracking off the walls and forty women kowtowing to a six-foot-four, knobby-faced guy in white pajamas.

"Miller." Ah, geez. Why couldn't Master Choi be here when I need her? Choi was the only reason I endured these sessions. Choi and the fact that my contract with Tony specified that I either carry a gun or achieve at least red-belt status in the defensive arts. So far, I've managed to drag myself up to green with a blue stripe. Fifth grade. I still have three grades to go. Choi tells me that my belt signifies the earth, that I'm like a plant first taking root, my leaves just beginning to stretch to the sky.

Rhee looked like he wanted to trample me.

"Charyot sogi!" My limbs shifted into the attention stance. "Now we practice *dollyo chagi.*" Why couldn't he use the English like Choi? I got ready for a turning kick, and landed on my ass before I had even shifted into a neutral stance.

Rhee's ankle was inches away from my mouth. I seriously considering taking a bite and hauling ass out of there. Then my eyes drifted past Rhee, to the buckled poster on the wall. The student oath. I didn't give a damn about respecting the instructor. But the next two items got me. *I shall be a champion of justice and freedom. I shall build a more peaceful world.*

I stood up, bowed, then chambered my leg and executed the kick, focusing on Rhee like he was the moon and I was Neil Armstrong zeroing in on the Sea of Tranquility. And for the rest of the hour, the Eagle kept landing right in Rhee's midsection.

I slept soundly, something that happens maybe four or five times a year. Only one dream. A field of flowers. Two women making love, their grass-stained bodies glistening in the late-day sun. I woke before the rain broke through.

In the morning, I took a steaming-hot shower, then rubbed Tiger Balm into my bruised elbow and knee joints. Geeja came tearing into the bedroom as soon as the minty ointment heated up and started giving off its scent. She has this mad passion for the stuff. Don't ask me why. So there I was, trying to put on my chinos while this black demon cat is bumping against me.

I finally succeeded in getting dressed and headed to the office. Tony was popping pills when I walked in. He looked like hell. I cleared my throat, startling him.

"What'd you do? Float in?"

"Good morning. Want a cup of coffee?" I was feeling too good to spar with him.

"Sure." I could feel his eyes on my back as I shook out yesterday's coffee grinds from the percolator. "I got a question for you." I turned toward him. "Nah, don't stop." He didn't want me to look at him. I went back to making the coffee. "Let's say something happens to me…" The room started to feel chilly. "Some perp takes me out. My car crashes." Concentrate on the coffee, Miller. One scoop. Two. "You'd still make this place work, right? I mean, you'd have to get a licensed partner or else you wouldn't meet the three-year apprentice requirement. But you wouldn't just clock out, right?"

I depressed the "on" button and stared at the red light. Tony's been a lot of things in the past two years. Preachy. Irritating. Occasionally amusing. But never maudlin. If he started this now, he'd be dead in no time. I turned around. "Tony, you trying to push me out?" He looked puzzled. "Because it isn't going to work. You can go on and croak tomorrow, but we have an agreement." A glimmer of recognition entered his eyes. He knew I was trying to bust his chops. "SIA is fifty percent mine, license or no license. So don't think you can take it away from me, you old flat ass."

He let out a good, healthy laugh. "Fine, fine. Just don't burn the goddamn coffee this morning, okay, Miller?"

We were back on familiar footing.

I poured us both coffee, then followed him into his office. His feet were on the desk, his hands clenched behind his head. I glanced at the framed serenity prayer on the wall behind him and said, "I met O'Donnell last night."

He swiveled his feet down and picked up his mug. "Where you gonna start?"

"The guy was registered at the hotel under the name Mike Weber. He paid cash and didn't provide a license number for his car. O'Donnell saw the car once. A white Grand Am. She also said he seemed relaxed answering to his name."

The best liars mix their falsehoods with a hint of truth, just to make it easier for them to keep track of their lies. I knew this from personal experience.

"I figure the name means something to him. Maybe the initials match his own. Maybe the first name's real. Or it's the name of his favorite dead uncle. He also told O'Donnell that he was a PR man for Dassler snacks. You know the company? It's up in Fort Lee, New Jersey." He nodded. "So I start there. Checking the employee directory for a close match."

"Good thinking." He passed me a sheet of paper. "I did that yesterday. Took me five hours to assemble this list. There are twenty possibles. Run them all by the DMV. See if anyone owns a white Grand Am."

I was about to protest, explaining that I had my work cut out for me with the Ross case. Then I remembered that as far as he was concerned, the case was open-and-shut. As if he were reading my mind, he slapped the copy of the *New York Post* jutting off the corner of the desk. 'By the way, did you read the paper this morning?" I never read the *Post*, which Tony knew full well. "The autopsy report on David Ross was leaked to the press. The damn bullet evaporated. Doesn't look good for that greenhorn T.B." He chuckled. "The whole case depends on the Korean guy now. Reverend Whaley is having the time of his life. Hear he's planning to organize a demonstration outside the custodian's house. Should make for some heavy fireworks." He tossed the paper over to me. "Just think, if you had been on the ball, none of this would have happened."

I walked out, holding the paper in front of me. The page was folded down to a picture of Thomas Emerson and his mother. The shot must have been taken a while ago. Thomas looked younger without the burn mark on his cheek. And his eyes were different. Even through the gray ink I could see the spark. Something like joy. His mother was in profile, beaming over him. I skimmed the photo caption. "Another victim of the inner city.

The twelve-year-old suspect has been released into his mother's care, a nurse at Kings County Hospital. Last year, her youngest son was killed when a bullet from a gunfight between rival gangs crashed through the kitchen window and struck the youngster in the head. The suspect was present at the time."

The suspect was present at the time. So matter of fact. A twelve-year-old boy saw his younger brother blown away just a year ago, and now he was being accused of doing the same thing to his teacher. Only there was no gun, no bullet, and, as far as I knew, a witness whose story had more holes than a pair of teenager's jeans.

I stopped in my office to make a couple of phone calls. The first one went to my friend Michael Flanagan. Michael's a computer whiz and my ace in the hole. Tony doesn't know he exists, and I like it that way. I keep waiting to hear that Michael's been hauled off to jail for penetrating the Pentagon's inner computer sanctum, but the guy seems to have this knack for crawling into files he should have no way of entering and crawling back out without so much as a bleep. That's where his nickname comes from. The Roach. Michael deems it a compliment. Come to think of it, so do I.

I read off the twenty names to him and bribed him with a token payment and the promise of a date with Dinah's cousin Joan. It was the second time I had used that bribe, but Michael has a tendency to forget anything he doesn't see on a screen. The bottom line is that Michael has more fun breaking into other people's files than most people have in bed.

The next call went to Virginia Savarin. Before I started dragging the city for traces of David's murderer, I had better make sure that Thomas Emerson, a.k.a. Pooley, was not the real thing. Last thing I wanted was to give Tony or Zack the opportunity to accuse me of knee-jerk liberalism. I made plans to meet Virginia at noon.

Glancing at the paper again, I decided to do a background check on Hyung Kim, the custodian who pegged Emerson as the murderer. I put in a call to Master Janet Choi, my regular Tae-kwon-do instructor. In her soft, singsong voice, she asked, "Master Rhee told me about your session. Don't tell me you're calling to quit."

Rhee may have been a hard ass, but he was a good instructor. I assured Choi of my commitment, then filled her in on my case. She expressed concern, then began probing. I didn't resist. Choi has an almost magical clarity of vision. A number of times in the past, we've met after class for heart-to-heart discussions about some of my more difficult cases. Each time, she had helped me to unravel the intertwining threads. So now I readily detailed the events in the Ross murder. Finally, I asked her to check up on Kim.

"This is no small favor you ask," she said quietly. "This is no small murder."

She sighed and hung up without another word. I knew that meant she would do whatever it took to get the information I needed.

I finished up some paperwork, hung up on my ex-publisher twice (it was becoming a weekly ritual), then put in a call to Zack McGinn. As expected, he was in the field. I left a message and headed out for my appointment with Virginia.

I arrived a few minutes early. Time is precious, as my good partner always says, so I decided to not waste mine. I marched in the direction of David Ross's classroom.

As I had suspected, the school's overcrowding was too critical to allow the room to remain roped off. The police lines were down and the door open. Luckily, it was lunchtime and the room was empty. I stepped inside, shuddering reflexively. The desk had been removed, but the stains remained. I walked slowly.

Apparently, there hadn't been much bloodshed. A splattering below the blackboard, on the scuffed wooden planks around the desk. I knelt down for a closer look. I didn't have enough experience to read the stains the way a veteran detective could, but something struck me as odd. A few perfect circles of blood.

Smaller than the tip of a cue stick. Five perfect dots headed toward the door. I searched for similar markings and found none. I made a couple of notes, then headed toward Virginia's office.

The room was twelve by twelve, with one heavily-armed window and torn-out Sierra calendar pages tacked to the walls. Three puke-gray metal desks were crammed into odd angles so that the chairs could move in and out without slamming into either a wall or another desk.

We dragged two chairs into the center and faced each other dead on. It wasn't a real friendly arrangement. She stared at me, waiting for me to start, her arms planted on the sides of the chair. I was in therapy for almost a year after my ex-lover's death, so I knew the technique. I had even borrowed it for my detective work. I met her gaze and waited for her to break. I was granite. Mount Rushmore would get up and walk before I talked.

"I guess I should explain why I'm here."

Okay, I broke first. But I wasn't about to lay my cards on the table. Tony had taught me that. Always hold back. Pretend to know less than you do.

"I'm investigating David Ross's death. I've already talked to Kim, and frankly, his testimony doesn't impress me." What was happening to me? I was actually telling this woman the truth!

"You want to know if Emerson could have killed Ross?" She started swiveling from side to side in her chair.

I nodded. She looked relieved, which made me worry. I was on the wrong track here. She had expected a different line of questioning. "I've worked with Thomas for several years. Without doubt, he's a troubled boy." She stood up, crossed the room, and opened a file drawer. She had a nice butt. One of my favorite anatomical features.

She sat back down opposite me. "Well, most of this information is confidential. All I can tell you is his mother's name and phone number. If you get permission from her, I'll be happy to review the file with you." She took out a piece of paper, jotted down the information, and handed it to me. In her opinion, that concluded our conversation.

"Look. I could use your help here. I think this kid is being railroaded and I don't know why. You could save me a lot of time by just…"

"Violating my professional integrity? Surely, Tennessee mentioned that my husband's on the police force?" Her Southern accent thickened. "As a private eye, who no doubt spends plenty of time with the more tawdry segments of our society…" She pronounced every syllable in "society." Despite myself, I found it endearing. Brooklyn kids like me are used to hearing words slurred. "… you are probably used to people who feel no compunctions about breaking a rule or two." She rose and walked to the door. "I, on the other hand, still find a modicum of self-respect in being able to tell you, and others like you, that I still play by those rules." She was waiting for me to leave, but I liked hearing her talk.

"The day David Ross was killed," I started, "I saw you comforting him in his classroom. He sounded pretty distraught."

Her nose flared. Got ya, I almost shouted. She closed the door. "Are you trying to tell me that you were spying on us *before* David was killed?"

"Us?"

She realized her error and rushed past it. "Will you tell me *why* you were following innocent people that had done nobody harm?" Unexpectedly, she lifted her hands in astonishment, as if her own words had just sunk in. "You were actually slinking around here, watching us?" A shiver ran down her body. I followed it with my eyes. The woman really was appalled. Or else she was just a good actress.

"Why was David so upset?" I persisted.

"I have no intention of standing here and answering your questions…"

"Then sit down."

"My husband…"

"Is a police officer. I know. That doesn't intimidate me. A lot of my good friends are cops." At least one was. "If he's a good cop, he knows how important it is to disclose any information pertinent to a murder. That's the bottom line here. You don't have to talk to me. But once I tell the police what I saw, you will have to talk to them. So make your choice." I've used this dare a dozen times. It never fails.

Her smooth cheeks flushed with indignation. "Why, Miss Miller, I believe I will take my chances with the recognized law enforcement in this state. That is, if they bother to listen to anything you have to say." She called my bluff. The cops wouldn't care two diddley-squats about colleagues talking together in an empty classroom about God knows what–especially when the information source was an apprentice PI.

If they ever make *Gone with the Wind III*, Virginia Savarin will be my first choice for the lead role. In less than fifteen minutes, the woman had tarnished my lifelong fantasy of yielding, blossom-scented Southern belles. I was sorely disappointed and only somewhat aroused.

I was heading for the basement exit when I sniffed the distinct musk of meat loaf and mashed potatoes. After breaking up with Cathy, sublimating my sexual urges with comfort food had become a favorite pastime. I immersed myself in the fork-and-knife clanging of the student/teacher cafeteria and checked out the display. The food looked better than the T.V. dinners I had been consuming lately. I passed myself off as a sub and walked away with a tray loaded with items that carried me back to a not-so-pleasant childhood.

"The jello's not so bad. Not half as bad as the meat loaf, in any case." I glanced up at a woman with coal-black, shoulder-length hair swept to one side. The sultry, thick waves almost covered her left eye. She gestured to the seat next to her. "You were looking at your food with a measure of distaste. I thought you could use some encouragement. C'mon, sit down."

I slipped into a lie and the chair at the same time. "Thanks. Subbing is tough work."

"Who are you subbing for?"

I was dumbfounded. "You know, I can't remember the guy's name."

A balding man on the opposite side of the table jumped in. "Must be Ross's class. Damn shame, that was. Emerson was a handful, but who would have thought the child was capable of cold-blooded murder? I've heard the kids say it was a drug deal gone sour. Now that wouldn't surprise me. Ross always seemed so edgy. Liked the man, but never trusted him." The woman's smile dropped off her face like an avalanche. She rushed out of the cafeteria, wailing uncontrollably.

A warning signal went off in my head.

Throw a black fishnet veil over her face, add some art-nouveau funeral wear, and you'd be looking at the woman Marion Ross had snubbed at David's funeral.

The meat loaf suddenly smelled like filet mignon.

Chapter 6

I found her in the bathroom, mascara running down her cheeks like clown makeup. She was wiping her nose with toilet paper when I walked in. "Sorry. I'm okay. Really," she said, waving me away.

Automatically, my hand swept her hair away back from her face. Feature by feature, she wasn't much to look at. But something about her eyes and the set of her mouth was deeply sensual. Right now, she reminded me of a woman who had spent a night dancing in the sheets, her skin flushed, her breath escaping in small bursts.

"Shhh," I said, stroking her back.

"Oh God!" Her sobbing intensified. She snuggled against me, wrapping her arms around my waist. I hadn't been that close to a woman in six months. Not since Cathy. My luck, they both wore the same perfume. I recognized it immediately. Passion.

It was time to get back to business. I drew back and asked,

"Was this guy Ross your boyfriend?"

She snorted into the same piece of toilet paper. "No, no. David was just a wonderful, kind man. My brother is...was his best friend. Jesus!" More wailing. This time I waited for her to stop on her own. "I don't know how he's going to..." She darted into a stall for more tissues. When I turned around, she was sitting on the toilet, blowing her nose again.

"You were talking about your brother," I prompted her.

"Yeah. Poor Joey." She opened her purse, pulled out a compact, and snapped open a mirror. "God, I'm a mess." Just then, an elderly woman walked in. I must have looked pretty weird, standing there staring into the stall while the occupant was moaning. The woman backed right out. My friend was still on the john, fixing her face. She seemed a lot calmer. "David didn't deserve this." She was talking more to the mirror than to me.

"How'd he die?"

She looked at me over the mirror, truly focusing on me for the first time. "You know, I don't even know your name."

"It's Robin."

She cocked her head, looking suddenly confused. "You were at the funeral."

Uh-oh. How do I get out of this one? I shook my head.

"No. You were there. I saw you. You were in a beat-up Plymouth Duster, driving right behind Ginny and her brother."

Now, I was getting mad. No one talks about Bella that way. "The car's not beat-up."

"What? I don't care about the car. What the hell are you doing here?"

"I was visiting Virginia."

"No one calls her Virginia."

"I do."

She rammed a battery of questions at me. Why had I pretended to not know about David's death? How come Ginny hadn't joined me for lunch? Why did I say I was a sub? She finally exhausted my previously boundless capacity for deception.

"All right. Back off. I'm a private investigator checking into David Ross's death."

She narrowed her eyes. "Why don't you try the truth?"

"Okay. I'm the Emersons' lawyer," I said. "Pro bono. This is a high-profile case. I figure if I can prove Thomas innocent, my career will be made."

"Finally." She glanced in the mirror and then grabbed my elbow. "Let's go for a walk."

I spent the next twenty minutes circling the block at breakneck speed. Terry Fasani spewed information in the same way she sobbed. Like a machine gun. Thomas Emerson was certainly innocent. The boy had been a top student until his brother's death last year. Since then, he had withdrawn. Started fighting with other kids. Just five months ago, a gang jumped him outside his building, pumped a lighter up like a torch and held it to his cheek. Soon after that, he started carrying the lead pipe with him.

If she was trying to convince me that Thomas was innocent, she was doing a lousy job. I told her just that.

"I can't help what preconceptions you may have about black teenagers. All I can say is that Thomas wouldn't kill anyone."

I started to defend myself against her accusation, but decided to let it pass. "So who do you think killed David?"

She stopped and stared at me with disbelief. "Take a look around here, will you? We are surrounded by crack houses, squatters who can't think beyond the next hit, gang wars, and God knows what else. Murder is commonplace in this neighborhood. Anyone could have killed David. But not Thomas."

I watched her scramble up the front steps. Stretching down from a hip-hugging paisley skirt were well-defined calves. She wore a thin gold chain around a bony ankle, and the kind of high-heeled shoes that could double as lethal weapons. She wasn't my type, but without question my hormones had kicked in. Must be premenstrual, I thought. PMS makes me as horny as hell.

"Hey, Terry," I shouted at her back. She turned around, her

hair and her too-close-to-sheer blouse billowing in the breeze. I climbed up after her. "I'm on your side. Cross my heart. If Thomas is really innocent, I may be his only out. But you have to help me. You have access to information I can't get."

"I really don't want to get involved in this."

"You owe it to Thomas." That didn't seem to move her much. "You owe it to your brother." Bingo. Her eyes snapped. "You said David saved your brother's life. The least you can do is to make sure that whoever took David's life doesn't get off scot-free. And that's exactly what will happen if you let them convict Thomas."

Somewhere along the line I had lost her. Maybe it happened when the wind changed direction, her blouse shifted, and my eyes unexpectedly discovered her undeniable cleavage. In any case, her face shadowed with doubt. "I've told you all I know. The rest of it is up to you," she said.

"At least take my card. In case you change your mind."

The card disappeared from my hand.

So far, I wasn't having a very good day. And it was about to get worse. The Emerson family lived in one of the city's worst housing projects. Barruda Gardens. Better known as Barracuda Houses. The kind where the gunfire sounds like the Jolly Green Giant's popcorn machine gone haywire.

I grew up in the projects in Coney Island, before they had really earned their reputation for violence. Even so, I have vivid memories of dimly lit corridors and elevators where you could end up pinned to a corner like a bug in a roach trap, the tip of a knife tucked under your chin.

I've done lots of stupid things in my life. But walking alone into Barracuda Houses was not one of them. I stopped at a pay phone and dialed Curtis Taylor. The grunt on the other end told me that getting Curtis out of bed after a long night of bartending was not going to be easy.

"Morning, handsome."

"Who the fuck is this?" Curtis didn't mince words. It was hard to imagine this ex-football star with the body of Adonis dressed up as Betty Davis. But that's exactly how we met. Curtis l... ... next door to me while I was attending the University of Virginia. One night his stove caught on fire while he was practicing a scene from *What Ever Happened To Baby Jane?* I smelled the smoke and pounded on his door till he finally opened it and I fell into his hairy arms. He looked at me through the longest false eyelashes and said, "My food wouldn't be burning if I were a real femme." And I replied in my best Betty Davis voice, "But you *are* Blanche, you are."

So now I said, "It's Jane, dahling."

"Ah dammit, don't you have any decency? I was working at Scarlet's till four o'clock in the morning."

"I need your help, Blanche."

"Bad timing. My head's pounding from that damn disco music."

"So get a real job."

"Thanks for the advice. If I didn't own the place, I'd think about it." Curtis inherited the bar when an ex-lover died last year. Just two months before that, he had lost a cushy job with an investment firm. He was still struggling to make the transition from Wall Street to Christopher Street.

"So what do you want?" he asked, inhaling what was probably his first cigarette of the day. His voice was raspy.

I explained my situation. Before I had gone too far, he stopped me. Curtis had seen the papers. He didn't want another project kid going down in flames any more than I did. Probably more so. We may have both grown up in the projects, but Curtis had to fight a lot harder than I did to get out.

"You've done it again, Jane," he said. "Give me two hours."

"Thanks."

He grumbled something under his breath. Something about crazy white women.

"And Blanche, dear," I said, smiling. "Don't wear the red dress."

At first glance, the project didn't look so bad. There was a small fenced-in garden and a primary-color playground equipped with a slide, jungle gym and swing. It was just after three, so a few kids had already reached home. I paused to watch two small girls do "choosies," pitching one or two fingers to decide who got the swing first. Curtis gave me a little push toward the Emersons' building. I started wondering if Barruda Gardens was as bad as the press says when something shattered under my foot. I looked down. A crack vial.

"Hey Jane. I don't want to stand around here with a white girl for a single second longer than I have to. So move it."

The Emersons' apartment was on the sixth floor. Curtis and I stood at the elevator, perspiration beading up on our brows. I was about to break the tension with a joke, but Curtis lanced me with a sharp stare. It suddenly struck me that he was more nervous than I was. Great. Then I saw what was making him so edgy. Down the corridor, in the shadows, two guys were watching us intently. I couldn't see their eyes. I checked the ceiling. Two of three bulbs were broken. Recently. The glass was still on the floor.

Curtis put his hand on the elevator door. "Shit." He looked at me, a warning in his voice. "I don't think it's working." The stairwell was about two feet away from our friends down the hall. "Let's get out of here."

"I need to talk to Emerson and his mother."

"Not today, you don't. This is a set-up. We go into that staircase, we're not…"

"The elevator's outta orda." It was one of the goons. "Betta take the stairs." His friend laughed.

Curtis grabbed my arm and started moving me toward the entrance. Our two friends stepped in our direction. They were both wearing black leather jackets, green T-shirts, torn jeans and high-top sneakers with the laces untied. The Bobbsey twins from hell. Only difference between the two was that the guy on the left had a small gold ring through his right nostril. "Whatsa matta? You don't like the stairs?" They moved around the corner with the swiftness of jaguars and cut off our path to the entrance. "Who you here for?"

I felt Curtis stiffen. He tilted his head at me. "I bring her here to make a deal." Oh, great. Now Curtis was going to pretend to be some tough, drug-dealing dude. Up to now, the toughest part he had ever played was Joan Crawford.

"What kinda deal?" The leather twins were so close, I could smell their hot, sour breath.

"What do you think, man?"

The one with the ringed nostril flipped out a blade. "I think maybe I'm gonna cut you ass. What do you think?"

There was no time to think. I executed a turning kick to the guy's stomach. He crashed against the front door. I saw his friend reaching into a pocket, and at the same time felt Curtis yank my arm. He was running toward the stairs, our only way out. I tore after him.

"Fucking crazy," Curtis was screaming at me on the way up. "Next time, call someone else."

"Shut up and move your ass!" I heard the door downstairs slam shut. There were two pairs of footsteps slamming up the steps. I ran up to Curtis's back. "Dammit. Move."

He picked up speed, cursing. "I gave up football because of a bad knee. It's going to give, I know it."

I was next to him now, urging him on. "C'mon, Curtis." I could hear the demon boys just a flight below. They were talking a language I could barely understand. But I got the important part. They were going to skin us like rabbits.

"Where the hell are we running?" Curtis finally spat out.

Good point. Project buildings don't have fire escapes. If we made it to the roof, I had a feeling we'd soon find out exactly how Icarus felt when his wings melted. I imagined us careening down to the concrete. Not a pretty picture.

I pulled ahead of Curtis and hit the fifth-floor landing, my lungs burning. I swung open the door, Curtis on my heels. No time for talking now. I just hoped he'd follow me. I ran down the hall, praying this building was similar to the one I grew up in. I was in luck. There was a second staircase. I darted inside, noticing that the boys had just exited onto the floor.

"Now, Curtis!" I headed upstairs. I saw a flash of puzzlement in his eyes, but he followed me anyway. Bless his trusting soul. We reached the sixth floor in record time, and then I stopped, easing the door shut behind me just as I heard the door below us open. I crossed my fingers. Let them head downstairs.

"Find six-A. Now." My whisper was tight. If the Emersons weren't home…

"Here." I ran after Curtis and started pounding on the door. No answer. Damn. Those goons would be back this way any minute. "Please open up! It's a matter of life and death."

Curtis joined me, banging on the door with his baseball-sized fist. Suddenly he stopped. "They're not home, Robin." His eyes were sad. Resigned.

In the distance, I could hear the sound of feet stomping on the stairs. They were headed up.

Chapter 7

A door to our left opened. "Quick. In here."

Curtis and I didn't have to be invited twice. We darted into the apartment next door. "Shhh. I don't want them knowing where you run to." At the moment, I thought our rescuer was the most beautiful woman I had ever seen. She was at least sixty, with short-cropped hair the color of moonlight caught behind clouds. She had smooth, mahogany skin and deep brown eyes.

All at once, I heard the bastards pounding down the hall. My breathing turned ragged again. I searched for Curtis. He was off to my left, leaning over the kitchen sink and looking like he was about to puke. I edged away from the door.

The woman turned around and shook her head at me, one long commanding finger tapping her mouth. I got the message. The only sounds in the apartment were the refrigerator's hum and a low moan from Curtis. We stood in the same positions for what seemed like hours. Then, finally, the voices faded away.

"You two be one sorry sight." She lowered Curtis into a chrome and red plastic kitchen chair that had to date back to the fifties. I watched as she poured two tall glasses of iced tea. Her hands were steady. Mine were still shaking. "Want to tell me what that was all about?" she asked, handing each of us a glass.

Curtis was downing his tea, pointing at me. I told her the truth. She stepped closer. "You really want to help Thomas?"

"If he's innocent. Yes."

She nodded, then led me back into the living room. The room was rectangular, with windows on the far side and cutouts leading to the kitchen. A narrow foyer on the left led back to the bedrooms. The layout reminded me of the apartment I had grown up in. If I wandered down the hall and into the master bedroom I was sure I'd find the closet in which I had killed my sister. My hands began to tremble again.

"C'mon, honey," the woman said softly. "Sit down. By the way, I'm Clara."

I told her our names, dropping into a brown corduroy couch bearing the thickest cushions my tush had ever encountered. I closed my eyes. Someone sat down next to me. It was Curtis. His color had returned to normal. "Let's make this quick. I'd like to get out of here before sunset," he said.

"Sunset don't make a difference. It's dangerous night and day." Clara was sitting opposite us in a tan recliner. Above her was an elaborately framed family portrait. I recognized Clara as a young girl, holding desperately onto the folds of her mother's thick skirt. Now she rubbed her index finger over the side of her nose and said, "I've been here twenty years…and this is the worst. It's like everyone just gave up. There are good folks living here. But you wouldn't know it. They all so scared, they live behind locked doors. Like me. I used to sit outside warm summer days, listening to the radio. No more. If I leave here, I get on a bus and go somewhere else. It's got so bad, I'm afraid to sit by my window catching a breeze. 'Fraid a bullet's going to get me this time." She seemed lost in thought.

"Are the Emersons good folk?"

She smiled at me. "Some's good. Some's not. Martha's a fine woman. A nurse at Kings County. But she's got her hands full. Her husband died back in 'eighty-six. Drug overdose. She's had one boyfriend since then. Bastard beat her and the kids. But Martha's no fool. She got rid of him quick. She's done real good with the kids. Best as she could. Still, she couldn't save Gordy. Gordy's the one that got killed last year. She was real broke up. The boy was…" Her eyes misted over. "Gordy was a real charmer. A seven-year-old charmer. Bright as wildfire, and just as hard to keep still. Martha got real depressed after that. Started staying home, laying in bed, drinking bad booze and crying for days. Must have been three months before she pulled herself together. I'd like to think I helped. But by then, the other boys were drifting bad." She paused, then continued.

"Clay's the real problem. Just fourteen years old, but he thinks the world's out to get him. I actually seen him slap his mother. He hangs out now with the same gang that killed Gordy. Don't understand that. Met him in the elevator one day last summer and he flashes this wallet at me. 'Got it off a white kid in the city,' he says all proud to me. Well, I gave him the back of my hand without thinking twice. Martha thanked me. Not that it made any difference. 'Cept, Clay don't talk to me anymore."

"What about Thomas?" Curtis was getting antsy, bouncing his leg up and down like a rabbit with a bad itch.

Clara directed her answer to me. "Thomas is a good boy. He's had it hard. But he's good. I twisted my ankle this winter. Couldn't get out to buy myself food. Thomas took it upon himself to do my shopping. Boy bought all the wrong things, like frozen pizza," she said, smiling. "I asked him to buy me some pita, you know, the flat bread? So he buys me pizza." She laughed, her affection for Thomas clear in her eyes. Then, abruptly, her gaze clouded over. "But the gangs pegged him. Seems sometimes they got more hate in them to a boy like Thomas than they do to anyone. It's like they know he can make it out. Do something good. And it makes them mad. The past few months, the boy's got downright sullen. But not mean."

"He's been carrying a lead pipe with him."

She looked at me hard. "You almost got killed in this building. If you had to come and go from here every day, what would you be carrying?"

Curtis jumped in. "A goddamn grenade launcher. Now, can we get going?"

"He's probably right, chile. This here is no place for the likes of you two." Clara walked back to the bedrooms. Curtis and I exchanged glances. When she came back, she had a thirty eight Smith & Wesson in her strong hands. I shuddered involuntarily. Her sharp eyes didn't miss a trick. "I never fired this. Never want to. Clay give it to me before we stopped talking. You better take it with you." I started to object, but Curtis went right up to her and started asking questions about the safety pin.

"Curtis!"

The look he gave me was one I had never seen on his face before. "I know how you feel about guns, Robin. Right now, I don't care. You got problems with this, go back to therapy. The only thing that matters to me is getting out of here with all my pretty, red blood still in my veins. Do you understand?"

I understood more than he realized. If just a few hours in this place could make one of the gentlest men I know pick up a thirty eight and plan to use it, what effect could living here day after day have on a young boy who had already had the threat of the projects burned into the very skin on his face? I was more determined than ever to prove Thomas Emerson innocent. I handed Clara my business card and asked her to urge the Emersons to contact me as soon as they could. Then we went out into the hall, my heart beating so fast I hardly heard Clara praying as she bolted her door behind us.

We opened the staircase door and listened. Then we headed down, taking one step at a time, pausing at every landing to take a breath and wait for sounds. Curtis and I didn't talk. We reached the first floor and sighed. "We're almost home," Curtis mumbled more to himself than me.

Then the door opened. "We was wondering when you'd show up." The bastards had waited for us.

Curtis pulled the gun up. The goons' eyes went wide. "Move your asses into the corner." His voice had a hard edge to it. I put my hand on his back. He shrugged me off, cursing. "Back off, Robin." Then to the boys, "Strip." I could feel the fire ripping through Curtis. His rage scared me. So did the way he was playing with the trigger. He wanted to shoot.

The leather boys were spitting warnings. "Gonna get you ass for this, man. No nigger gets away with dissing the Razor. You pork out on us, we gonna buck you one day. My posse gonna buck you."

The muzzle of the gun never wavered. When the boys were butt-naked, their blades and clothes thrown in a pile at our feet, Curtis called me over. "Pick their stuff up."

"Gonna buck the white broad, too. Gonna fuck her first, then we gonna…"

Curtis moved closer. He towered over them by a good two feet. Looking at them naked, I realized that they really were just boys. Horribly twisted boys. They couldn't be more than fifteen. Curtis put the cold metal against the temple of the boy that called himself Razor. "Feel that," he said in a tight voice. "Feel that." The kid tried to narrow his eyes into a tough street look. It didn't work. The fear kept them wide open. "One day someone's going to pull the trigger. Pop!" The kid jumped. "And it's going to be all over. That's it for your goddamn, stupid life. You'll be seventeen, eighteen tops. And that's it. All your tough talk and all your drug money gonna mean shit. You're going to be lying in the gutter, with bugs chewing on your dumb ass. And your posse won't even remember you were ever alive."

"Curtis." I wanted to be out of there. I wanted to see Curtis wearing a red gown and high heels and laughing.

"You got the stuff?" he asked over his shoulder, his eyes still boring into Razor's.

"I got it. Let's go. I need to see Blanche, real bad. Please." My voice cracked.

He nodded, my words getting through the rage. "Me too, Jane."

We backed out and ran toward our cars. When we got there, I dropped their clothes into a garbage can.

"Burn them."

"Curtis, I..."

"Just burn them."

"I don't have a match."

Curtis cursed again. He pulled out a disposable lighter then he lit the clothes. "I'm going home, Robin. Don't call me for a while." He turned on his heels and headed for his car at a fast clip, but not so fast that I couldn't hear the sobs beginning to break from his body.

I got home around six and downed two bottles of Yoo-Hoo. Some people turn to booze, I turn to junk food. I rummaged through my refrigerator for a lost package of Twinkies, then retrieved a bag of taco chips tucked behind a stack of Nine Lives, and headed for the living room, the cats hot on my heels. Luckily my metabolism keeps me thin, otherwise, after a few days like today, I'd end up a small, dark-haired blimp.

There was a knock on the door. "Is it safe to come in?"

"Sure."

Dinah and Beth stepped in gingerly. They were a striking couple. Dinah is a stocky five-six, with dark curly hair, green eyes and olive skin. Aside from our body types, we could pass for sisters. Beth, on the other hand, is my height, shaped like a pretzel stick, with spiky blonde hair and caring blue eyes.

"Uh-oh. She's junking out," Beth said with mock horror. "Maybe we should leave."

"Naw. We're just what she needs. A therapist for her head and a nurse for her body."

Despite my foul mood, I smiled. "Are you guys going to sit

down?"

Dinah folded herself into my favorite chair. "Twinkies and taco chips. Must have been a really good day." She looked at her watch. "You have forty-five minutes before my next client shows." Beth sat on the arm next to her.

I hadn't seen them since last Friday. I started to bring them up to date, but Beth interrupted me before I could get too far. "Wait. You mean you actually met K.T. Bellflower?"

Dinah laughed. "I don't think that was her point, honey."

"But K.T. is terrific." She feinted a punch from Dinah.

"Beth's got a crush on her," Dinah explained. "She tapes the show every day and drools over her while I'm busy saving the pained and weary every night." They kissed. After four years, you'd think the honeymoon would be over. I started to regret my decision to let them in. "Matter of fact," Dinah continued, "I'd think K.T. was right up your alley. Blonde hair, Southern accent, great body, tremendous cook…" Dinah smirked. "What's wrong with her? Did she seem too available?"

Anger kicked in. This was one of Dinah's favorite subjects. She insisted that I was only attracted to women who were inaccessible or dangerous.

"You have junk-food taste in women, Miller. If it doesn't look like it's going to give you indigestion, you shy away. It's time…"

I stood up. "I don't want a lecture from you today."

Beth headed to the door. "I have a roast beef waiting for me." Beth doesn't like conflicts. She slipped downstairs.

"Robin, look at what happened with Cathy." Dinah was using her therapist tone on me now, her eyebrows lifted in that I-care look that drives me nuts. "You were wild for her, but only as long as she kept playing push and pull with you. Once she started to get serious, you panicked. You deserve…"

"I deserve some peace and quiet." Dinah was going to tell me I deserve better. I must hear that from her once a week. She acts like I purposely pick ice queens or women on the edge of emotional disaster. I can't control where my libido leads me.

"Fine. I'm sorry. Why don't you finish telling me about this case?" Dinah's face was expressionless. Sometimes that was worse than the I-care look. I threw myself on the couch, noticing that Geeja and Mallomar were observing the whole scene from their respective window sills. They looked annoyed with me.

I finished recapping the case, feeling pretty damn contrite by the time I ended. Dinah brought me another Yoo-Hoo from the kitchen, kissed my forehead the way my mom used to do every night before my sister's death, and then left me alone with my cats.

The room suddenly felt unbearably cold.

I closed my eyes and instantly I was four years old again, caught in the bedroom I had shared with my older sister Barbara. It was one year after Carol died. July 4, 1963. Ronald was just two months old. The kids in the neighborhood were blowing up M-80s in garbage cans. The explosions rattled the windows. I broke into a sweat, the vision of Carol's bloody chest swelling before my eyes like a nuclear mushroom. In the other room, Ronald began to wail. Through the thin walls, I could hear my mother crooning to him. You are my sunshine, she sang softly. My body shook so hard, the metal joints of the high-riser bed started to whine.

For months after Carol's death, I woke screaming from nightmares. The first few times, Barbara would crawl into bed with me and hold me. But then my parents made her sleep on the couch until I learned to bear the nightmares silently. So that night, when the dark, summer air detonated around me and the bile shot into my throat, and my hands and feet started to feel like ice laced with needles, I bit my lip till I tasted blood, till the shivering stopped.

Even now, crying shakes me to the core.

The peal of the phone brought me back home. I jumped to answer it, suddenly hoping that Beth was calling to invite me to dinner. I snatched up the phone. It was Marion Ross. She wanted an update. I shifted mental gears and filled her in.

"That's it? That's all you've done?" Her voice shot up two octaves. "I expected some progress."

I started to smell smoke. For a second, I wondered if Marion's high-pitched squawk was burning the phone wires. Then I remembered that I had a cordless phone.

"Marion, I've only had one day. I have to start by making sure Thomas Emerson is innocent."

She didn't want to hear it. "I want more than that. Let Reverend Whaley and the press prove that Emerson is innocent all on their own. I want you to concentrate on what really happened."

"I am. But you haven't been real helpful. I have no leads."

"Am I paying you so that I can do the work?" She sounded so wound up her springs had to be close to breaking.

I ignored her question and fired one of my own. "Did David ever talk to you about paying off a cruiser?"

"Excuse me?" I had a feeling she knew exactly what I was talking about.

"A beat cop."

The line went dead quiet. Then abruptly she said, "Of course not."

I didn't believe her.

"Ms. Miller," she continued. "Apparently, you've forgotten our roles. I'm not here to answer your questions. You're here to answer mine—"

I heard fire engines in the distance. "Marion, can you hang on?" I scooted to the front windows, lifted up the screen, and stuck my head out. "Christ, not again."

There was an interrupt on the line. I pressed the flash button. A woman's voice sang into my ear. "It's Terry Fasani. Can I speak to Robin Miller?"

Terry Fasani? Then I remembered. The curvaceous woman from David's school who couldn't believe I was a private eye. I bumped my head against the screen on the way back in. "It's me. Can I call you back? I have someone else on the line."

"No problem." She hesitated. "Is that a fire engine?"

I explained that some punk had been setting fires to cars in the neighborhood for the last three weeks. Tonight, Bella was just two cars away from the blaze. I took Terry's number down and switched back to Marion.

"If this is the way you treat clients, I'm not surprised Mr. Serra has doubts about your capabilities."

After the day I'd had, I wanted more than anything to tell Ms. Ross to stuff her six-pronged candelabra where the sun don't shine. Instead, I calmly explained to her that there was a distinct possibility that my beloved car was about to be blown to smithereens. She didn't care.

"Find out what was making David so miserable before he died. That's what I'm paying you for."

"I thought you were paying me to find out who killed him?"

But maybe she already knew who that was?

"I know exactly what I am paying for." I heard her swallow on the other end. More booze? "And it's not for you to go slumming in the projects to satisfy some liberal do-gooder impulse. My husband was in trouble. I want to know the how, what, where, and most importantly, the who. Can you do that?"

I crossed my eyes at Geeja, who was assertively stretching a front leg in my direction. I was afraid she was trying to tell me that Bella was doomed. I answered Marion in the affirmative.

"Good. Now, when can I expect results?" She sounded like she was ordering Chinese food. I started to answer, but there was another interrupt. I hesitated, wondering for a second if I shouldn't just toss the phone into the burning car. I decided to take the call, apologizing to Marion who hung up before I could finish.

I recognized the voice on the other end immediately. "What can I do for you, Virginia?" The background noises made it sound like she was in the middle of a party.

"Today's my birthday."

"Happy birthday." I moved Geeja off the sill and stuck my

head back outside. The flames were almost out. Bella was safe.

"What's that sound?"

"Water. Some firemen are dousing the flames on what used to be a station wagon. It's a new neighborhood fad. Do you have any other news for me besides the birthday flash?"

"I saw Thomas and his mother today. After school. I just wanted to tell you that he swears he didn't do it."

"Thanks. I guess that solves everything."

"Tennessee said you tend to be sarcastic."

"Is T.B. there?"

"He just arrived a few minutes ago with K.T. By the way, she asked me to invite you to a dinner party she's giving Saturday night."

My stomach kicked. "I may be busy, but give me the information anyway." I had planned to spend Saturday night the usual way. Rent a video, order Chinese and buy two pints of Haagen Daaz vanilla ice cream. But my hot plans didn't stop me from writing down the address.

"One last thing." She must have moved into another room because all the background noises abruptly disappeared. "Thomas said a friend of his saw a man and a woman heading up to David's room after three o'clock. He wouldn't tell me more than that. The poor boy was terribly shaken. His mother wasn't doing much better. I know you've tried to contact them. My professional opinion is that you should just leave them be. Pressing them won't help anyone."

My suspicion shifted into high gear. I had the sense she was holding something back. "He didn't tell you his friend's name?" I asked.

"No."

"Did the friend recognize the couple?"

A deep breath. "No."

"What about the guard...what's her name?" The name badge flashed before me. "Juanita Morales. Maybe she'll remember this couple entering the school."

"I thought the same thing. Juanita said that whoever it was didn't come in the front entrance. At least, not while she was on duty."

"You sure?"

The party sounds returned. Plus a male voice telling her to come say hello to some guests. It wasn't a voice you'd ignore. "I have to go now. Sorry to interrupt your evening. Hope I've helped some."

Her Southern accent had thickened as she became more distressed. By the end of our conversation, her voice was practically sashaying around her words. One thing was certain. The woman knew a lot more than she had told me. But what was she hiding?

Then I remembered the look in her eyes last Friday as her hand rested on David's shoulder. The tenderness with which her thumb drew a circle into a knot of muscles.

With a sudden conviction, I would have bet a year's worth of royalty checks that Virginia Savarin had been in love with David Ross.

Chapter 8

My mind was still connecting the dots between Virginia, David Ross, and T.B.'s lost bullet as I dialed Terry's number. I wasn't happy with the way the picture was turning out.

Terry answered on the third ring. She was on her way to some gym in Bay Ridge called the Body Shop. She asked me to meet her there at eight. Considering the nutritional value of my dinner and the fact that the Stairmaster in my basement was shrouded in spider webs, a workout wasn't a bad way to end the night. Neither was the sight of Terry Fasani in tight biker pants.

I changed into sweats, poured the cats some dry fish-shaped food, then slipped into Bella and drove toward Eighty-Sixth Street and Fourth Avenue, the pizza capital of the world. I was hoping to squeeze a slice in, but Terry was standing outside the gym when I got there. The first thing she said was, "You really are a PI." She was holding my business card.

She was sexy and she could read. Not a bad combination at

all. As we headed toward the locker room, I gave her a synopsis of my detective career to date.

She looked impressed. "When I realized you were serious about being an investigator, I was shocked." I watched her spin the wheel on the combination lock. She had great fingers. "I never met a real PI before." She tossed me a sultry smile. "It's kind of exciting."

Maybe today wouldn't be a total loss.

She pulled out a canvas bag and began rummaging through it. Then she stood up and pulled off her top. Uh-oh. My eyes shot across the room to the water fountain.

"I was pretty rude to you earlier. I'm sorry about that," she said, touching my arm. I brought my eyes back to her face. At least I tried to. She had designer tits. Just a soft handful, with erect brown nipples. I prefer pink, but brown was more than acceptable. I felt myself get wet.

She shimmied out of her jeans. Her legs were muscular, her stomach so flat and hard I could have used her abdomen as an ironing board. Which is not what I had in mind.

"You okay?" she asked.

A tiny curl of black pubic hair peeked out of the top of her black bikini underpants.

I raised my eyes. Terry was pulling her hair back from her face. "I was asking you if you're single. This is a great place to meet guys, if you are. Much better than the damn super-spa they opened up around the corner."

"Look. I think I better tell you that I'm gay. So maybe I shouldn't be in here at all. Not right now. You know what I mean?" I was stammering.

She laughed. "I thought so." She lifted one heartbreaker leg onto the bench and started stretching. I was so excited, it hurt. "Don't worry about it. I have lots of gay friends."

"But you're not?" Please don't say no.

"No, I'm not." She straightened up and lifted her arms above her head. Her nipples were staring at me. "Not that I haven't

76

toyed with the idea. Before I got married…"

I winced.

"You didn't know I was married?" She sounded upset, as if she somehow expected me to know her marital status. I checked her hands. How'd I miss the ring?

"No. I didn't." I was almost whining.

She put her hands on her waist and started stretching to each side. Her breasts hardly bounced. I wondered if she noticed that my eyes were bobbing back and forth in time to her exercise.

"Sam just got back from the Gulf. It's been a hard adjustment for all of us. I've been spending most of my nights here. But Sam wants me home, cooking dinners, listening to his war stories." She smirked. "I guess you don't have to worry about those things."

No. I just have to worry about getting trapped in a locker room with a luscious straight woman with stand-at-attention nipples. She started doing pelvic thrusts.

There is no God, I moaned to myself.

"Maybe you should tell me why you called." I strained to make my voice sound controlled, professional. What I really wanted to do was whimper.

"Sorry." She finally slipped on a black midriff-length T-shirt and black biker pants. My relief was palpable. "Don't you want to stretch?" she asked me. Wrong question.

I shook my head and followed her out of the locker room. The gym was surprisingly quiet. Terry and I had our pick of the equipment. We started with the Life-Cycles. I climbed on and started pumping. I glanced down at the gauge. At this rate, I was going to melt the gears.

"It's about David," Terry started. "If you're serious about investigating his murder, then I want to make sure you're looking in the right directions. David was a great guy, but he wasn't a saint. Not by a long shot. My brother Joey says David was doing drugs. He's part-owner here so you may want to ask him about that…" She adjusted the resistance, glancing in my direction. "I like it hard." There was something about the way she said the words that told me she knew exactly what affect she was having on me. I pedaled faster.

"The balding guy at lunch today…" I began.

"Webster Bainbridge."

I repeated the name with raised eyebrows and she laughed.

"The gossip king of P.S. 189," she added.

"He said there was a rumor about a bad drug deal."

"Webster probably started the rumor. I wouldn't put much credence in what he says." She sounded disgusted. I figured she had been burned by Webster sometime in the past.

"But David was involved in drugs?"

"That's what Joey thinks."

"What does Joey think?" a tenor voice asked. I turned around. A thin, smooth-skinned man with well-developed pecks and Terry's sensual eyes was standing between us. Terry introduced him as her brother. She didn't have to. The resemblance was striking.

"So you're the investigator?" he asked in a tone that managed to be both delicate and gravelly at the same time.

I stopped pedaling. Joey was the guy at David Ross's funeral who had looked so familiar to me. I could feel my memory bank buzzing. The two of us had definitely met somewhere. I glanced down at his smooth calves, and suddenly thought about Scarlet's, the bar my friend Curtis owns. I raised my eyes to Joey's full lips. With instant certainty, I knew I had seen Joey there at least once. I made a mental note to call Curtis, then asked, "Was David involved with drugs?"

His mouth curled into an angry pout. The expression made his face look even more feminine. "Look, I don't know what Terry's been saying to you, but I won't have anything to do with sullying Dave's name. Terry's got it in her head that the kid they arrested…"

I started to give him the name, but he waved my words away. "I don't want to know who he is. All I know is the kid's no innocent. Okay? The custodian said this punk mugged his wife a few months back, so we're not talking about some wide-eyed boy with a bright future. The cops seem satisfied. That's enough for me."

"The kid is innocent, Joey."

He looked like he was struggling not to cry. "How do you know, huh? If that kid killed my best friend, I don't want to see a bunch of liberals get him off."

"Joey." Terry hopped off the bike and put her arms around him. He shook her off.

"Everything okay here?" A new voice broke in. I turned and found myself staring at a body builder from hell. I recognized him instantly. The mismatched midnight blue silk and hunter green polyester guy from the cemetery parking lot. Tonight, he was wearing a chartreuse T-shirt with a monogram over his chest. V.S. Up close, he was even more imposing. A redwood version of a human being.

Joey nodded. "Vic, this is Robin Miller. Private Investigator." Turning to me, he added, "Vic and I own this place. We've been dreaming about this since we were twelve, right Vic?"

The Hulk stepped around Joey and said, "You talk too much, Little Joe." He sounded like an indulgent father. The indulgence didn't extend to me, however. He looked at me as if he had just watched me eat roaches, then snarled, "You bothering my friends?"

"I'm just asking a few questions about David Ross. Did you know—"

"Ross was a punk. If it weren't for Little Joe, I'd never have let him come within a hundred yards of this place. Far as I'm concerned, Ross got what was coming to him. Case closed. You got more questions to ask, ask them somewhere else. This is my place, and I don't need no lady dick bothering my clients."

I smirked and pointedly scanned the room. Business wasn't exactly bustling. My look implied as much.

"What you trying to say?" Vic barked at me, his face reddening with anger.

"Not many clients to bother," I said. Something in his eyes told me I was pushing him to the edge. For some reason, I wanted him there. "So what did you have against David Ross?"

His lips curled in disgust. "The guy was a freeloader. Sponged money from Joey like he was a goddamn Rockefeller. Calling in some stupid 'Nam chit." He stopped suddenly. I sensed that he had said more than intended.

"Was David involved with drugs?"

"You think that's why someone offed him?" He smiled. "I like that." Christ. He really looked pleased.

"If you hated David, why'd you go to his funeral?"

I watched his hand ball into a fist. I took a step back.

"I know Joe since we were five. I went for him. You got a problem with that?" He looked like he wanted to slam my head against the Life Cycle.

Terry put her hand on Vic's arm. His biceps were twice the size of her palms.

"It's okay, Vic," Joey said protectively. "Let's get back to those books."

Vic glared at me, then turned and followed Joey toward the management office. Unexpectedly, Joey stopped and muttered something to Vic, who squeezed Joey's shoulder before striding away. Watching them, I wondered if their relationship was entirely platonic. I filed the thought for later.

Joey walked back to me and asked, "Tell me why you think the black kid's innocent." It was almost a dare. But there was something else behind his eyes that I couldn't read. He was really troubled. I had the feeling he wanted me to prove him wrong. What could I say? That I didn't trust the custodian's story? That an old lady who saved my life told me Thomas Emerson brought her frozen pizza when she twisted her ankle? That I had looked into the kid's eyes and seen a scared boy trying hard to stay tough?

"I don't know. It's just a gut feeling."

He shook his head, apparently disappointed in my answer. "That's it?"

"That's enough for me right now. There has to be another reason why David was killed. Maybe he was in trouble. Maybe he crossed the wrong line. If he was involved with drugs—"

"Let me tell you something, David and I did a tour in 'Nam. If he didn't get hooked back then…" The sadness in his eyes deepened. You could almost see the memories flickering over his face. A chill swept over me.

"Dave the Brave. That's what we used to call him. Know why? One night we got pinned doing a zippo raid." He grimaced, his face flushing with the vividness of the memory. "Good old Uncle Sam ordered us to burn down a village. Only this time, it was a setup. We broke out of the green and next thing we knew, Charlie's spilling kill-fire over us like it was rain. Two guys in our company made it through that night. Me and Dave. I was on my knees, shaking in my boots, just waiting for the hit. David had a goddamn grenade frag in his hip, but he picked me up, dragged me over to a hidey-hole, and covered us with a couple of dead guys straight out of boot camp." The pain in his eyes made me wince. "David held his hand over my mouth the whole night so the gooks wouldn't hear me crying. He survived all that, but not…not…" His voice broke, as if his own words had suddenly sunk in. He walked away without another word.

"Sorry about all that." Terry's voice surprised me. "He's been having a rough time. On top of David's death, he's worried about the business. The gym's been going downhill ever since they opened up that new Santa Fe Spa." The concern in her eyes was articulate.

Deep sibling love was an alien concept to me, but apparently not to Terry. For some reason, the realization heightened my attraction to her.

I blinked at her. "It's okay."

She looked like she was ready to start wailing again, but stopped herself. "Why don't we get out of here and get a cup of coffee?"

I waited outside the gym for Terry, since I wasn't up to

another striptease. Then she followed me and Bella back to the Slope. We parked near my house and walked over to Cousin John's on Seventh Avenue. I ordered a couple of cappucinos and two raspberry tarts. Terry didn't have much of an appetite, so I ended up eating both tarts. It wasn't much of a sacrifice.

"So tell me more about Joey's relationship with David. Did they see a lot of each other?" I asked as I stirred my cappucino. I was trying hard not to blurt out the real question on my mind. I was almost certain Joey was gay. The intensity of his feelings for David made me question the nature of their relationship.

"They were still close," she said, her lips tightening with tension. "But they led pretty separate lives. Keeping the gym afloat takes up a lot of Joey's time. I mean, Vic's the show piece… and he certainly knows his way around the equipment. But Joey's the brains. Does all the marketing, the bills—" She cut herself off and turned those bruised eyes on me. A tingle ran over my skin. I was right. I couldn't help where my libido led me. Right now it was shoving me hard toward Terry. "Can we talk about something else? I don't want to talk about David or Joey right now."

"Name the topic."

"You."

"Sure you don't want to talk about the oil fires in Kuwait?"

"I get enough of that at home. When did you first realize you were gay?"

I've had my share of straight inquiries into the origins of lesbian sexuality. They usually end with, "Will you show me?" As a rule, I draw the line at married women. If they want to experiment, I point them in the direction of the nearest gay bar. Terry was different, though I'd have a hard time getting that line pass Dinah.

I told her my coming-out story, which any self-respecting lesbian has memorized and embellished for special occasions like this. Tabatha Adams was working her way through college by managing the Carvel ice cream store on the corner near my high school. She knew things about ice cream that would have made Tom Carvel blanche. She was a petite woman with a golden blonde shag and a size D cup. I'll never forget the day she took me into the freezer and showed me how to make the sweetest, smoothest ice cream this Brooklyn girl has ever licked.

Terry was listening to me, rapt.

"How about you?" I asked. "Have you ever been with a woman?"

She leered at me, knowing full well why I was asking. "No. Can't say that I have." She sipped her cappucino, gazing over the top with amusement in her eyes. "You know why?"

She had never found the right woman. I've heard that one quite a bit.

"I like the power of sleeping with men," she said.

"Excuse me?"

She leaned forward, conspiratorially. "There's this incredible high that comes with making it with a man. All that matters to them is that little stick of theirs." She wagged a spoon for emphasis. "You know how to handle that, and they're like putty. I get myself on top, you know what I mean?" Unfortunately, I did. Imagining Terry riding a spoon was not enhancing my sex drive. "Sometimes, I pretend I'm riding a bronco. It's a real trip."

Check.

"But I'd like to try a woman. At least once." She was looking at me intently. There was an invitation in her words. I figured we better get out of there before I found myself in more trouble than I needed.

I walked Terry back to her car, which was just a few doors past my brownstone, a fact she didn't let pass unnoticed.

"Didn't you say this was your place?"

I nodded and kept walking, a fever sweeping over me.

Terry stopped. I heard her footsteps heading toward my home, then the whine of a gate swinging open. I spun around in time to see her striding toward the second metal gate outside Dinah's garden apartment door.

"Whoa." I ran back. "That's my housemate's domain. See." I pointed to Dinah's buzzer.

Terry just smiled, a sinister I'm-going-to-get-you smile that made my knees weak. She moved close. "Is she your lover?" Her voice shot little waves of heat over my face.

"No, just friends." I had trouble swallowing. Terry licked her lips provocatively, a gesture that told me she must have watched her share of straight porno flicks. At that moment, however, I had no objections. One long finger drew a line from her chin, down her neck, to the center of her chest. It rested there, drawing circles. So did my eyes. She was dressed now, but I could still feel those nipples staring at me.

"I'm serious about taking a trip to your world. Maybe for just one night. Maybe longer." She had lowered her voice into the deep, husky range. The woman was an artist.

"Look, I'm flattered, but as a rule—" Her soft, full lips cut off my words. Suddenly, her tongue was exploring my mouth, a hand flickered over my breasts. She pressed me against the metal gate. Oh, what the hell. I wrapped my arms around her and pulled her tight body against my own.

"Hey, Sherlock!" It was Dinah, standing in the open doorway behind me. She was wearing a Mickey Mouse nightshirt and beach thongs. There was just enough streetlight for me to see that her eyes were two angry slits. "You want to make out in front of the whole goddamn neighborhood? Fine. Go park yourself on Seventh Avenue. But not on my doorstep, okay? I have clients who walk by here just to see if I turn my lights on when it's dark. I don't need them seeing two sex-crazed broads grinding on my gate." I saw her eyes flick to Terry's wedding band. "Ah geez...you're pathetic, Miller. Go home. Your cats need you." She closed the door and locked it behind her.

Dinah sure knows how to kill a moment.

My insomnia kicked in that night. I played fetch with Geeja, but she got bored after the first forty-five minutes. Then she stalked over to Mallomar, who had been watching her with undisguised admiration. The two of them bumped heads, then turned their tails up at me and strutted off toward the upstairs bedroom for their nightly licking ritual.

"Sure, abandon me," I yelled at their retreating butts. They didn't miss a beat.

I dropped onto the couch, succumbing to the noise in my head. On some level, I knew Dinah was right. There was a time I would never have allowed myself to get into such a compromising position with a straight woman, never mind a married woman. But since I bumped Cathy out of my life, something's been askew.

My thoughts drifted back to New Year's. Why the hell had I reacted the way I did when Cathy said she'd move East? For the year-and-a-half we were together, I had been urging her to make the move. But I never thought she would. She seemed too cool, too level-headed, too controlled. Safe. After all, you don't have to worry about being abandoned by someone who was never really there.

The proverbial light went on over my head.

The only woman I've ever lived with was Mary Oswell. After we broke up in 1986, she moved to San Francisco. Three years later she was dead. Something had happened to me while investigating her death. Something I still didn't understand. It was as if someone had held up a mirror to me and I had seen my face for the first time. For years, I had clung to the myth of Mary as the snow queen. During the investigation, I uncovered the truth not only of her passion, but of the depth of her love for me.

Contrary to what people say, the truth had not set me free.

The truth scared me. It made me face the fact that I had held Mary at arm's length, never allowing her to come as close as I had always demanded, blaming her and feeling sorry for myself for the distance between us.

Had I done the same thing with Cathy?

A knock at the door made me jump. Dinah's head appeared around the door frame. I glanced at my watch. It was close to three in the morning. "Come in."

She drifted to the couch, tucked her feet under the edge of her nightshirt, and smiled uneasily. "I couldn't fall back to sleep. You okay?"

Dinah could be a real pain in the ass, but she was more like family than my family was. "Sure. Got a spare vibrator?"

She chuckled. "Nah, we burned out the spare over the weekend." A cold hand squeezed my ankle. "I'm sorry I came on like Attila the Hun."

I sat up. "Don't apologize. You were right."

"So who was she?"

I gave her the play-by-play, beginning with Terry's appearance at the funeral and ending with the bump-and-grind on the gate downstairs.

"And I interrupted that? Ouch. Think I'll go downstairs and wake Beth up," she quipped.

"You're not going to warn me that I'm playing with fire?"

"Do I have to?"

We both knew the answer. Married women are strictly taboo.

Dinah sat with me for close to an hour. Most of the time, we just leaned against each other in silence. At one point, I almost nodded off. That's when Dinah returned to her domestic bliss, leaving me suddenly and irrefutably wide awake. I spent the rest of the night cleaning out the refrigerator and listening to old Janis Ian records till I got annoyed. Why was she complaining about learning the truth at seventeen? Learning the truth at thirty-one is a lot harder. The way I saw it that night, Ian had a head start.

I exchanged Janis Ian for Tina Turner, and sat down with the remains of what used to be macadamia nut ice cream.

As soon as the sun came up, I showered, changed, and strolled to the office. The first thing I did was call my friend Curtis. If Joey was a regular at Scarlet's, Curtis would undoubtedly know him. I got an answering machine—a new purchase for the technophobic Curtis. I left a rather sheepish message pleading for help, then hung up feeling even guiltier about our close call in the projects.

Afterwards, I was more than ready for a break from the Ross case. I quickly dialed my computer sidekick Michael Flanagan, the Roach. He's the only person I know who sleeps less than I do. I suspect he naps right at his computer desk, while running hard disk checks. He didn't have good news for me on the O'Donnell case. There was no match for any of the possibles at Dassler, Inc., in Fort Lee, New Jersey.

When Tony came in, we decided the next step was to introduce O'Donnell to Victoria Vichas, an ex-police artist Tony dated a few years ago. He made the arrangements.

I spent the morning typing up case notes and trying to tie up loose ends. O'Donnell and Vicky showed up around noon. The two women couldn't be more unalike. O'Donnell looked even frailer today, her short-cropped brown hair almost colorless, her eyes shielded by tortoise-frame glasses, and her thin, pale lips tight with tension. She was wearing an oversized beige cardigan, a man-tailored ivory shirt, and a navy blue pleated skirt. I wanted to drag her out and buy her a new wardrobe with screaming neons and sharp edges.

Vicky, on the other hand, was a tall, overweight woman with a long, auburn perm, bright red lipstick, and a kelly green dress too small for her size twenty-two frame. She had smiling eyes, a Brooklyn accent, and a knack for drawing portraits with an almost photographic quality. I watched Tony escort them into his office and start to close the door. I took that as an invitation.

"Hi Vicky, Ms. O'Donnell," I smiled at them, saving my widest grin for Tony. "Hey Tone, why don't you brew up some coffee?"

Tony actually looked relieved. I could tell he was having a hard time being around O'Donnell. Her case hit just a little too close to home for him. Without a single sarcastic remark, he headed into the waiting area. He didn't come back until Vicky had almost finished her first sketch.

Vicky took a coffee mug from him and said to O'Donnell,

"So how does it look?"

O'Donnell took her glasses off and leaned closer to the drawing. "His eyes were more round, and his cheeks fuller." She glanced up, her bottom lip trembling. "He looked really healthy. Robust." She pointed at the sketch pad. "But this may be closer to how he looks now."

Tony placed another mug on the desk, then walked out again without making eye contact with any of us. O'Donnell and Vicky were still discussing the portrait when I heard the front door close softly.

An hour later, they had finalized the sketch. Vicky went outside to try to find Tony, while O'Donnell and I talked about the next step of the investigation.

"Our best bet is for me to drive down to the Grand Palace Hotel in Atlantic City and see if any of the hotel staff remember him. They may, especially since he was a big spender. In the meantime, Tony's going to check the membership registers for a couple of public relations associations to see if his name, or a close match, shows up."

She squirmed in her seat.

"What's wrong?"

"I didn't think finding him was going to mean so much work." She hesitated. "I may have to bail out."

From her expression, that was the last thing she wanted to do. "I know it's discouraging, but…"

"It's not that. My company's not doing too well. Seems like word got out about my…condition. People are afraid to buy from us." She laughed bitterly. "Like you can get AIDS from opening a packet of Dixie's Barbecue Potato Chips. Jesus."

"So it's about financing?"

She tossed me a bitter smile. "Money makes the world go 'round. It's the only thing that may keep me alive long enough to fulfill some of my dreams. Like buying a house in the country. Seeing Ireland." The smile was real now, despite the tears in her eyes.

"Don't worry about the money."

"I'm paying you by the hour. When Tony called this morning, I asked for an estimate of the cost to date. I was floored. A trip to Atlantic City is just too much for me to handle."

Damn Tony. "Don't worry about the money. When the case is done, just pay us what you can afford."

She looked annoyed. "I'm not a charity case."

"And I'm not a social worker. You gave us an assignment. I'm going to finish it one way or the other, no matter what you say."

"You're not a very good businesswoman either," she said a glimmer of hope lingering in her eyes.

"No. But I am a good investigator."

I was feeling a lot less confident by the time I got home that night. Tony had never come back to the office, so after extracting some new facts about the mysterious Mike Weber (including his tendency to drink Scotch for breakfast and tip room service with crisp ten-dollar bills), I ended up doing all the footwork Tony had lined up for himself. After five hours of research and calls, checking various association directories, telephone books and city directories, I had come up with nothing.

To make matters worse, I found Marion Ross standing outside my brownstone when I got home. She was looking even less like a grieving widow, and more like an impatient, rich dowager standing last in a Broadway-theater bathroom line just as the house lights start to blink. It was one of those greenhouse-warm days in early June, but Marion was inexplicably wearing a winter-black dress and a sable wrap. I climbed the stoop and braced myself for another round of her lectures.

She checked her slim gold watch. "I expected you an hour ago."

"Did we have an appointment?"

"It's almost seven o'clock. I assume your workday ends at five, six at the latest?"

There was no appointment, just an impatient client out for my blood. I was starting to think Tony was smart for dropping her case. I unlocked the door and allowed her to follow me upstairs. "If that's what you assumed, why are you here now?" Without looking back, I could tell she had stopped midway up the stairs. "Come on, Marion."

As soon as Geeja caught a glimpse of the lady in sable, her tail flared up. "It's okay, sweetheart. It's not a relative." She wasn't appeased. A wicked hiss hurled past me. Marion stumbled backwards. "Don't worry. She rarely draws blood."

I pointed Marion toward the couch and hurried into the kitchen to offer the girls a can of tuna. "I don't have much time," she shouted at my back. "My father is hosting a reception for a new client. The Katsu Corporation?" The name was meant to impress me. It did. Katsu had recently purchased substantial real estate holdings in New York, not to mention a record company in Nashville and the Fortway hotel chain.

I came back into the living room stinking of pulverized tuna. "What's on your mind, Marion?"

"I wanted to talk to you about last night. After much soul-searching, I realized that your failure is partly my own." She started twisting the strap of her purse around one hand, and it struck me a little belatedly that the lady liked to tote handguns. She snapped open the purse and I jumped back. "I haven't been very…forthcoming." She pulled out a small, manila envelope and handed it to me.

"What's this?"

"A few recent pictures of David. The most recent telephone bill. Credit card statements."

"Why are you giving me this now?"

At long last, Marion sat down on the couch. I smiled crookedly, knowing that she had placed her black-wooled butt right on Mallomar's favorite spot. Mallomar is a big-time shedder, specializing in long white hairs.

"Circumstances have changed a lot in the past week," she began. "When I first came to you, all I wanted was to help my husband, to understand what was happening to him. Now…"

She looked up at me and, for an instant, I saw that David's death had hit her far harder than I had realized. "I want his murderer punished. I no longer care about discretion. I care about vengeance. Pure and simple."

"I still don't understand."

"My husband was having an affair."

Her directness surprised me. "Why didn't you admit that right at the beginning?"

She lifted her chin imperiously. "I was hoping you'd prove me wrong. Two weeks before David died, we had an awful fight. I accused him of having a mistress, and he swore to me that he was faithful. I didn't believe him. I told him that he had better get his life back in order, or I'd leave him. He was devastated."

"Thanks for the news," I said sarcastically. "Now if you're really ready to level, maybe you could clear up another concern for me. Did your husband have a drug problem?"

She looked sincerely surprised. "Of course not. Where did you ever get such an absurd idea?" Irritation crept back into her features. "Try to listen to me, will you." She rummaged in her purse again, pulled out a roll of toffee candies and popped one in her mouth. When she started talking again, she sounded a little bit like my Uncle Morty.

"My husband was cheating on me. But he was not a bad man. And I know the man loved me. I'll never forget how he looked that night..." She stood up abruptly and crossed to the front windows, leaving a trail of rose perfume. "My husband loved me. I think he threatened to break off his relationship with his mistress and that she killed him in a jealous rage."

I was just about to tell her that she could have a promising career as a writer for the daytime soaps, when she spun around, her hands punctuating her words in a Betty Davis staccato.

"Find his lover, and you'll find the murderer. Find her..." She swept past me. "Before I do."

Chapter 9

I didn't make much of Marion's threat. Maybe if I had, things would have turned out differently. But the woman looked so damn silly swinging that sable wrap around her elegant cat-furred back that I couldn't take her seriously. I shoved the manila envelope into my briefcase and headed into the kitchen to whip up dinner.

A little while later, I curled up with the cats, a bowl of Kraft macaroni and cheese, and a lesbian novel. After a half-hour, I threw the book down. The last thing I wanted to read about was well-adjusted lesbians in the throes of first love. I spent a few hours reviewing my case notes and checking out the contents of the envelope Marion had brought me. The photos didn't mean much to me.

I laid the phone bills out on the table and scanned through them. A series of phone calls made to and from Smithville, New Jersey, caught my attention. I pulled out the credit card statements to see if I could find any correlation, but after a few minutes the numbers began to blur and I nodded out. I woke around midnight, leaping from a wicked dream about Jodie Foster, Candice Bergen and me, to the sound of fire engines charging down the block.

I tried desperately to fall back asleep, but my body was in full rebellion. Then I remembered the magazine I had rescued from Marion's trash. I pulled it from the coffee table and retreated to the bedroom. The magazine had your standard modern-woman fare—self-help articles on losing weight, coping with husbands addicted to alcohol, gambling or sex, and psychological quizzes to help readers determine whether or not they were emotionally ready for success. I tried to prevent myself from gagging as I flipped to the article on Candice Bergen.

The story began with a double-spread of photographs. She has the kind of smile that promises good-natured mischief. Half-reluctantly, I realized that something about her reminded me of K.T.

I fell asleep by the third page.

Another dream. A frozen lake. I'm walking around its edge, shivering. Out in the middle of the blue ice is a magnificent flower. An African daisy, brilliant orange. But no. The flower is rare. Never seen before. A heat seems to pulse at its core. I'm drawn to the flower like a magnet. I put one foot on the ice, and the crack echoes through the air like a gunshot. Backing off, the ache inside me grows unbearable. I plunge ahead, running just ahead of the shatter line, the broken ice nipping at my heels. Then my arms fold around the flower, its petals growing, curling around me. I sink.

Gulping for air, finding lips instead. Soft, full lips. Sucking my own, running along my neck. I open my eyes and see only her hair. The color of sunset. The downy, untamed curls sweep along my body like feathers, like a woman's breath. Her hands reach up to me and I take one finger in my mouth. Skin soft as rose petals, the taste salty and clean. She finds my nipples, circles them with her warm tongue, then gently flicks the tip. A stone tossed in water, the ripples pass through me, reaching my core, turning me wet and hungry. I dip my hands in her hair, press her head to me. Yes! I scream, the ice crawling back in. Take me, give me, I want, I want.

The ice fills my mouth.

I jerked awake, my heart racing.

Next morning I made a few strategic calls, then headed back to David Ross's school, the dream trailing my consciousness like a shadow. I shook my head and blasted the radio. By the time I reached East New York, the shadow had begun to pale and the case took hold again.

Marion Ross was a tightly wound snob, but she was right about one thing. The jealous-lover scenario had a certain compelling logic to it. And there were two possible candidates in David's school: Virginia Savarin and, despite her protests and my own, Terry Fasani.

It took some fancy dancing to get past the security guard, who unfortunately remembered what had happened the last time I made an unscheduled visit to the school. To make matters worse, my so-called son Tito had been expelled last week. I angled my hands on my hip and acted indignant, but the narrow-eyed guard wasn't buying. I ended up flashing my I.D. and spilling the beans. She smiled, satisfied that she had broken me. We briefly discussed the murder, but she couldn't shed any new light on the case. With the chip on her shoulder significantly smaller, she guided me up to the man I wanted to see—Webster Bainbridge, guidance counselor and gossip extraordinaire.

"A lady's here to see you, Web."

Bainbridge was outside his office, pinning anti-drug ads onto a bulletin board. A ring of thin, brown hair circled the back of his head, making it look a little like a donut. He turned around and shifted his thick glasses up the bridge of his nose. "Thank you, Miss Morales."

I put out my hand and introduced myself.

"A female detective, how delightful." Bainbridge sounded like he meant it. "Come on inside. I just brewed some coffee. Sumatra decaf. Interested?" I was starting to like the man.

"I suppose this is about David Ross?" he asked as he filled two mugs. "That's why you pretended to be a sub the other day, wasn't it? From the way Terry reacted, I gather you were successful."

"Not really."

He handed me a mug that warned, "Don't let the turkeys get you down." I took a sip. The coffee was superb.

"What do you want to know?" he asked.

I smiled. "What do you want to tell me?"

"In other words, you want the complete run-down. Fine. First, David was a very complex man. He could have worked at an exclusive prep school in Manhattan, but preferred the inner city. Yet he loved his luxuries. At our last Christmas party, he sprung for two bottles of Dom Perignon." He paused, obviously savoring the memory. "He was a war hero, but was distinctly anti-American. Nevertheless, during the Gulf crisis, each time we played the anthem, the man's eyes filled. I once interrupted his class during the pledge of allegiance, and he almost bit my head off. But I guess you don't care about all this..."

"Go on." I had a feeling if I gave him a long line, he'd lead me right to my target. He proved me right with his very next words.

"The marriage was troubled, of course. A typical Montague—Capulet romance. You know, Romeo and Juliet? Marion is strictly upper-class white bread. Rich, prominent WASP family. Her grandfather was a shipping magnate. David, on the other hand, was strictly working-class Brooklyn. The two families clashed from the first."

The news didn't surprise me. "How do you know the marriage wasn't working?"

Bainbridge adjusted his glasses again and shook his head indulgently. "I have a reputation in this school of being a gossipmonger. In fact, I'm just the lucky recipient of everyone's confessions. Maybe it's just psychological residue from their childhoods, but for some reason the staff loves to unburden themselves around me. I don't object."

His honesty was unexpected.

"David Ross was an abysmally distressed man. His wife is chronically depressed, jealous, cloying, and I tell you this from first-hand experience at several end-term parties, downright boring. Perhaps they had great sex early on, but I got the distinct impression that Marion retreated into the igloo quite a number of years ago."

"Did David take lovers?"

A pleasant laugh shook his frame. "Did he take lovers? Who didn't he take is a better question. In one year, he hit on my intern, the resource room teacher, the school psychologist and even the cafeteria administrator. I dare say he was successful with most."

"Virginia Savarin?"

"You'd have to be a fool or worse to not pick up on the chemistry between David and Ginny."

"But did they have an affair?"

"Unfortunately, I was never in the position to observe them 'dancing in the sheets,' as they say. Still, it's a distinct possibility. That is, if Virginia could put down her morals long enough." He snickered.

"What about Terry Fasani?"

A gleam in his eyes told me what his answer would be. "Again, I cannot claim first-hand knowledge. But I would bet my collection of Judy Garland records that they got it on. My lord, Terry just oozes sensuality. As a woman you may not be able to appreciate this, but she can make a man's blood boil with just one glance. She's also a loose cannon. Very volatile. Frankly, I find that exciting," he smiled. "Now, the rumors about Terry run the gamut, from sleeping with her brother to being born a hermaphrodite. The last one is hard to believe, but beneath every rumor is a kernel of truth, you know."

Remembering my suspicions concerning David's relationship with Terry's brother, I asked, "Any rumors of homosexual affairs?"

"David was a freethinker. A little perverse. He once told me that he'd had a wet dream about Boy George. He may have been pulling my leg, but I had the sense he would've been interested in pulling a different part of my body, if I may be so direct," he responded coyly.

My coffee was getting lukewarm, and so was my tolerance for Bainbridge's banter. I stood up.

"Not so fast, my friend. I've saved the best for last. You've seemed to miss out on one of the more interesting aspects of David's life. I alluded to it at lunch the other day. Without question, David Ross was addicted to cocaine. I saw him buying from a local dealer. I tried to approach him about it, but he was totally resistant."

I felt a headache coming on. Wearily, I asked, "Do you know the dealer's name?"

"I know his moniker. D.J. Cruiser."

The fatigue dissipated instantly. I flashed back to the day David was killed. His frantic telephone conversation. Something about paying off a cruiser.

I had a feeling my meeting with Bainbridge had just paid off.

Back at the office, I read through my early case notes. Assuming Bainbridge was right about Cruiser being a coke dealer, the jealous-lover theory had just slipped out of first place.

"Is that the Ross file?"

Tony's voice startled me. According to the office schedule, he was supposed to be presenting the results of an employee security check to one of our corporate clients. "Just doing some paperwork," I said awkwardly.

He snapped the file off my desk. From the way his nose flared, I knew I was in for a lecture. "'No servant can serve two masters: for either he will hate the one, and love the other, or else he will hold to the one—'"

"In English, Tony."

"Your loyalty is to me. To this agency."

"What about the client?"

"The case is closed, Robin. Understand?"

"But…"

"Look, there are elements to this case you don't understand. I'm telling you, it's over. Ross is dead, his murderer's been pinned, and Marion Ross just has to come to terms with that. So does that lunatic Reverend Whaley. Now, I don't need arguments on this. The case is a hot potato, and I want it dropped. Now!"

I gritted my teeth and nodded.

"Good." He slipped his flat butt onto my desk corner. "Torstar Brands was thrilled with our work. They just signed a contract for a similar security check for one of their affiliates. I'm going to be on the job fulltime, which means you better start working on the case I assigned to you."

"O'Donnell."

A shadow passed over his eyes. "Call her Christine, for chrissakes. She gets enough of that O'Donnell business at the hospital."

"Sorry, Tony."

"I spoke to her this morning. Justway dropped her insurance coverage. Don't matter she paid every dime on her policy for the last fifteen years. Without coverage, she won't be able to afford medication much longer, so let's move fast on this." He picked up the Ross folder and slipped it back into the file cabinet. "She also told me about your little act of generosity. Seems she didn't feel comfortable with it. So I made a deal with her. We find this guy, she pays us what she can now and the rest from whatever's left from her estate, if anything. We don't find him, she don't owe us a red cent. Okay with you?"

He didn't wait for my answer. He didn't have to.

"I want you to head out to Atlantic City today. Take the sketch. Don't bother calling in until you have a lead."

The door closed with a dull thunk.

Bella's a fine car for tooling around Brooklyn, but seven

months ago she started rebelling whenever I tried to make her leave the borough. So I stopped at home, packed an overnight bag, replete with the Candice Bergen magazine and a bottle of Yoo-Hoo in case I needed a late-night fix, and headed over to the car rental place on Union Street.

I liked Atlantic City a lot better in the old days, when the real excitement was finding an overweight boardwalk hawker who sold Veg-o-matics or ninja kitchen knives just like the ones advertised on TV. Today, the town's been Trumpized. Everything is pushed to extremes. The Grand Palace is no exception. I reviewed the Palace a few years ago. The staff was superb—I even developed a friendship with the convention services manager–but the review didn't win me any waves of gratitude. The place is a logistical nightmare. To get to the hotel lobby, you have to pass through thirtyfoot-high gates, cross a moat, climb a steep flight of stairs, and then bulldoze your way through a wall of wheezing tourists, dismayed hotel registrants, and tight-bunned bellboys dressed in outfits last seen on one of Disney's animated princes.

I checked in, changed into my best Wall Street drag, then ripped a few pages out of the room's Yellow Pages and headed back out. There were six major car rental agencies in town. From what O'Donnell told me, I had a feeling "Mike Weber" was not the type to rent a wreck. The first place I tried was the airport Budget.

The woman behind the counter had drooping, watery blue eyes, a mouth that turned downwards and a chin the length of my ring finger. Her hair was unnaturally black and pulled back into a shapeless bun. I checked her name badge. Selma Schneimec, manager. Great.

It was just after six and there were seven or eight people ahead of me. I waited while Schneimec painstakingly wrote up each contract, asking every customer the same questions over and over in the same exact nasal whine. I looked around, positive her loud squeal would attract every canine in a six-block radius.

By the time I got up front, my nerves were frayed. I took a

deep breath and shifted into gear. "Ms. Schneimec, may I speak to you privately for a moment?"

She raised one eyebrow into a thick, inverted V and glanced past me.

"I know you're busy, but this is very important." I flashed one of the fake business cards Tony had printed up for me. I just hoped it was the law firm card and not the one for J & R Gas and Oil.

"I'd like to help, ma'am," she said, sounding like she could care less. "But the only reason I'm out here at all is because of the rush. We're trying to minimize the customer wait time, so if you don't mind…"

"This is about an inheritance." I was banking on her greed potential. She didn't disappoint me.

"Joan, I have to take care of this lady. Take my line."

She lifted a portion of the counter and led me into the back office. There were two cloyingly pink Care Bear cards propped on either side of a five-by-seven frame. I smiled at the photograph. The two slack-mouthed kids were obviously Schneimec's. So were the birthday cards.

"That's a new picture. Mory and Miranda gave it to me for my birthday."

"Great kids," I said enthusiastically. Perfect casting for the new Munster family. "Can't wait to get home to my own children. How about you? Do you get off soon?"

She grimaced. The lady obviously hated her job. "Not soon enough. The night manager called in sick. On my birthday. So now I'm stuck."

"Tough break."

I watched her blow crumbs off the desk. "Tell me about it. I promised the kids a night out. Pizza. A movie. Now they're stuck with my mother."

"Sorry." I pulled up a chair. "I'll try to make this fast. My client is a single, elderly woman. Very well-off."

"Do I know her?" she asked hopefully.

"No."

Her face fell.

"But you may be able to help her. Last September, she was here on vacation. As she was getting out of a taxi, she fell and broke her hip. A gentleman driving one of your cars helped her out. Now she's dying and would like to leave him something in her will. As a thank you."

Schneimec's interest was fading fast. "What does this have to do with me?"

"She needs the man's name. Of course, she'll be very grateful for your assistance. His name was something like Mike Weber and she thinks he was driving a white Grand Am. Unfortunately, her memory is not very reliable, so the name and make of car may not be entirely correct. Here are the dates in question." I passed her a sheet of paper.

"I still don't get it."

"All I need is for you to check the records and confirm his name."

"That's confidential information. I can't—"

"I'm not asking you to break any company rules." I smiled broadly. "Remember, I'm a lawyer. My license is at stake. All I'm asking is for your help in locating this Mike Weber. You don't even have to give me his telephone number. Just ask him to get in touch with me at the number on my card."

The wheels were turning. "Can't do." She stood up. "Company policy, you know. As manager, I can't very well violate—"

I interrupted her by waving a hundred-dollar bill under her nose. I was walking a thin line between success and a cell block. "My client is very adamant about obtaining his name."

The money disappeared into her skirt pocket. "Just a minute."

One hundred dollars and fifteen minutes later, Schneimec announced that no Mike Weber had rented a car from them in September. As a matter of fact, she smiled for the first time, they stopped offering Grand Ams at this location over a year ago.

I struck out at the next five car rental companies as well. I dragged myself back to the hotel around ten. After four hours of lying, bribing and playing Sybil, all I knew was that Mike Weber had either used a different name entirely, driven his own Grand Am, or rented the car from any one of the hundreds of agencies on the East Coast. The possibilities had narrowed significantly.

The next two hours propelled me from casino tables to security guards to three hotel restaurants. I flashed Mike Weber's sketch so often, he was becoming animated. Finally, I gave up and retreated to my hotel room. I stripped, bathed, and fell into bed. The hotel had a twenty-six-inch TV with a super remote. I flashed through the channels till I found *The Invisible Maniac*, a movie about an invisible scientist who escapes from an asylum and teaches high school physics.

Next morning I made a one o'clock appointment with Angie Pardalos, my friend in convention services, then I tucked the sketch into my briefcase and made the rounds of some of the neighboring hotels. Around eleven, I came back to the Grand Palace and started mugging the chambermaids and room service team. One woman said the sketch reminded her of a guy who tipped her a twenty for changing the sheets two times in one day. That was it.

I ended up in the hotel bar, the soles of my feet sweating inside my pumps. Since they were all out of Yoo-Hoo, I settled for a Molson Draft. I had an hour to kill before my scheduled meeting with Angie, so I pulled out some notes and placed my briefcase on the counter top. Two seconds later some beer-bellied jerk with a thick wad of bills bumped my briefcase onto the bartender's side. The guy disappeared without a word.

"Sorry about that," the bartender said as he started picking up the papers that had fallen out of the briefcase. "Some of the people here are damn rude." He was a pink-cheeked, clear-eyed man with buck teeth and a boyish grin. "Hey, that's my Davey man!"

Right away I lurched for the sketch. "Him? This guy?"

"Nah. The other one." He picked up one of the pictures of

David Ross. "Dave the Brave. He's a war hero, you know. You and him…"

I felt my pulse quicken.

"You know David Ross?"

"You bet. Him and his lady friends come here all time. 'Specially the redhead."

Chapter 10

The temptation to grab the bartender by his red velvet lapel was almost overwhelming.

"Hey Ray! Another Bloody Mary." It was the Big Wad again.

I watched Ray mix the drink, adding an extra splash of Worcestershire sauce, a leafy celery stick and a pink plastic Palace guard. When he was done, I signaled to him.

"When was the last time you saw David?"

Ray leaned over the counter conspiratorially. "You ain't his wife, are you?" His smile told me that he considered it a distant possibility at best.

"What do you think?" I asked with a wink.

"Right." His laugh was embarrassingly rich. "Well, you sure don't look like some uppity bitch from the East Side of town."

I winced. The description of Marion Ross was on target, but I still hated knowing that the characterization had to come straight from her husband's mouth.

"How Dave got stuck with a lady like that, I'll never figure.

I mean, he's a real man's man." He took my glass and refilled it without asking me. I gathered it was meant as a compliment. "Matter of fact, he's a real woman's man too." He obviously assumed an intimate relationship between me and David.

I laughed. "No doubt about that." The beer was frothy. I took a quick glance in the mirror behind Ray. Sure enough, I had beer foam on my upper lip. I licked it off. "So who was the redhead? She in any of these pictures?"

I turned to find Ray fixated on my mouth. He blushed when our eyes met. "Dave's one lucky man," he said with a tentative smile.

Since I had a case of raging hormones myself, I couldn't very well blame the guy for looking. "The redhead, Ray?" I asked.

He shrugged his shoulders sheepishly and shuffled through the pictures. "Don't know any of these people." He handed the photographs back to me. "You the jealous type?"

"Would Dave have time for me if I was?"

"Guess not. He gets enough of that at home." He wiped down the bar with a piece of gold felt. "Besides the redhead don't have anything on you. She's tall, nice shoulders, but no boobs or hips. Pretty eyes, though. And great legs, down to there, with spike high heels..." The crimson snuck back into his cheeks. I started to wonder how far out of adolescence he was.

"Did she have a name?"

He hesitated. "Joanie...you know her?" A wave of discomfort passed over his face. He scratched the right side of his jaw, looking more and more like a schoolboy. "Look, I like Davey. I don't want to get him in any trouble."

I dug in my bag for a ten and slipped it under my mug. "Dave and I have an understanding. What we do when the other one's not around is our own business."

A woman sat down at the far side of the bar. Ray scurried over to take her order. If he was hoping I'd be gone by the time he served her, he was wrong.

"Do you remember Joanie's last name?" I asked.

105

"Why do you want to know?" I could tell I was wearing out his bartender congeniality.

"The woman you were describing sounds like my sister. Now, that would sure be a kick in the head, wouldn't it?" I tried to sound brave and wistful, all at the same time.

Ray looked genuinely upset. "Nah, she don't look like you at all." He tapped the back of my hand gently. "You know, I'm not even sure the two of them were together."

I was surprised to find my eyes going moist. Damn, I was starting to get misty over my own lies.

"Aw, don't do that." Ray dashed for some fresh cocktail napkins. "Seriously, most times when Joanie was around, so was this other guy. Quiet type. Damn." He was desperately trying to comfort me. I started to feel bad for him.

"It's okay, Ray."

"No. I'm telling the truth. Sometimes the four of them would come down on the weekends…"

My interest jumped. "Four of them?"

Ray misunderstood the point of my question. "Doesn't mean they're two couples, could just be friends."

"Who were they?" The urgency in my voice was real.

"I'm trying to remember their names. Besides Joanie, there was this man and woman. A good-looking couple. Dark hair, nice bodies. But they always hung back, drank juices mostly. And gave lousy tips." His easy smile returned. "That didn't make me real fond of them."

"When was the last time they were here?"

"Let me think," he said. "Sure, I remember. They were here Monday and Tuesday the week before last. They never came down on a weekday before. Davey said it was his birthday. Tell you, he drank like it was his last."

A grunt sounded from the other side of the bar. Big Wad was back and waving his plastic Palace guard. "You working the bar or the broad?"

"Sorry…" Ray was fishing for my name. "Margaret."

A full-beam grin now. "That's my mother's name," he said as if he had suddenly discovered a reason to marry me. "Maggie."

"Hey, bartender man!"

Ray looked torn.

"Go on. I have an appointment soon anyway."

He looked crestfallen. I dropped another ten on the counter and ambled back to the hotel lobby, leaving another broken heart in my trail.

Angie was on the phone when I arrived. I stood outside for a few seconds, trying to shift gears. Now I knew where David went on the days he disappeared, but I still had no idea why. If he was having an affair with this Joanie, there were certainly hotels a lot closer to home. Unless Joanie and her companions had something to do with the drug deals Webster Bainbridge had referred to. Finally, I shook my head, knocked on the door, and walked in. Angie hung up and smiled at me. She had her Syrian mother's dark, exotic features and her Greek father's ebullience. Her smile was practiced, but nonetheless spectacular.

The office was pretty damn impressive too, if you were into early palatial style. Her desk was a good eight feet wide, a cherry wood monster with gilt edges. The wallpaper was forest green with gold tracings that looked suspiciously like the hotel's exterior. Under my feet, the rug felt like an unmowed lawn.

"What happened to your office?"

She hiked around the desk. "A promotion. It's good to see you again."

"You too." We hugged. Her arms felt distantly familiar. Four years ago, we had a magical weekend affair. Although we've seen each other a few times since then, neither one of us has ever tried to replicate those few days.

"You planning on reviewing us again?" Her tone implied that she considered the prospect about as appealing as a root canal.

"Was it so bad the last time?" I asked, following her over to a high-backed couch upholstered in a fabric that reminded me of antique tapestries in the Met.

She slid into the couch and grinned. "As a matter of fact, it was pretty damn good." I had the distinct impression she was not referring to the review.

I changed the subject. "I'm doing some private investigative work these days."

Her face dropped. "Why? How…" She was stumbling over her words. The reaction didn't surprise me. Most people couldn't fathom how I could move from Laurel Carter, international best-selling author, to Robin Miller, apprentice private eye. Maybe that was exactly one of the reasons the work appealed to me. It kept people off-balance, and put me in control.

"Do you remember my fifteen minutes of *Entertainment Tonight* fame? 'Laurel Carter, Queen of Romance, searching for her own princess. Tonight at seven-thirty.' Something like that?"

"Sure." She looked puzzled, but a glint of amusement was growing in her eyes. "But I still don't get it."

I provided my standard explanation, but Angie wasn't known for her patience or easy comprehension.

She began twirling one long strand of auburn hair around her index finger. "Sorry, but to me, PIs are grubby men wrapped in dirty raincoats. And they earn about one sixtieth of what you can making writing a single romance."

Angie also wasn't known for her lack of materialism.

"It's not about money, it's about satisfaction," I answered, irritation sneaking into my tone. Angie looked perplexed again. For her, satisfaction and money are inseparable.

"Well, if you're happy," she said, sounding doubtful.

We spent another few minutes catching up. It turned out that Angie was living with a woman now, for the first time ever. They had met at one of the hotel's media conventions. Apparently, Cathy Mae Johnson had moved in with Angie just four months ago. She dropped the name with purposefulness. It took a few minutes before the name registered. Cathy Mae was a 1981 Miss America runner-up who now had her own show on one of New Jersey's biggest radio stations. I know the program pretty well.

Silky Sounds, the best of the big singers. Judy Garland, Mel Torme, Nat King Cole.

I complimented her on her "catch," which made her smile a little more warmly. "So what can I do for you?" she asked.

We got down to business. I gave her an abstract of the O'Donnell case to date.

"There's not much I can do for you," she said, lifting the Mike Weber sketch for a closer look. "You're talking what? Eight, nine months ago? I'm good with faces, but I see hundreds of convention-goers each and every week. There's no reason why this man would stand out for me."

"It was the annual food and snacks exhibition."

A delicate laugh spilled from her mouth. "Not everyone is as fond of snack foods as you are, Rob. Believe me, the chips and dips crowd doesn't make for a very memorable convention." The putdown was subtle, but stung nevertheless. My mother was a checker for A&P. She used to sneak home bags of Oreos and other snacks that customers had ripped open and left on shelves or dropped at the checkout counter. Snacks were one of the few ways we still related after Carol's death.

"The man in question said he worked for Dassler," I said. "If that's true, he may have been one of the exhibitors. Don't they have to register with you?"

"With one of my staff assistants," she corrected me.

I was starting to wonder how the two of us had ever ended up in bed together.

"I'll ask Maureen to check her files..." She crossed to the desk, hit an intercom button, brusquely summoned a Maureen Febonio, then sat back down next to me, crossing her long, tanned legs right under my nose. Ah yes, I remembered suddenly, that's how it happened. Four years ago, she had sat on the edge of her office desk and crossed her legs in the same way. Except that back then she was wearing a tight, black leather miniskirt that had shifted up to mid-thigh. The weekend had started right then and there, on top of her desk.

The door opened, stopping my throbbing memory in its track. Angie introduced me to Maureen. Despite the corporate masquerade, replete with makeup, a double braid of pearls, and high heels, I recognized her as a member of my club. "A pleasure," she said, shaking my hand with confidence. She was a heavy woman with broad shoulders and generous, sensual lips that looked swollen from kissing.

Angie explained the situation to Maureen, who nodded once or twice to indicate that she was following her lead. "You want me to check my records," she said abruptly, interrupting Angie's all-too professional description of my case.

They stood silently for a moment, staring each other down. I checked out their body language. In an instant, I realized that these two had once had more than just a working relationship. Maureen turned around and closed the door with a quick wink in my direction. It never ceases to amaze me how lesbians and gay men can announce their sexual preference to each other with no more than a glance. Maybe we emit some secret scent or high-pitched tone that only other gays can pick up. Or maybe it's just the depth of interest you catch in someone's eyes, a look that says I see you.

"Robin?" Angie was sitting next to me again.

"Were you and Maureen lovers?" I asked, surprising myself.

With a corporate smile, she said, "Why do you ask?"

"Body language."

"She's involved," she said defensively, spinning her diamond pinkie ring.

"I'm not interested." Maureen struck me as the type that would lead in slow dances. And I've never been able to follow.

"Oh." She flicked the edge of a manila folder, sounding vaguely disappointed at the lack of dyke drama.

We spent the next hour checking out various records and flashing the sketch of "Mike Weber" to various staff members. Again, I came up empty. I was packing up my briefcase to go when Maureen knocked peremptorily and opened the office door. She ignored the glare of indignation Angie fired at her and walked up to me. "I have an idea of how we can locate this guy, but it's going to require at least another pair of hands."

I stretched mine out. "Able and willing."

She took one of my hands and led me out. We left Angie standing in the middle of her grand office looking a lot like a spoiled child who had just dropped an ice cream cone on her foot.

Maureen's idea was so simple, it bordered on brilliance. At every Palace convention, the hotel sponsors a contest booth. The first prize is a one-week stay at any Palace property in the United States. To be eligible, conference attendees have to drop their business cards into a glass fishbowl. The names were entered into the computer for future promotional mailings. But Maureen's efficiency was impressive. Not only did she save the cards, but they were divided up by conference and arranged alphabetically—first by company and then by the individual's name. The food and snack convention had two separate binders.

Before we started searching through the business cards, I sketched out a "template" for potential matches using my notes from the O'Donnell interview. Mike had told O'Donnell that he was a public relations executive for Dassler, who had risen through the ranks by focusing on the "3-F" line–pretzels, potato chips and popcorn. He also had an accent that O'Donnell identified as being distinctly New England. We decided to search for companies with similar names and products, individuals with comparable names or initials, and job titles that indicated middle management or higher.

After three hours, we were cross-eyed and bordering on delirium. There were over six hundred cards and at least sixty-five of them ended up being possible matches.

"Here's another one," Maureen said, picking up a card. "Maury Wyskowski. Sales Rep. Frozen Bagels. 'As good as the real thing, including the hole.'"

We both burst out laughing,

"How about Michele Treber, 'The best chips to touch your lips?'" Maureen asked, tears rolling down her cheeks.

"We're looking for a man, silly."

"Maybe you are, but I'm sure as hell not."

By now, my stomach muscles were starting to spasm from laughter. Mercilessly, Maureen grabbed another card and read, "Fred Fallick, VP for Sunday Sausages."

"Ow, ow." I clutched my stomach and signaled for her to stop.

"Or how about Mike Weaver, president, Weber Pretzels. 'The best twist in the East.'"

We both stopped, the laughter dying in slow motion.

"Let me see that one," I said, taking the card from her.

Weber Pretzels, Georgetown, Massachusetts. I strode over to Maureen's desk and tried the number. A secretary answered. "Sorry, Mr. Weaver is out of the office."

"Do you know when he'll be back?"

There was an uncomfortable hesitation on the other end. "I don't have that information at hand, but if you'd like to leave a message…"

I took a deep breath. So did Maureen. She was standing so close to my back that I could feel her exhalation blow down my neck. "My name is Angie Pardalos," I said. Maureen's groan echoed in the receiver. She started to pace behind me. "I'm with the Grand Palace in Atlantic City."

"I'm dead," Maureen whimpered.

I ignored her. "It's very important that I talk to Mr. Weaver directly. He's won a one-week trip to any U.S. Grand Palace location, including the new twenty-five-acre property in Maui. But I have to speak with him to confirm the prize."

"Hold on please."

From across the room, Maureen hissed at me.

"What are you doing?" She was frowning, but her eyes were still glistening with amusement. She's too good for this place, I thought.

"Don't worry," I whispered back. "I'll take responsibility for whatever happens."

"Hello?" The secretary was back on the line. "Yes, I'm still here."

"I'm afraid we will have to get back to you." She sounded increasingly unsure.

"That's not possible. The way this prize contest works, the recipient must accept the award immediately, or else we move on to the next person in line."

From the muffled three-way conversation on the other end, I gathered she had summoned assistance. Finally, another woman got on the phone. She seemed older, more self-assured. "Unfortunately, Mr. Weaver will have to decline this offer. He was hospitalized recently for a minor operation and has asked that we do not disturb him during his stay."

Chapter 11

A tremor of excitement passed through me. I was certain that we had picked up Mike Weber's trail.

"That's a shame," I said, feeling slightly embarrassed by how electrified I was by the news of Weaver's hospitalization. What if it wasn't the same guy? What if O'Donnell's story was less than honest? "Perhaps we can make an exception in Mr. Weaver's case. Good will, and all that."

Hesitation. "Well, we don't want Mr. Weaver becoming the focal point for some publicity stunt by the Grand Palace."

I expressed indignation.

"If it can be done discreetly, I'm sure that Mr. Weaver would appreciate your flexibility," she said, mollified.

"Fine. Now, all I need to do is confirm his eligibility for the prize. Do you have a copy of his plane tickets for the trip he took to Atlantic City last September?"

"If I remember correctly, he drove down to Atlantic City."

"He drove down? That's quite a drive." I felt feverish.

"It was a combined business trip and vacation."

I audibly flipped some papers on the desk. "Funny, we don't have a record of his license plate number on the hotel registry."

"I'm sure you must have it. I remember the trip quite well. His wife's car was in the shop, and he didn't want to leave her without some mode of transportation, so he left her the Mercedes and took the company car. A Grand Am. Hold a minute…" She read me the license plate number.

"Thank you. You've been very helpful." More helpful than she would ever know. "Now, all I need is his address so that I can mail him the voucher."

"Just send it to the office."

"Why don't I just send it directly to the hospital. It could be a great pick-me-up. I'm assuming he's in Boston General."

"Mr. Weaver is not in a local hospital. Believe me, the office is the best choice. I will handle this personally."

I explained that we needed his signature or his wife's upon delivery, but the secretary wouldn't budge. She refused to give me the address of either his home or the hospital. Finally, I disqualified Weaver from the prize, winning a sigh of relief from Maureen, who by now had a thin line of sweat along her upper lip and a sparkle of intense interest in her eyes.

"It's him," I said. "I'm sure of it."

"How the hell do you do this for a living?" she asked, seeming far more intrigued than perturbed. I suspected that our brief detective episode had cast a pall on convention services.

I stood up and hugged her. "Are you kidding? I feel terrific."

We celebrated by taking the elevator down to the hotel coffee shop and sharing a slice of strawberry cheesecake. Before we parted, I gave her the photographs of David Ross and asked her to find out what she could about him. I had my suspicions about why Ross and his companions had frequented Atlantic City, but I needed confirmation.

Afterwards, I headed back to my room, sat down at the desk and began dialing. The first call went to Tony. After updating him, I called Michael the Roach. Armed with a license plate number, he could probably find out what brand of underwear Mike Weaver prefers. What I wanted was a lot simpler: his address. Unfortunately, Michael wasn't home. I didn't bother leaving a message and moved directly to Plan B.

Despite what Weaver's secretary told me, I started with Boston General, then worked my way through most of the major hospitals in the Boston area. An hour later, I had irritated staff at medical facilities north and south of Georgetown, Massachusetts. Then it struck me. If Weaver was seriously concerned about his illness being leaked to the local business community, maybe he wasn't in Massachusetts at all.

The next call went to Alice Lewis, head of the AIDS clinic at St. Vincent's Hospital in New York. "Hey Mouth, it's Miller."

A gritty laugh floated through the lines. "If you're calling to wish me a happy birthday, you're five months late."

"What are you talking about? I took you out to Henry's End for your birthday."

"Yeah?" I could hear her sucking in cigarette smoke. The only time she didn't have a cigarette in her hand was when she was feeding her eight-month-old son. And that's only because her lover Sandra would kill her if she did. "Wait, I remember you now. You're the tall, skinny one who owns stock in Yoo-Hoo."

"Okay, okay. I know I haven't called in a while. Things have been crazy."

"This is going to be a professional question, isn't it?"

I hesitated.

"You know, when Sandra and I decided to have a kid, all our friends were remarkably supportive. We got baby-sitting offers from people who didn't know the difference between a diaper and a sanitary napkin. Now we have little Alfred in our lives and no one calls any more. Including your friend Beth."

Alice and Beth had been lovers back in prehistoric times, before either one of them ever met their current partners. But Beth became involved with Dinah only two months after breaking up with Alice. She still hadn't forgiven her.

"It's like we have the plague," she continued. "Sure, an eight-month-old boy can be hell on wheels, but he's certainly not the plague. More like a bad case of the croup."

"I never promised to baby-sit."

Her laugh transformed into a hacking cough. "That's for damn sure," she said when she finally caught her breath. "So what's happening in the dick biz?"

Alice is a fervent believer in the confidentiality rights of AIDS patients. I had to step carefully or I'd end up with no information, or worse, no friend. "I need to find out what hospital an AIDS patient is in. I could use your contacts."

I barely heard her breathing on the other end. "Robin, what is this about?" She had dropped the banter and shifted into her professional persona. "It's not what you think."

"I'll tell you what I think. If you're working for one of those self-righteous assholes who are trying to make a case for prosecuting AIDS patients who sleep around..."

"Whoa. Give me a chance. I'm working for an individual client."

"Legal implications?" she asked abruptly.

"None. She just wants to confront this guy face to face."

"Right. Wake up, Robin. You find him, she finds her lawyer. Sorry, you can count me out of this."

"The woman is sick. She can't afford lawyers." I took a deep breath and provided her with the details. I could hear the assurance in her tone waver.

"Just tell me this much," I asked, exasperated. "If prominent businessman from the northeastern part of Massachusetts had to check into a hospital outside of Boston, where would he go?"

"Theoretically?" I could tell her rigid code was about to bend. I grunted yes.

"If he had the bucks and wanted to disappear into a sea of sickness in a city that won't take notice, he'd come here."

The very next phone call told me what I wanted to know. I

sent Mike Weaver a.k.a. Mike Weber a dozen roses.

I was home by ten o'clock Friday night. The first thing that struck me was the blinking light and digital counter on my answering machine. Twelve calls. I hadn't been away that long.

I stepped over Mallomar, who was splayed on the floor belly-up, paws kneading the air in a desperate attempt to attract my loving attention. Geeja, on the other hand, hadn't deemed me worth an appearance. I hit the play button and knelt down to rub Mal's white stomach. The first call was from Zack McGinn. A recently fired twenty-two caliber handgun had been found in the Emerson home. Thomas's fingerprints were all over the muzzle. Great. I plopped down on the floor next to Mallomar.

After a call from my sister, there were two in a row from Marion Ross, each one more virulent than the last. She wanted results. I guess she figured if she tortured my answering tape long enough, David's murderer would materialize faster. Next up was Terry Fasani. She invited me to see the documentary *Paris is Burning* with her brother and some friends of theirs.

I smiled to myself. All at once, I remembered exactly where and when I had seen Terry's brother before. During the annual Joan Crawford Drag Queen Festival that Curtis stages at his bar. Joey had come in second in Miss Scarlet's beauty contest. When the results had been announced, Curtis and I had hissed like disgruntled cats. The guy deserved to win.

Coincidentally, the next message was from Curtis. "Joey Pisano's the guy who should've been Miss Scarlet. The one with the great gams. He's a regular here Thursdays. Drag night. Real friendly. I don't think he's attached, though he could be. I'd have grabbed him a long time ago, but he prefers the Stallone type. You know—big, white macho guys with thick, hairy necks." Curtis could have been describing Joey's partner Vic. Or David, for that matter.

What if Joey had been involved with both men? If so, it wasn't hard to imagine Vic killing someone in a jealous rage.

"We're all crazy about Joey," Curtis continued. "He's a great girl. So, whatever you're doing, leave him alone. Okay? As a favor to me. After all, Jane, you owe me."

Curtis was still hurting. I closed my eyes tight as my messages continued to play.

Another call from Terry, but this time she sounded wired. "I need to speak with you urgently. Beep." In the background was an angry male voice. I couldn't tell if it was television or real life. In either case, it was not a pleasant sound.

I rolled over onto my belly, stroked Mallomar behind the ears, and waited for the next message. "Hey Rob. It's Tony. Guess what? The Weaver guy didn't lie about his public relations background. I checked some association registries for his name. I'm staring at it right now, in bold print. Address and all." He read off the address and phone number. "Good work kid."

A compliment from Tony was pretty rare. Surprisingly, I felt myself start to beam.

"Hi…uh. This is Kentucky. Not the state. The person. K.T." I stood up and stalked to the answering machine, my face flushing. "About tomorrow night, I have a feeling dinner parties may not be your style. But I'd really like you to come. I promise, it will be low-key." Her voice was deep and melodious, with just a hint of the Southern drawl. It filled the air like the smell of baked bread. Suddenly, it dipped into a whisper. "I just know there's a reason we met. It was like a spark that just needs some breathing on. I felt like that just one other time. I was standing in an open field down in West Virginia and the air began to moan around me. Low and powerful."

Her voice was mesmerizing. I closed my eyes and listened to her like she was a song I had never heard before.

"I knew something magic was 'bout to happen, if only I stayed still and open." She paused. "Lord, listen to me. You'd think I was back home sitting on some old rocker and sharing stories with a wide-eyed dog. Sorry. The point is, I want you to come tomorrow night. Simple. Clean. I'll be standing still and open. Bye."

I was slightly breathless and my throat bone-dry. I missed the next message entirely. The spell wasn't broken until Terry's panicked voice filled the air. "Look, if you're there, please answer. I really need to speak with you. Shit. Call me." At the end, her voice broke. Her message was followed by another one from Marion. The woman's impatience crackled on the tape like a downed electrical line.

I called Terry first, but her line was busy, so reluctantly I tried Marion. I confirmed the dates David was missing the week prior to his death and told her about the weekends in Atlantic City. Gently, I mentioned Joanie's name. "The bastard, the bastard…" she shrieked into the phone. I remained silent until the howling stopped.

The first couple of times I investigated extramarital relationships, the intensity of a client's grief upon learning about the affair they paid us good money to discover unnerved me. I tried to comfort them, or defend myself against their accusatory tirades. In the end, I learned that the best course of action was to let them cauterize the pain in whatever manner they deemed fit. When the howls simmered down to a whimper, I began talking again. "I'm sorry, Marion…"

"Sure, sure. Everyone's sorry for Marion." A crash reverberated on the other end of the phone. It sounded like glass exploding.

"I need to ask you some more questions. Perhaps tomorrow?"

"No. Not tomorrow. If this woman killed my husband…" She left the sentence unfinished. "You want to know who Joanie is? I don't have a goddamn clue. You have the phone records, the pictures. Find out. That's why I'm paying you."

"The name doesn't mean anything to you?'"

She laughed bitterly. "Now it does. It means a lot. It means my marriage was a sham. It means…damn." I could hear her fighting back the tears.

"You said you were convinced David planned to call the affair off," I ventured.

"Yes, yes. That doesn't make me feel any better. You know what

David told me he was doing all those weekends he disappeared? He said he was going on veteran retreats, so he and his damn war buddies could exorcise all the demons. I believed him. The first couple of months, I actually believed him. The Gulf War had just started and I figured it had stirred up old nightmares for him." I heard another crash. "I'm an idiot."

There was no use questioning her further. I muttered a few lame words, then hung up, the weight of the day pulling me into myself. If O'Donnell and Weaver and the Ross marriage were any indication of what relationships were like these days, I was better off alone. I tried Terry again, but the line was still busy.

I gave up and headed upstairs. A few minutes later, I lowered myself into a steaming bath. My head was spinning. I focused my attention on the air fern hanging above the tub and tried to sort out the facts. David Ross probably had an affair with someone named Joanie. Correction. David probably had affairs with several women. And maybe even a man, if Webster Bainbridge could be believed. One of his lovers, possibly Joanie, may have visited David shortly before his death. But why did she bring another man with her? Could it have been a jealous boyfriend or husband?

Despite Marion's protests, I had serious doubts that David had intended to break off his extramarital affairs. What was more unsettling was that I couldn't entirely rule out Marion as a suspect. Nor could I explain the significance of the missing bullet, or the Atlantic City trips. Then there was the drug angle. If David was tied into some East New York drug ring, the list of suspects was more than I could handle alone.

I was just about to sink my head under the water and hold it there when the phone rang. I sprang from the tub, grabbed a towel and raced to my phone.

"Miller?" It was Zack.

"Who else would be answering my phone at the stroke of midnight?" I asked.

"How the hell am I supposed to know what goes on in your

lesbian den? You could be having wild orgies for all I know."

"Dream on, Zack. Look, I'm standing here dripping wet. Did you call just to be social?"

"Nah. When you didn't respond to my call, I got worried. I still think you're too soft for this business." It was a standard line, one he had used on several occasions in the past—mostly when he needed to talk police business with someone who wasn't a cop or his wife.

I whipped off the towel, tucked the phone under my chin, and started digging through my dresser drawer. "Can it, Zack. You may like me a lot, but you're laying the concern on a little bit too thick."

He chuckled. "You're a pretty good read."

"Thanks. What's up?" I dragged on a pair of sweat pants.

"Couldn't sleep."

"I know what that's like. Hold on." I dropped the phone on my under-utilized bed and slipped an old polo shirt over my head. "I'm back. It's the Ross case, isn't it?"

Silence. "I'm starting to think you're right on this one," he muttered somewhat reluctantly. "Something about this whole thing isn't kosher"

What bothered Zack most was the missing bullet. There was something else, but he was holding out. I pulled on some socks and waited till he broke. It didn't take long.

Reluctantly, he revealed that everyone from the D.A. to the mayor himself was breathing down Lt. Sergeant Rodammer's neck for results. Since Zack was heading the investigation, he was the one that the Hammer decided to come down on. Worse, the Hammer wanted Zack to *use whatever means possible* to nail the case closed within forty-eight hours. He was thinking out loud and I could hear his doubts gaining strength with each word.

"Then, all of a sudden, there's the handgun Hollerman suddenly discovered in Emerson's apartment," he said. "I mean, what the hell does 'recently fired' prove? I could point the gun at the nearest mailbox and pull the trigger. That's recently fired.

But that's not murder."

"Have you talked with Emerson?"

"Yeah. He says it's his brother's gun. If his prints are on it, it's because they keep the damn gun in the silverware drawer. Can you imagine?"

Unfortunately, I could.

"Talk to the neighbor next door," I said.

"The old lady?"

I shook my head impatiently. "Her name's Carla. She knows the family pretty well. She may be able to corroborate Emerson's story. Now, I have a question for you. Have you checked Marion Ross's alibi?"

"Solid as a jail cell. She was at a P.A.L. fundraiser. The Hammer himself vouches for her presence."

"Zack—" I hesitated. "You sure you can trust the Hammer?"

"Don't start, Miller. You sound like the damn IAD. Despite what you think, most cops aren't one step up from scum." His tone wasn't as confident as his words.

"Do me a favor. Double-check her alibi anyway. Indulge me."

"Yeah, yeah. I'll think about it." All of a sudden, a woman's voice called to Zack from a distance. "Damn. I must've been talking too loud. I'm going to get off, okay? There's no way this marriage is going to end up another casualty of police life."

He disconnected without another word.

About an hour later, the phone rang out again. Obviously, my popularity was at an all-time high. This time it was Terry Fasani, talking so fast her words derailed. The only point she was clear on was her address. Her last words were, "I'll be outside when you get here." The buzz of a dead wire sang into my ear. Without thinking, I put on my sneakers and headed out to the car.

It was after one o'clock and the street was unnaturally still. In the distance, I could hear the wail of an ambulance, the throbbing bass of a blasting car radio, the rickety thunk of a truck bobbing over pot holes, but on my block the only sounds were a paper bag gyrating past darkened brownstones and a lone car starting up down the block.

I unlocked Bella, slid inside, and turned the key in the ignition. There was a dull rattle and then a shudder. Terrific. I pumped more gas and leaned forward over the steering wheel as if I had X-ray vision and could see right through the hood. I turned the key again. She kicked over, but something was wrong. I cocked my head and sniffed. Smoke. I turned on my lights, expecting to see smoke wafting up from under the hood. Instead, the smell intensified. Inside the car. I whirled around and glanced over the headrest. A tongue of flame was running along the edge of the back seat. Even as I watched, it moved in rapid spurts. I lunged for the door lock. Damn. Jammed again. Already, the car was filled with a gray, noxious smoke. I covered my mouth with one hand and jammed the other against the horn. Suddenly, the right side of the front seat caught, the fire moving my way fast. I turned and began kicking the door, my throat stripped, and a sickening dizziness beginning to take hold. A tongue of flame jumped to my sweatshirt and I batted it with my hands. I raised my legs and kicked with all my heart, just as the car went black.

Chapter 12

I regained consciousness with a jolt, vomiting onto the sidewalk where I lay. The air was crackling with sound, the pounding rush of water against metal, the harried shouts of firemen, the sounds of doors and windows opening and closing in rapid succession. I wiped my mouth and tried to stand.

"Take it easy." It was Beth. Her cool palm was stroking my cheek. "Small, steady breaths."

I sucked in some air and starting vomiting again. Whatever was coming out of me was coal black.

Beth lifted my head, urging me to sit up. I raised myself halfway and fell back against her. We were sitting on the sidewalk, about two car lengths from the burnt-out shell that used to be my car. That could have been me.

"How'd I get out?" I asked in a ragged voice.

"You kicked the door open. When Dinah and I got out here, you were out cold and your hair had just caught." My hand shot to my head. I could feel the singed edges along my left side. The remaining hair was about a half-inch long. I shuddered, an acrid odor filling my nostrils.

"Is that what I smell? The burnt hair?"

"And the burnt rubber, the charred metal, the smoke…"

"Am I burned anywhere else?" I interrupted, instantly patting myself down with my right hand.

"Minor burns on your wrist and left ear."

I stood up shakily and took in the scene. Dinah was talking to a cop and two firemen. "I don't have time to deal with this," I said.

Beth didn't say a word. She led me inside to the shower then bandaged my wrist, and made me drink two glasses of water. I greedily accepted three Advils and a clean pair of sweats. By the time Dinah came back inside, I was almost steady on my feet.

"I need your car keys." The words were out of my mouth before I realized it.

Dinah stared at me in disbelief. "You've got to be kidding."

I shook Beth's hand off my shoulder. "The hell I am. Look, I'll take the old Volvo."

"What you're going to take is a good night's sleep. I'm not going to let you drive after what happened." Dinah's tone was adamant.

"Dinah," Beth said cautiously, having the good sense to realize no one was going to stop me.

"I got a call from someone in trouble. By now, she probably thinks I'm not going to show." I stepped past Dinah.

"Where are you going?" she asked.

"Car service." I said, my hand already on the front door. I paused, a wave of nausea curling into my throat.

"Damn you." Dinah rummaged through her backpack and tossed me a pair of keys. "The Volvo's on Fourth Street, near Seventh Avenue. Call us when you get where you're going."

I grunted and shuffled outside.

Terry lived in Bay Ridge, close to the gym we had gone to the other night. I parked outside a modest brick home, the car windows wide open, cool air sweeping over me like a balm. After a few minutes of steady, grateful breathing, I stepped outside. True to her word, Terry was sitting on the top step, trembling like a lost child and bleeding from the corner of her mouth.

I bent over and raised her gently by the elbow. "What happened?" At my touch, she cracked, her body jerking with soundless cries. Up close, I could see a greenish purple bruise forming under her right eye. I opened the front door and led her in. The apartment was definitively male. Brown tweed rugs, walnut-trimmed Early American furniture straight out of an Ethan Allen catalog, and a beige recliner positioned in front of a twenty-six-inch television. My eyes flicked over the framed Gulf War news clippings above the couch. I lowered Terry onto a love seat and went in search of the kitchen.

It didn't take long to realize where the battle had been fought. Two kitchen chairs lay on their sides, a pot of spaghetti had been thrown across the room and ended up under the table. Pasta and tomato sauce were splattered all over the floor. I stepped over a broken glass, opened the freezer door, and emptied an ice tray into a dish towel.

A bottle of brandy was on the counter near the refrigerator. Normally, I drink hard liquor at weddings and bar mitzvahs—about three times a decade—but right then the amber liquid promised an oblivion that suddenly appealed to me. I pulled out a tall glass, took three long, shuddering gulps, refilled the glass and retraced my steps. Terry was curled into a ball when I walked back into the living room. I pressed the ice against her cheek and offered her the glass. We took turns sipping.

"Who did this?" I asked, the fury I felt dulling the sting of my burns.

Her eyes closed.

"Terry, you can't let him get away with this. Tell me. I can help you."

She stared up at me, indecision shadowing her face. Then she touched a finger to the corner of her mouth, where the blood had already dried. "Sam," she said weakly.

"Sam who?"

She looked away. "My husband."

"Where is he now?" I asked through clenched teeth.

"Airport." She finished the brandy in one ravenous swallow.

My pulse quickened. "I'm calling the police." I headed toward the phone.

She jerked me back. "No. It's over now. Let him go.

I sat next to her, the need in her eyes pulling me in.

"What happened to your hair?" she asked, touching the side of my head. Reflexively, I leaned back. "And you smell like smoke."

I told her about the late, great Bella.

"And you still came," she said in wonderment, a new expression snapping into her gaze. Before I knew what was happening, her mouth was on mine, exploring my lips with her tongue. Her arms wrapped around me, her firm breasts pressing hard against mine.

"Terry, Terry," I repeated, trying vainly to disengage myself.

"I need this, this tenderness. Please. Erase the memory."

As soon as I moved one hand, the other one was on my back, pulling me closer to her. "This isn't right," I said. But even to my ears the words were unconvincing.

She stilled my mouth with her tongue. I could feel her hunger. An echoing voracity rose inside me, mixed with the heat of the brandy and the need to simply disappear into sensation. Suddenly, desperately, I wanted to feel uncontrolled passion.

Her mouth slid along my neck, biting, sucking, her chill, sweet breath raising goose bumps along my arms. I lifted her blouse and ran my hands over her slender back, the ridges of her spine, the angular edges of her shoulder blades. She felt fragile and powerful at the same time, her muscular body responding to my touch with a deep tremor.

All at once, she paused. Her eyes locked on mine and then, without hesitation, she lifted my sweatshirt over my head. I shivered with the sudden cold, my nipples hardening instantly.

For a split second, I felt excruciatingly shy. And then her mouth was on me, my hand entwined in her dark, thick hair. At first, her touch was so light it felt like wind. Gradually, she took more of my nipple into her mouth, sucking insatiably. Electric shocks of pleasure shot along my nerves, my vagina throbbing in time to the rhythm of her lips.

We undressed feverishly, rolling onto the floor blindly, knocking into the coffee table, the leg of the recliner. The world had disappeared. No. The world had contracted to the beat of my need, to the taste of her salty skin, the soft prickle of her recently shaved legs, the musky smoothness of her inner thigh. I could feel her opening up to me, pulling in my tongue, fingers. I anchored my hands on her hips and let her take me into the wetness. The world constricted into a single unbroken moan, the delicate arch of her back, the pressure of her body against my mouth. I held on till she collapsed in silence, then I crawled up next to her and nestled her while she wept.

Flames circled my ankles. I was running from the fire, but it surrounded me, the heat singeing my face. Outside the blazing ring stood my father, and in his arms was the limp body of my sister Carol. Blood ran , from her stomach in a slow, thick flow. Only Carol wasn't a child, she was a woman. She lifted her hand to me and cried out my name. I stretched out my arms to touch her, then froze as my father's face darkened and he tossed the body into the flames.

I lurched from the dream. For a moment, I was totally disoriented, like swimming in a sea of oil on a moonless night. Seconds later, my eyes adjusted to the dark and the edges of the night table became visible. So did a framed picture of Terry and her husband. I covered my eyes and groaned.

"Mmmm." Terry rolled over sleepily and draped her hand over my thigh. I leaned against the headboard, the knot in my stomach intensifying with each click of the digital clock. I had to get out of there. I started to shift my legs off the bed, but Terry clung to me, suddenly awake. "Don't go," she murmured. "I need this." Her fingers were inside me. My response was immediate and infuriating. I closed around her fingers, my arousal so deep it bordered on pain.

"No, Terry." Even to me, the protest was unconvincing.

"I need this," she said again, this time the words more determined. She kept her fingers inside me and moved her head down my body, sucking like an infant taking its first milk. I spread my legs wider. Then a truck passed by the bedroom window, its headlights illuminating the room for an instant. The instant was long enough. Too long. I saw Sam's p.j.'s slung over a hook on the back of the door. Sam's boots next to the wardrobe. Sam's Army-issue fatigues tossed over a chair. My hip suddenly spasmed and I reeled away from Terry in pain.

She switched on a small night light and looked up at me, puzzled. I made some lame excuse about my hip and started looking for my clothes. I tried not to notice the distressed expression on her face as she recognized that I had more than a foot out the door.

"Your clothes are all over the place," she said. "Why don't you just put on one of my sweats? They're in the right-hand dresser drawer." Her voice was flat. I wanted to disappear into a bolt of lightning.

I leapt at a sock I mistakenly thought was mine and said inanely, "You're too skinny."

"Then slip on something of Sam's."

I looked at her in astonishment, but her face was blank. Still I hesitated. She was kneeling in the center of the bed, the bruise around her eye already beginning to bloom, and her mouth swollen from lovemaking. A barely discernible moan emanated from her, the sound of a pup whimpering over the body of its dead mother. Her wounded yearning drew me back. Then I lowered my gaze to the floor. The bed springs squeaked. "I'm going to shower," she said coldly. "I'll lock up after you leave."

I found most of my clothes in the living room. But my socks were definitely MIA. I headed toward the bedroom to find a pair I could borrow. I was moving fast, dressing as I walked. The shower had been turned off, and I was not prepared for another flash of the steel-gray darkness in Terry's eyes. Rushing, I pulled out a dresser drawer too fast, dropping the drawer and its contents on my foot. In the bathroom, the toilet flushed. I swept the contents together and went to upright the drawer. I stopped mid-motion. A Photomat envelope was taped to the bottom of the drawer. Glancing over my shoulder, I peeled the envelope off and stuffed it into my pants. Two minutes later, I was sprinting down the steps, sans socks or a clear conscience.

The sky was turning plum as I approached home. Every light was on in the brownstone. I winced. I had forgotten to call Dinah. As soon as I put my hand on the gate, the two of them bolted outside, shouting questions at me simultaneously. I waved them off, muttering apologies, and retreated upstairs. I never made it to bed. I fell onto the couch and slept for four hours straight. I woke with a jackhammer headache and a mouth so dry my tongue felt that it could crack. The cats were curled up on my butt and back. I untwisted myself, put on a pot of coffee, then dragged myself into the bathroom. I tore my clothes off, spiked them into the laundry basket, gargled, showered and dressed. All the time, there was a dull squeal in my head like a car careening around a corner on two wheels.

I was having a hard time accepting the fact that I had crossed a line I had set for myself years ago. Sleeping with a married woman was bad enough, but sleeping with her just for sex and waking up with her husband's picture staring me in the face bordered on reprehensible.

I gulped down two mugfuls of black coffee, then headed out to the avenue for breakfast and a haircut. It was just after noon when I returned home. I unlocked the downstairs door and went in search of Dinah and Beth. I figured an apology was due. Unfortunately, no one was home. Then I noticed Beth's nursing uniform folded on a pile of laundry on the kitchen table. An idea clicked into place.

Time to visit O'Donnell's Mike Weaver. Dressed as a nurse, I'd have no problem gaining access to his room—even if Weaver had specified no announced visitors.

Twenty minutes later I was in the Volvo, dressed in white and driving over the Brooklyn Bridge. It was then that I remembered the photographs lying wrapped in my sweats. I almost turned around, but the prospect of examining the stolen pictures revitalized the memory of Terry's bruised face, as well as my guilt.

Closing the O'Donnell case would be just the antidote my system needed, I rationalized.

I parked four blocks away from St. Vincent's. The most inconspicuous entrance was the emergency room. I snuck in behind an ambulance crew, then weaved through the plastic benches lined with huddled bodies. The sights registered like a kaleidoscope of illness: gauze held against a child's bleeding scalp, an elderly woman sobbing into a soiled handkerchief, the uncomfortable rush of a covered gurney scraping over tiled floor.

I found the elevator bank, pressed the button, then leaned against the wall, inhaling deeply. The air carried with it the distinct medicinal smell and taste of hospital corridors. I shuddered deeply.

It took me another half-hour to find the right wing and room. When I finally got there, I hesitated outside. Next to the door hung a sign reading, "Respiratory Isolation." A box of face masks sat on a small table to my left. I took one out, then glanced into the room. A woman and two children were clustered around the bed, blocking my view. I could hear their voices, tight, muffled whispers that barely carried over the clicks and whirs of the machinery keeping him alive. All of a sudden, the woman lifted the smaller child, a four- or five-year-old girl wearing denim overalls and a pink turtleneck, so that she could reach above the rail to kiss her father's cheek.

I backed away from the door. My job ended here, I told myself. I didn't have to confront this Mike Weaver. Christine O'Donnell did. The pay phone was back near the elevators. I headed in that direction.

O'Donnell's first words were, "He's here? In New York?"

I answered in the affirmative, gave her his hospital room number and said, "So that's it. You can work out the payment schedule with Tony."

"Can he speak?" she asked.

"I didn't talk to him."

"Tell him I plan to take the case to court."

I closed my eyes and fell against the wall. "Christine…"

"I'm going to sue the bastard. Tell him I'm going public. Civil court, criminal court. One way or another, I'm going to get him."

Her words faded as Alice's warning reverberated in my ears. If this went public, she'd never forgive me.

"Look, you never said anything—"

"Right. Would you have taken my case? Would you have tried so hard to find him? You have a problem with my decision, that's your personal business. But for now, I'm still your client and I'm instructing you to convey my message to him."

I shook my head resignedly and asked, "Why are you doing this?"

She exhaled heavily. "It's not just primal revenge, if that's what you're thinking. What he did was wrong. I want him to pay for that. Figuratively and literally." Her voice broke. "I'm going to spend my last days in style. At the bastard's expense. Tell him that."

"A lawsuit will take too long. There's no way—"

She cut off my words again. "Don't tell me there's no way. There has to be. I need money. I don't care if you use blackmail, just get me what I'm due." She left me with a dial tone buzzing in my ear.

I stared at the phone for a good five minutes, then dialed Tony whose instructions were brusque and to the point. Do whatever O'Donnell wanted. No discussion. I hung up and groaned. I shuffled back to Mike Weaver's room. Before I was ten steps from the door, I knew something was missing. I glanced at an orderly, whose eyes darted from me to the half-closed doorway.

"Hey, man," he said in a heavily accented Jamaican voice, "Don't worry. It's good news, for sure. The man's been moved to another ward, that's all. The pneumonia's done, and he's starting to breathe on his own." He slapped my back and happily told me where I could find Mike Weaver.

Whatever energy was left in me suddenly escaped, like air wheezing out of a balloon in one rush. I leaned on an empty gurney and wiped my palms heavily over my face. I can't do this now, I admitted to myself. I straightened up and started down the hall. A now-familiar click and whir caught my attention. I peeked into a darkened room two doors down from where Weaver had been. The bed closest to the window was empty, the sheets stamped with the hospital's name folded down as if waiting for the next nameless victim. The room was alive with noise, warm air flowing from the window vents into a room already heated to greenhouse temperature, the whoosh of a plastic wrap expanding and contracting around a blue-veined ankle.

"If you're going in, honey, you're going to have to wear a mask."

"What?" I turned around to find a nurse at my elbow. She was a tiny woman, with a flattop Afro and a broad smile.

"I haven't seen you on the ward before. Are you friend, family, or a new hire?" she asked, checking out my nursing uniform with uncertainty.

"New hire."

Her smile darkened. "I thought so. The poor guy's had one visitor since he was admitted. A tall, frail guy. Looked like he wasn't doing too well himself. This one," she inclined her head to the doorway, "won't last the afternoon." She clucked her tongue and ambled away.

I tied the mask around my head and walked inside.

Despite the sunken cheeks and lesions on his face, I could tell that he must have been a handsome man. He had a strong chin, a Roman nose and chiseled lips. All at once, his eyes shot open.

They were the color of cobalt glass. For an instant, something akin to joy leaped into his gaze, then the fear closed in. I stepped closer, moving around the IV stand to a black, plastic chair. I sat down, my own breath suddenly thin and ragged. Each time his chest puffed up with a tortured breath, my own lungs tightened.

Painfully, he angled his head toward me, his eyes focusing on my face, the need in them articulate and unrelenting. I touched his cheek tentatively, as if I were reaching out to touch all the people who had already left. Carol. My father. My ex-lover Mary. I grasped at his hand.

I sat there until he died at 3:45 pm, Saturday, June 8. I know because I checked my watch. It wasn't until then that I realized what day it was.

Six years exactly since my father's death.

Chapter 13

I clicked the remote. The three networks were broadcasting reports on the Operation Welcome Home festivities in Washington, D.C. After fifteen minutes of Schwarzkopf adulation, I switched to cable. I found a "Cagney and Lacey" rerun, and hunkered down onto the couch with both cats and a bag of chocolate malted balls I had purchased on the way home.

Cagney was unbolting her front door just as mine swung open.

"Hi gorgeous," Beth said as she walked in with a laundry basket under her arms. "You don't happen to know how one of my nursing uniforms disappeared from my kitchen, do you?"

I offered a half-assed explanation and she shrugged.

"Life was a lot simpler when you were writing those sappy romances." She put the basket down on a stool and turned around. "Your answering machine is blinking." Without waiting for a response, she hit the "play" button. K.T.'s voice sang into the room, reminding me once again of her seven-thirty dinner party. It was already after six.

Beth frowned and pressed herself in between me and the cats. "Don't tell me you're not going."

"Okay," I said sullenly, wishing she'd leave me alone with Sharon Gless and my fantasies. I increased the volume.

She reached for a malted ball and said, "I watched one of K.T.'s cooking shows last night. She kind of reminds me of Sharon Gless."

"But her smile looks more like Candice Bergen's," I said.

Beth stood up. "Yeah. And who'd want to spend the evening with a cross between Sharon Gless and Candice Bergen who can cook...in probably more ways than one." She opened the door. "By the way, you don't have to thank me for doing your laundry."

I grumbled thanks ungraciously as the door clicked behind her.

Then I glanced at the basket. Christ.

I ran downstairs and bolted into the downstairs apartment. The sliding doors to Dinah's office were sealed shut, which meant she had a client in there. I cut off my incipient holler and silently zipped through room after room, finally finding Beth in the basement where she was humming show tunes and folding laundry. I groaned when I saw the pile in front of her.

"Decided to venture into the world of civilization?" she asked. Somehow even Beth's sarcasm came off pleasant. It always astounded and unnerved me.

"Where are the sweat pants I borrowed last night?"

She pointed to the carefully folded pile to her left.

The envelope of photographs had been scrubbed into a sheet of discolored nubbles. I gingerly pulled out the photographs. From the corner of my eyes, I saw Beth wince.

"Uh-oh," she said, sounding like a five-year-old or Lou Costello. "Did I do a bad thing?"

I smiled at her. Beth was the most even-tempered, consistent person I know. She sure didn't deserve to be the recipient of my moodiness. Surprising both of us, I hugged her, apologized for last night, this afternoon, and half of my life, then left her humming "I've Grown Accustomed to Her Face."

The photographs were in pretty bad shape, reminding me of Silly Putty imprints of the Sunday comics. Colors and faces were distorted. But on one photograph, two faces were absolutely clear. Terry Fasani laughed at the camera, squirming the way you do when someone touches a ticklish spot. And the man licking the ticklish spot behind her ear was David Ross. I spent another ten minutes examining the rest of the photos. There was one shot of David and Terry making out on a bench. I sighed and tossed the picture down on the coffee table.

A redhead appeared in a number of the remaining shots. I could just make out the woman's features, but the face looked an awful lot like Terry's. I guessed the wig was a small act of discretion on her part. Or just part of her sexual foreplay.

I cupped my hands behind my neck and stared into space dumbfounded. All the hints had been right in front of me, and I had ignored them. I let the facts sink in. Not only had I slept with a married woman, but I had also slept with one of the prime suspects in a murder investigation.

Reluctantly, I dialed Marion Ross. I was relieved to get her answering machine. Foregoing all principles, I left her the news and promised her more information within twenty-four hours. Then I finished the malted balls and searched my closet for something to wear. K.T.'s dinner party might be just the diversion I needed.

Greenwich Village reminds me, at times, of an animated cartoon drawn by someone on drugs. The frenetic air of unreality alternately energizes and terrifies me. Tonight, my nerves on edge, the burns on my wrist and ear beginning to itch, and my head throbbing, it felt assaultive. I got lucky and found a parking spot near Bleecker and Sixth. Then I double-checked the locks and headed toward the park.

A tall, thin man wearing a torn Army jacket and long, dusty cornrows was working the line outside the Waverly theater. As I waited on the corner for the light to turn, I could hear him shouting, "It's a bird, it's a plane, no, it's Homeless Man." A teenager with a cracked front tooth and hair spiked into a rainbow rooster's comb threw a cup of coffee at him. His friends thought the scene was hysterical.

I retreated into my New Yorker's unseeing cocoon and jogged across the street between blaring taxi cabs, exhaust-spewing buses, and New York drivers cursing the cars with New Jersey plates. I walked biy the seething basketball courts on West Third, squeezed through the crowd surrounding the incense-and-belts street vendor, then collided with some middle-aged man wearing an old waiter's suit. It wasn't till he moved passed me that I realized he was carrying a black-and-white television set in his left hand. I could hear him muttering, "Black-and-white TV set. Five bucks." I shook my head and decided to get off Sixth Avenue.

The night was warm and a thin sweat was forming on my back. I felt almost feverish. The blasts of car horns and boom boxes mingled with the muted roar of the subway below my feet, making the sidewalk reverberate. I rushed across Fourth Street to the park, away from the New York cacophony that was making my own thoughts more dissonant. My mind played flashes of my father's face, the coolness in his eyes as he turned away from me just hours before he died, the wounded anger in Terry's gaze as I left her bed, the childlike way she angled her head away from David's teasing mouth as they posed for the photograph. I checked K.T.'s address again, and entered the cobblestoned mews where she lived. It was like diving below water on a stormy day and discovering incandescent coral.

The street sounds subsided to a dull hum somewhere behind me. A narrow courtyard lined with quaint carriage houses and overgrown oak trees invited me to walk slowly, breathe deeply. I stopped outside K.T.'s building, a slender house painted French blue with shutters the fragile pink of a winter dawn. The window boxes overflowed with brilliant impatiens, African violets, and geraniums. In the upstairs window, a single candle burned in an old-fashioned holder. From the street-level window wafted the smell of fresh-baked breads and piquant spices, and the tinkle of silverware and polite laughter.

For a long while, I hesitated to ring the doorbell, afraid to challenge the magic of the moment, afraid to suddenly find myself back in the dissonance I had just escaped.

Suddenly, the door swung open, spilling the buttery smells of home cooking over me. K.T. stood in the doorway, smiling. The foyer light bent around her silhouette. I said nothing. A question flickered in her eyes, but subsided instantly.

"I saw a figure lurking outside the dining room window," she said. She stepped over and hooked her arm through mine. I shivered at her touch. "You look like a lost child," she added softly.

We passed the dining room and the chatter of her other guests and walked down a foyer to the den. I stopped in my tracks and turned to her. She smiled at me, and I felt my face answer in kind.

The room was a treasure trove of American memorabilia. A fire engine red flying horse from an old gasoline station sign hung over the fireplace. Posters for B-movies from the fifties and sixties hung over a jukebox and pastel ice cream parlor stools. I sat down on one and spun myself till I started getting dizzy, then stood up, automatically steadying myself by placing one hand on K.T.'s back. My eyes settled on a collection of brightly colored tin wind-up toys which lined a shelf running the length of the whole room. I picked up a mechanical carousel, turned the key and watched the figures spin. Enchanted, I dropped into a dentist's chair stationed next to a coffee table made out of an old red wagon covered with plexiglass. On it sat a phone built out of Lego blocks. I laughed out loud.

K.T. nodded, seeming satisfied with my reaction. She brushed a hand over my cheek with exquisite tenderness and then reached for my hand. "Good," she said. "Now we can eat."

I followed her back out to the dining room, amazed at the transformation in my mood. I felt almost giddy.

If I had known then how short-lived the mood would be, I would never have left that room.

We entered the dining room to find that the other guests were already eating salads at a long, knotty pine table that looked as if it had been lifted directly from a farm kitchen. The table settings were eclectic, Mexican Fiesta ware mixed in with crockery and Depression-era glasses. When we entered, they raised their heads expectantly. K.T. introduced me to the people I didn't know—T.B.'s girlfriend Paulina, Virginia's husband Larry, a couple from New Orleans whose names I didn't catch, and a dark-haired young man named Salvador who was too busy breaking off a hunk of bread to acknowledge me. From the seating arrangement, I gathered that the famished Salvador was with K.T. I shook off my surprise and sat down between Virginia and K.T., intensely aware that the table apparently broke down into four couples—and me.

I made a brief attempt at joining the small talk in progress, but the men were fixated on speculation about whether the Minnesota Twins or Cleveland Indians would win tomorrow's baseball game, while the women were stuck on Julia Roberts's upcoming marriage to Kiefer Sutherland. I gave up conversation without a struggle.

K.T. walked around the table, pouring each of us a glass of wine. Larry made a point of abstaining. I gratefully accepted a goblet of perfectly chilled white wine and took in the rest of the room. It reminded me of a country home you'd find nestled in a thick forest, with darkened pine beams running along the ceiling and an old-fashioned riverstone fireplace occupying almost the full length of the wall leading into the kitchen. Dried flowers hung upside down from the beams. A miniature wicker rocker sat in the corner near the fireplace, a threadbare, one-eyed teddy bear propped up against its back.

K.T. glanced behind her, then back at me. "He's from the old days. Robbie Roger." She was gazing at me intently. I focused on the teddy bear, my appetite waning with each second. Why did she have this impact on me?

I sprinkled some balsamic vinegar on my salad and asked, "What's Robbie holding under his arm?"

Virginia and T.B. halted in mid-conversation.

K.T. glared at both of them and said defiantly, "A model airplane."

I could feel the tension crackling among the Bellflower clan. Over a model airplane?

One of the New Orleans guests, a fat man with long gray hair tied back into a ponytail and a face that belonged on a Michelangelo statue, chuckled good-naturedly. "Now, don't go ruining a foot-stompin' good meal like this one for some old family squabble. K.T., why don't you go fetch us the next course. I've had enough of this here arugula to feed half a herd of cattle."

As soon as he spoke, the recognition sunk in. Winston J. Hawkins. He was known as *the* cajun cook. I've dined in every one of the fifteen Hot Hawkins restaurants in the country. The man's secret recipe for jambalaya has burned and jolted my tongue into ecstasies in at least seven different states. I blurted out my praise as K.T. swept out of the room. Her delicious laugh made my arms break out in goose bumps.

And then dinner was served. Hot tortilla soup, followed by lobster fajitas with a potpourri of fillings, dirty rice, black beans and finally, fried bananas served in a bourbon sauce that sizzled under a wallop of homemade vanilla ice cream. When I put down my spoon at last, I almost cried.

T.B. pushed himself back from the table, rubbed his belly, and uttered a badly mispronounced, "*Bellissimo*. You've done it again, sis."

K.T. smiled indulgently and began clearing the table. Winston's wife, whose name seemed to be Cindy Sue Lynn or Cindy Lynn Sue or some combination of the three, rose up with purpose. "Let me take care of the dishes."

"She's one fine woman, that one," Winston said admiringly.

T.B. must have seen the look on my face, because he rapidly

changed the subject. "How's Serra Investigations doing these days?"

"What's Serra Investigations?" Salvador asked, wiping his mouth with a now-greasy cloth napkin. T.B. filled him in. Salvador's eyes instantly darkened with distrust.

"Sal's a cop," T.B. explained, glancing over at Larry, who had turned suddenly silent.

Great. I could feel my status as *persona non grata* take root.

"Robin is investigating David Ross's murder," Virginia added with a sideways look at Larry. Sure, I thought, throw another shovelful of dirt over my head.

I scrambled to change topics. "Hey, the final episode of 'Twin Peaks' is airing in just a few minutes. Maybe we can—"

"What's to investigate?" Larry asked. His voice boomed across the table. I leaned forward and looked in his direction. He was wearing a navy blue police T-shirt that strained across his pets and biceps. The man was big and ruggedly good-looking. He was also staring at me with unmistakable distaste. "From what I hear, the case is sewed up solid. Except for T.B.'s disappearing bullet."

T.B. jumped to his own defense. "How many times do I have to tell you, it's not missing. I don't think it was ever there."

"You're making us look stupid. You should hear the guys razz me. 'If your dumb, cracker brother-in-law hadn't fucked up the autopsy, the papers wouldn't be tearing down the NYPD again.' One guy in my precinct thinks Reverend Whaley paid you to dump the bullet."

Salvador underscored Larry's words with a snicker.

T.B. shot him an angry look and said, "I'm telling you, there was no bullet. It must have been something else, something that can make the same kind of markings…"

"Forget it, T.B." Larry said, returning his attention to me. "The kid's guilty. Whoever's heading this investigation must have shit for brains if he can't close the case."

"There are extenuating circumstances—" I started to explain.

"What circumstances?" Larry asked, ignoring Salvador's

continuing tirade.

After ten minutes of verbal battery, I blurted, "Ross was having an affair with a married colleague, for God's sake." Then I bit my lip.

Virginia's eyes flared for an instant. "Larry, I've had enough of this. We better go before this gets out of hand."

"Aw, Ginny, this just getting interesting." Winston chimed in, leaning forward with heightened curiosity.

T.B.'s date obviously didn't agree. She pushed back from the table impatiently and left the room. I considered following her.

"Who? Who was it?" Larry demanded.

Virginia was staring at me with an intensity that I didn't fully understand at first. Then it sunk in. She thought I was talking about her. Impulsively, my eyes snapped back to Larry. "Terry Fasani."

I could almost feel the air escape from Virginia's lungs.

"That's your friend," Larry said, grabbing his wife's elbow.

"Yes," she said quietly, not moving her eyes from my face.

We fell into an awkward silence that lasted until K.T. and Cindy Lynn Sue came back into the room.

"What lovely guests," K.T. remarked. "So well-behaved."

Virginia stood up abruptly. "Let's go, Larry."

This time there was no argument. The two of them strode out of the dining room, barely acknowledging K.T. on the way out.

"I've heard of people who eat and run," K.T. said, vainly attempting to restore good humor.

"Whatever happened?" asked Cindy Lynn.

T.B. grunted. "Me and my big mouth. Sorry, sis." The next thing I knew, the rest of the guests were making a beeline to the front door. I made a quick pit stop at the bathroom, then headed after them.

"Wait." K.T. grabbed my arm. She said good-bye to Winston and his wife, who were apparently flying to France the next day.

"See you at the opening of the LeClerc's Culinary Academy…"

Winston bellowed from the street.

Then K.T. closed the door, momentarily resting her forehead just above the lock. She shook her head. "Some low-key party," she said. When she turned around, her hazel eyes zeroing in on me, I became intensely aware that no one else was in the house. Not even Salvador.

"Where's your date?" I asked.

She cocked her head, then smirked. "Please don't tell me that you thought Sal was with me."

I nodded hesitantly.

Her smile broadened. "My brother-in-law's basically a good guy, but he still thinks that the only reason I'm gay is because I haven't met the right man. God knows why he thought Sal would be the one to turn me around. Matter of fact, I can think of a number of my straight woman friends who'd sooner turn gay than sleep with a man like that. Besides," she said, taking a step in my direction. "The only reason I planned this party was so that I'd have an excuse to see you again."

"What?" I could feel my cheeks begin to steam.

"As soon as you left my restaurant last week, I grilled T.B. about you. Then I decided to convert my plans with Winnie and Cindy into a small dinner party."

Her honesty was disconcerting. "I'm sorry things didn't work out," I said, edging my way to the door.

She stepped aside and said, "I had a cat like you once."

My hand froze on the doorknob. "Excuse me?"

"Skittish. Anyone try to pet her, she'd arch her back and hiss till her throat was sore." She lifted my hand off the doorknob, and lowered her voice. "See, one of the Crutchfield boys got hold of her when she was just a kitten. He slipped her into a pillowcase, spun her around his head and pitched her into the creek just down from our house. I ran after her. The way I recall, it was one of the bloodiest rescues on record. Took a good two years before she'd let me stroke her. But then she never left my side."

For some inexplicable reason, I felt mildly annoyed. "Nice

story," I said, my neck muscles starting to spasm. I rubbed my thumb into the knot under my jawbone.

K.T. pursed her lips, her eyes still inviting. "You're a tough one." She sounded as if she meant just the opposite.

I felt like I was traversing thin ice, a rumble beneath my feet warning me to get back to terra firma fast. I opened the door.

"At least tell me what happened in there tonight," she asked.

I gave her the short version. When I mentioned Terry's name, her eyes narrowed with concern. "No wonder Ginny got upset. She and Terry are pretty close."

"Did she know what was going on between her and David?"

"Sure she did. From what Ginny told me, she spent a lot of energy helping them cover their tracks."

Virginia's evasiveness was suddenly starting to make sense. "Why did she put herself in that position?"

"What would you do if your closest friend was sleeping with a man whose wife is a manic-depressive and carries a handgun?"

"Marion Ross is a manic-depressive?" The veins in my temple began to throb.

"Hell yes. And she's not a real fan of Lithium either. When she's off medication, she can be downright scary. She once threatened to kill anyone who so much as looked twice at David. She even showed up on Ginny's doorstep one night, threatening to blow her away just because she and David had gone out to dinner together. If it hadn't been for Larry, who knows? Maybe she would have pulled the trigger."

An alarm went off inside my head.

If K.T. was telling me the truth…

I bolted down the street, leaving K.T. standing open-mouthed in her doorway.

146

Chapter 14

From the moment I left K.T., nightmare visions had swamped me. Now I double-parked the car outside Terry's apartment in Bay Ridge, Brooklyn, chiding myself for being melodramatic. The living room lights were on, and from the way the windows flickered blue-gray, then white, I decided she must be watching television. Sitting there in the Volvo, I let my heartbeat return to normal. After a few minutes, I put the car in drive, eased my foot onto the gas, then immediately moved it back onto the brake.

It wasn't enough to know that Terry was all right. I owed her an apology for last night, for letting things between us get out of control. And no matter how reluctant I was to admit it, I owed Marion Ross some information about Terry's affair with David.

I switched on the hazards, locked the car, and headed up the steps to the front door. Breathing deeply, I pushed the buzzer. I heard it ringing inside, but there were no answering footsteps. No shout of acknowledgment. Instantly, I felt the blood drain from my face. The damn TV's too loud, I muttered to myself. I pushed the buzzer again. Still no response.

She's showering, I thought.

Not with the TV on, an unwelcome voice inside me warned. Unless Sam had come back home.

Somehow, the possibility wasn't comforting.

I knocked on the door, and as I had feared, it swung open under my fist. Electricity sparked along my spine. There's an explanation for this, I thought. There has to be.

I walked inside, every nerve in my body on fire. Automatically, my hands angled into a defensive position. The television was on and the credits for 'Twin Peaks' were just rolling. I scanned the room. Nothing was disturbed. Except the phone, I noted with a jolt. It was on the floor by the couch, the receiver off the hook.

From somewhere in the back of the apartment, I heard a click. I froze. The rattle of venetian blinds repeated. I released my breath. This is crazy. My imagination's just running wild, I tried to convince myself as I headed for the kitchen, my heartbeat accelerating. A bitter odor struck me. It reminded me of last night's car fire. I stepped around the corner guardedly, doubting that Tae-kwon-do could measure up to a twenty-two caliber.

A stainless steel teakettle on the stove had turned black, the plastic handle starting to melt. I turned off the burner, all doubts evaporating in an instant. Something was drastically wrong.

Another noise in the back of the apartment made me jump. A light footstep. Unmistakable. My limbs went stone cold. I eased open the silverware drawer. Hefting a butcher knife into my right hand, I slithered toward the hallway. My throat was so tight, I couldn't draw in air.

The bedroom light was off.

I flattened myself to the wall and moved closer to the doorway. The knife was heavy in my hand. The thought of what I might have to do with it weighed even heavier.

"Terry," I whispered desperately.

A faint moan. So faint, the light before my own eyes dimmed. Not again. Not another death.

I kept my back to the door and edged inside. The room was black. But the air crackled. Someone was in there with me. Pale light from a street lamp outside the window glinted off the knife as I took another step away from the door. A car passed outside, illuminating the room like a bolt of lightning. Something glimmered just a few steps from my feet. My eyes wouldn't focus. Then, all at once, my vision cleared.

Terry was lying on her back, a stream of dark, viscous liquid running off her forehead.

I felt the movement before I heard anything.

Someone was rushing at me. I dodged to my left stumbling over Terry's leg. The knife slid into the darkness. I scrambled over the bed and heard the whoosh of metal slicing the air. My hand grazed fabric. The next second all sensation disappeared. The last sound was the sputter of breath being knocked out of my lungs.

A crimson glimmer alive with amoeba-like shapes floated in front of me. This time I'm dead, I thought with something akin to relief. Then reality hit me. No, I'm not ready for this. I have too much work to do. Too much reparation.

I struggled to open my eyes.

"Larry! Her eyelids are flickering."

I knew the voice. K.T.

Water flowing over rocks.

I let the darkness cover me again. The next time I woke, I was in a hospital bed. I knew because when I extended my hand, I felt the cool steel of the bed guard.

"Robin, don't let go again. You have to stay awake."

I forced my eyes into a thin slit. Through the blur, I recognized Beth.

"Don't tell me," I slurred. "A bad concussion, right?"

"You're lucky that's all it is. The woman they found in the room with you is dead."

I closed my eyes, too drained to cry.

"Shhh," a new voice murmured. "You're going to be all right." K.T. was standing to my left.

"Anyone want to fill me in?" I asked. My mouth was as dry

as New York's reservoirs in late August. I ran my tongue over my cracked lips.

"I figured out where you were going," K.T. said. "It wasn't too hard after I saw how white you turned when I told you about Marion Ross's threat. I called Larry and Ginny since they live near Terry, but they hadn't arrived home yet, so I left a message and hailed a cab. When I saw your car double-parked and the front door wide open…" Her voice cracked.

I examined her face. Her eyes held more tenderness than I could bear.

"Larry and Ginny live about ten blocks from Terry," she continued. "I ran and got them. Luckily, they were just pulling up to the driveway. Larry's the one that found you."

A question squeezed its way through the daze. "Why did it take them so long to get home? They left before me."

"Traffic. Now shush. The doctor—"

"Where's Terry now?"

She paused. "She died in the ambulance."

I felt myself drifting again. This was the second time in my life that I had received a blow to my head severe enough to cause a concussion, but I didn't remember the first one being so utterly overpowering. All I wanted to do now was sleep. Or heave over the side of the bed.

A moist cloth moved over my lips. I looked up to find Beth bending over me. "The hospital agreed to release you into my care, so as soon as you can convince Dr. Gonzalez that you aren't about to lapse into a coma, we can take you home. Dinah's taking care of the paperwork."

I nodded and felt the room move with me.

Nearly ten hours and four police interviews later, I was back home in bed. K.T. hadn't left my side for more than five minutes at a time. But her presence was making me edgy. I needed to be alone.

I wanted to be unconscious.

"You're driving me crazy with all this crap," Dinah complained as she tucked me into my own queen-size bed and stuffed pillows behind my back. "Go back to writing romances. I'd rather be embarrassed by your politically incorrect trash than terrified daily by the very real prospect of your death."

I glanced at K.T. over Dinah's head. "She loves me."

"I can tell," K.T. said.

We spent the next five hours playing Monopoly and Trivial Pursuit. Needless to say, I lost every game. At some point, K.T. headed downstairs to make dinner for Beth and Dinah. They took turns eating and napping while I focused on not barfing. Finally, around eleven o'clock, Beth allowed me to do what I had struggled against doing all day long. Sleep.

When I woke up, it was just after eight o'clock Monday morning. The only one in the room with me was Tony. He was rocking back and forth on the bentwood rocker by the window, Geeja curled up in his lap and purring shamelessly to his stroking. As soon as my eyes opened a slit, the two of them sprung at me. I groaned and pretended to lose consciousness.

"What the hell's been going on with you?"

"I'm feeling great, Tone. Thanks for asking."

"Kill the sarcasm. You put Serra Investigations smack in the middle of a high-profile homicide. I want to know how we got there."

I didn't have the energy to fight. I gave him a complete update. With just a few omissions—like the night I had spent with Terry. At the thought, my stomach turned over. Terry.

"Get me that garbage can. Fast."

Bile spilled out of me.

"Geez, Miller."

"Tony, get out of here. When I'm on my feet, we'll discuss the case. For now, I just need to be alone."

He looked like he was ready to leave, then something propelled him to open his mouth. " 'Be not slothful in business,'" he said halfheartedly.

"For chrissakes, I almost got killed twice in the last few days.

I'll be as slothful as I goddamn please."

Tony just shook his head and walked out. If I had felt stronger, I would have hurled my alarm clock at his back.

Instead, I dragged myself out of bed and into the bathroom. I splashed water over my face and then reluctantly raised my eyes. I looked like an escapee from a Freddy Kruger flick. My short, choppy hair was matted to my scalp and my jade-green eyes were shot through with broken blood vessels, resulting in a color combination that would have been ideal for Christmas. The *piece de resistance*, though, was the white gauze patch covering the shaved patch above my burned ear. *If I stay in this job much longer, I can kiss any hope of a love life goodbye*, I moaned to myself.

Then I remembered Terry. Again. This time, reality sank in.

I'm a goddamn black widow. Death follows me like a pit bull. I sat down on the toilet bowl and rested my head in my hands. The vivid memory of the way we had seized each other just three nights ago fiercely contradicted the horror of last night. How could she be gone so fast, so irrevocably?

Guilt and regret swept over me.

If in fact Marion Ross killed Terry, I had all but loaded the gun and helped her aim it. My body shook from dry heaves, shook so badly I ended up kneeling on the bathroom floor, my forehead against the cool porcelain of the tub. I sat there for at least a half-hour, till my stomach settled and my anguish metamorphosed into anger.

No time for mourning. By now, I knew the routine well. The case came first. Then the pain.

I made myself as presentable as I could, then headed downstairs to my office, turned on a classical radio station, pulled out my case notes and started weighing the facts. I had two deaths on my hands now, and possibly more than one murderer.

But how likely was it that the two deaths were unconnected? So far, I had at least two suspects with solid motives for killing *both* David and Terry. The betrayed spouses: Marion Ross and

Sam Fasani. Rut motive wasn't enough. At half past nine, I dialed Tony's office number. Jill Zimmerman, our part-time assistant, answered. I was relieved to hear her voice.

"How was the honeymoon?" I asked.

"Apparently not as exciting as the last week of work. Tony told me what happened while I was gone. How're you doing?"

"Peachy. Tell Tony I probably won't be in the rest of this week."

"I was afraid you were going to say that. Now I'll have to listen to one of his tedious sermons on the virtue of hard work. I've been here less than two hours and he already has me hopping."

"Sorry." I hesitated. "Look, I may need your assistance on a case Tony doesn't want to pursue…"

"The Ross and Fasani murders?" She didn't wait for an answer. "Tony's already warned me that those cases are strictly off limits. That's like telling a kid that he can't have chocolate before dinner. I'll be happy to help you any way I can."

I brought her up to date, then asked her to conduct an in-depth check of Marion Ross and Sam Fasani. Employment history, financial status, the works. Then, with a quick glance at my notes, I threw out two more names: Virginia and Larry Savarin.

A few minutes after we hung up, the phone rang. It was Zack.

"I hear you're trying to get yourself killed these days," he said.

"News gets around fast."

"You kidding? This case is the talk of the town."

"What have you heard?"

"You mean, besides the jokes about the female PI who almost bought it?"

I didn't answer.

"Sorry," he started. "Okay, here goes…Willie Jefferson, the detective on the case, gave me a call late last night. Seems like everyone knows you and me are friends. He wanted to know if you could be implicated in the case in any way other than professional interest." He hesitated. "You weren't involved with the vic were you?"

"Go on, Zack," I said impatiently.

"Aw jeez, Rob. You sure pick your dates."

I decided to make things easier for him. "We weren't lovers."

I could hear him drinking something. From the background noise, I guessed he was on the pay phone by the bodega across from the station. "I wouldn't care, Rob. It's just that these murders are a mess. Everyone's trying to cover his ass. Willie and I decided we better work together. You know, two heads better than one. That crap. Man, we blow these cases and we'll both end up working as damn security guards at the Dime Savings Bank."

Copland's *Fanfare for the Common Man* was reaching a crescendo on the radio. I leaned over and lowered the volume a notch. "What have you come up with so far?"

"We got two deaths. Both victims are teachers at the same school. The kid accused of the first death is out on bail. So the first thing this morning, some beat officers drive out to the projects. But the Emerson aren't there. No one knows where they've gone. The Hammer is livid. He still thinks it's open and shut, that we got some psycho juvenile on our hands. Willie, on the other hand, thinks the department's just trying to find some black face to pin this crap to."

"Willie's probably right."

"I'm not arguing. But it doesn't look good for the kid, his disappearing like this."

"Assuming it's not Emerson, do you think we're looking at two different murderers?"

"It's possible, but not likely. First of all, as far as we can tell both victims were shot with twenty-twos. Of course, without the bullet that killed Ross, we're working in the dark. But there's another connection, one that Willie picked up on when he read my notes. They found sawdust in the hallway carpet leading to the bedroom."

"Sawdust?" I didn't see the significance.

"You didn't remember either. Good. Now I don't feel so bad. We found some sawdust at the scene of the first vic. No one made a big deal of it then. Could've come from anywhere. A grocery store, bar. But it could mean a lot now. Like we're looking for one perp who's got sawdust on his shoes."

My thoughts were churning like white water. I had my own theories. "I know Marion Ross has an alibi for her husband's case, but what about last night? Did Willie check her out?"

"What's Marion Ross got to do with this?"

"The woman carries a twenty-two, Zack—and she just found out yesterday that her husband was sleeping with Terry. That means she had means and motive. Now, what I want to know is, did she have an opportunity?"

"Willie hasn't interviewed her yet. You sure about this affair?"

"Hell, I have a picture of David and Terry kissing. I can drop it off at the station, if you want."

"No. Just hold onto it. In a safe place."

Zack's wariness concerned me. "What else?" I asked.

There were a few seconds of silence, then he said, "I talked to my friend Roberta—she's in forensics. She was at that P.A.L. fundraiser. The one that Marion Ross was at when her husband was deep-sixed." He lowered his voice. "She says Ross and the Hammer *were* there. But only for the first hour. They left the hotel around two."

We both fell silent.

"She had time, Zack," I said, my chest tight with tension.

"I know. Leave this part of the investigation to me. Okay?"

By questioning the Hammer's honesty, Zack was putting his career on the line. I wasn't about to interfere. "Fine."

"Got a question for you. Do you think your car bombing is connected to all this?" he asked suddenly.

"It wasn't a bombing. But no, I don't. Some kook's been burning up cars in the neighborhood for the past month."

"But not with people in them. From what Dinah told me, you had to be set up. Someone must have seen you coming to the car

155

and timed it just right." I had a flash of a car starting up down the block as I entered Bella. Christ. Zack was probably right.

"Rob," he started. I knew what was coming. "I think this case is getting too hot for you to handle."

"It was a random act of vandalism. Let it go. I'm more concerned about what happened to Terry. Has anyone talked to her husband?"

"Willie tried to find him. The guy can't be located."

"Can't be located?" I repeated in disbelief.

"Joey Pisano, Terry's brother, told Willie that she and Sam had a fight on Friday afternoon and that Sam took off. He doesn't know where or why. Willie said the brother looked like he was on the verge of a breakdown."

I remembered how close Terry and Joey had seemed the night I met him at the gym. Reluctantly, I realized I should call him. For sympathy. And questioning. Damn. Pain blossomed under my collarbone, between my breasts. I breathed past it and asked, "Did he tell you that Sam used to beat Terry?"

"Where'd you get all this?" he asked, a trace of annoyance slipping into his voice.

I told him about what I had found at Terry's house on Friday night.

"Two plus two..." he said pensively. "If you're right about Terry and David Ross, Sam certainly had motive for both killings. And as far as we know right now, he could have had opportunity. Combine all that with the beating on Friday, his subsequent disappearance *and* the fact that he's a vet—"

I sensed that he was eager for any clue that would shift his focus away from Marion Ross and the Hammer. I interrupted him. "You said a twenty-two was used in Terry's shooting?"

"Looks that way. Hopefully this time the bullet won't mysteriously disappear."

"My friend Ryan once told me that a twenty-two is a woman's gun. Don't you think a macho guy just back from the Gulf would prefer something with more weight, like a thirty-eight?"

"A gun's a gun," Zack muttered.

The Copland piece finished, and the announcer came on explaining that the entire day was being devoted to patriotic music in honor of today's ticker-tape parade down Broadway for the returning Persian Gulf troops. An idea blossomed, but it was too farfetched to mention to Zack. Instead I asked, "Can you get the military info on Sam Fasani?"

"I already have. Willie copied his files for me." I heard him shifting through papers.

"You have the information with you?"

"I knew I was calling you. Okay. Sam was with the 3rd Platoon, 59th Chemical Company, 10th Mountain Division. Part of the psychological operations unit. They're the ones that faked the Iraqis out, made them think the troops were advancing from one direction while they were really out west, preparing to outflank them. If he is guilty, we're going to need hard facts. I'll tell you right now, the NYPD is not going after a war hero without irrefutable confirmation. We've got enough bad press going for us already."

"The first step is finding him, right?"

"Right," he said suspiciously. "I'm going back inside now to call Willie with an update. You sit tight in the meantime, okay? I'll call you within the hour."

I was out of the house by then.

Chapter 15

The blizzard on Broadway was exhilarating. It was like being transported into a Cecil B. deMille version of a homecoming celebration. Tons of ticker tape, shredded paper, and yellow ribbons floated down from the skyscrapers, all but obliterating the thin blue of the sky. Thousands of people lined the sidewalk, shimmied up lamp posts, climbed on top of construction scaffolding. The air reverberated with the shouts of onlookers and the thump of approaching drums. With my head pounding, I bulldozed my way to the front of the crowd.

I flashed my fake press pass at the security guard posted near the reviewing stand, then ducked by the photographers and hiked up onto a mailbox. The movement awakened my nausea, but I took a deep breath and held on till it passed. I sat on that damn mailbox for a good hour before I saw the banner announcing Sam's platoon. Then I took out my hastily drawn sign and ran over to a group of kids just outside the press area. Pressing ten bucks into each hand, I asked them to hold up the sign and shout Sam's name repeatedly.

I knew it was a long shot, but I had a gut feeling Sam would be there. I watched the troops pass. Recognizing Sam from his pictures would be impossible. They marched by in full regalia, helmet straps hooked under their chins. I decided to get into the action. I ran into the street and started shouting Sam's name. Finally, one soldier smiled at me. "You his wife?" he asked hopefully.

"You bet."

"Sam's carrying the American flag up front, near the platoon sign. You missed him. Better hurry up."

I caught up with him soon after the troops came to a halt before the reviewing stand."

"Sam Fasani?"

He turned to me, a surprised expression on his face, his eyes shining with tears of pride. "Yes ma'am."

Suddenly, I was at a loss for words. The crowd had spontaneously erupted into a chorus of "God Bless America." Sam stood expectantly in front of me, his shoulders straight despite the weight of the wooden flagpole hooked into the leather pouch on his waist, his forehead gleaming with sweat under the rim of his helmet.

"Ma'am?" he asked puzzledly. The thick lens of his glasses magnified the question in his brown eyes.

He had chestnut hair, just a shade darker than my own, and his weak chin was covered by a faint beard. The man was far heavier and faster than I had expected. I scrambled to keep up with his pace.

I took the plunge. "Your wife..."

Immediately, his eyes narrowed. "I don't have a wife." His head snapped forward. The troops started to advance.

"She's been murdered."

His head swiveled toward me briefly. I was jogging to keep pace with him. From the corner of my eye, I saw a young cop heading in my direction. "He's my husband," I yelled. The cop nodded and moved back. Sam never said a word.

"Did you hear me? Terry's dead."

"Who the hell are you?" he asked, the military politeness gone.

"A private investigator. The cops are looking for you. I wanted to talk with you first."

The parade paused again.

"You're serious then? Terry's dead?" His voice was thin. He nodded, as if I had confirmed something unspoken, then he asked, "You suspect me?"

"What do you think?"

"I think the bitch somehow managed to spoil this day too."

His words silenced me. I watched him march ahead, then gathered myself and ran after him. "That's your reaction?"

"Look, lady, I served in 'Nam. This is long overdue," he said, the sweat now rolling down the side of his face. "Just a few years ago I entered the reserves…we needed the money. I never expected to be called. And I never expected this," he said, swinging his chin to the crowd. "When I got home, I was bursting with pride. I figured I'd get a real hero's welcome this time. Instead, Terry tells me she's been seeing someone else. That's what I came home to. The threat of a divorce. I tried to make it work, but she couldn't be bothered."

"Is that why you beat her on Friday?"

Again, his head snapped toward me, his eyes burning. "I never beat my wife in my life. I know you liberals think anyone in the Army has to be a macho pig, but that's not what I'm about."

"You don't seem especially grieved—"

"Fuck you." The muscles above his jaw line were jumping erratically. "I'm sorry Terry's dead, but she left me a long time ago. Friday was the final straw. I asked her to go with me to Washington for the parade on Saturday and she told me to go to hell. She said she had met someone new." He shook his head, then glanced to his right and left. We had fallen out of line. He picked up his stride and fell into place.

"Where were you last night?"

Silence.

"I can call a cop over right now…"

"I don't know where I was."

"Look, this isn't a game. Your wife was shot to death—"

"I got drunk and picked up some whore down by the piers, okay? I don't have an alibi."

"Do you have an alibi for the night David Ross was killed?"

His head snapped toward me. "No. But I'll tell you where I was an hour after I heard the bastard was dead. Celebrating at a local bar." He smiled bitterly. "Lady, if the cops want me, let them come and get me. Makes no difference to me." With that, he stomped away from me.

I felt too sick to follow him.

When I got home, I gathered that Beth and Dinah had made an appearance at my bedside around lunchtime, only to find me missing. Apparently, in the attempt to locate me, they had called everyone in my phone book. The result was a series of frantic messages on my answering machine and a nasty note from my housemates threatening life and limb if I came home and disappeared again before getting in touch with them.

I gave the cats a treat, left a message on Dinah and Beth's machine, then turned my phone off and slept for seven hours. Concussions do wonders for insomnia.

When I awoke, the room was dark but not empty. I closed my eyes instantly, a fever of recognition sweeping over me. Above the sound of my own breathing, above the gentle snore of the cats, was the intake of another person's breath. I opened my eyes a slit, waiting for them to adjust to the dark. Instinctively, I knew the presence was not Dinah or Beth. The stealthy footsteps toward my dresser confirmed my suspicions. I heard a drawer slip open.

I shifted my head to the right. The person was wearing a bulky overcoat, with the hood up. In the dim light, I couldn't even tell if it was a man or a woman. I weighed my chances of pouncing across the room and reaching the stairs before the intruder could react. I moved one leg tentatively. Immediately, the person whirled around, the raised pipe catching whatever light existed in the room. I didn't wait for the impact. Bolting straight up, I kicked the gloved hand dead on and heard it rattle across the floor. The force of the kick threw me back onto the bed. I swung to on my feet just as the figure pivoted and sprinted out the bedroom door.

I raced down the stairs. There was a thud below me, then one of the cats screeched. I jumped past the last three steps to the landing. For an instant, the pain in my head was so bad it was blinding. I braced myself against the wall briefly, then ran outside and down the stoop. The figure had disappeared.

"Robin?" Dinah was staring up at me from her doorway, her eyebrows furrowed with puzzlement. I plopped down on the stairs. I heard her call for Beth and then the two of them came up to me. I gave them a weary synopsis.

"It's my fault," Beth moaned. "When I got back from the grocery store, I went straight up to Robin's to check on her," she explained. "I must have left the front door open."

"Whoever it was would have gotten in no matter what," I said. "Don't worry about it."

Then the memory of a cat's howl shot through me. I stood up suddenly and headed inside. I ran through the living room, kitchen and office shouting the cats' names. Beth and Dinah got the message immediately. I sat down on my desk chair and listened to them searching the apartment, the weight on my chest pressing my breath into a poison that chilled my limbs.

The black widow strikes again.

A few minutes later, Beth and Dinah emerged with both cats in their arms. Geeja's tail had a new crimp in it, but otherwise the girls were all right.

My tears broke.

We called the police, who made a cursory visit about an hour later. The front doors to the building and to my apartment hadn't been jimmied, nothing had been stolen, and the intruder had been wearing latex gloves. In other words, besides taking the complaint, there was nothing the cops could do–except lecture us about keeping the doors locked at all times.

I spent the night downstairs, mind and body being administered to by my favorite psychotherapist and nurse. After Dinah and Beth went to bed, I sat in their rocking chair and wept silently. The way I had been taught. I wept for Terry. For Mary and for Carol. And for myself.

Early in the morning, when the welcome numbness had settled back in, I wrote my housemates a quick thank-you note and slipped up to my apartment. My answering machine was blinking wildly from last night. There was an angry phone call from Zack, two from K.T., one from Tony and three hang-ups.

I ignored them all and roamed through both floors, checking for signs of any other unwelcome visitations. Then, satisfied I was alone, I went into the kitchen to make myself a half-pound of bacon, a three-egg Swiss cheese omelet and a pot of hot cocoa. After forty-eight hours of nothing but toast, farina, and Yoo-Hoos, I needed a real meal.

I was washing the dishes when the phone rang. I answered reluctantly. It was Master Janet Choi, my regular Tae-kwon-do instructor. All at once, I remembered that nearly a week had passed since I asked her to check up on Hyung Kim, the custodian at David Ross's school. She sounded uneasy. "Choi? What is it?"

"Your Hyung Kim is an angry young man," she said quietly. "He also lies. This mugging he speaks of did not happen to his wife. It happened to a neighbor. There is more." Choi's English became stilting, cold.

Her loyalty to the Korean community was strong, but her belief in justice was absolute. Reluctantly, she informed me that Hyung Kim, the D.A.'s sole witness, was related to the owner of a Korean grocery that had been torched last year by three black teenagers.

"He pledged revenge," she added. "You must know, such

pledges are not made lightly."

Choi had only confirmed what I suspected all along. Still, her news energized and enraged me. The trumped-up charges against Thomas Emerson hinged on the testimony of a single man with a year-old grudge to avenge.

As I sat down with my case notes, I realized that I was working for me now, for what I felt was right.

I had my job cut out for me. After a week and a half on the case, I had more questions than I had started with. And a second death to contend with—one that meant a hell of a lot more to me.

Sharing Zack's assumption that the same person murdered both David and Terry, I drew up a column of possible suspects. Marion Ross still topped the first column, followed closely by Sam Fasani. I hesitated to write down Virginia Savarin's name. Instinctively, I liked the woman. Remembering the way she stood up to me the day I confronted her in her office, I half smiled. The woman had guts. But despite what I felt, I still didn't know her well enough to rule her out as a suspect. Reluctantly I wrote down her name. I had no similar compunctions about adding her husband to the list.

For each suspect, the motive for murdering David Ross and Terry Fasani was identical. Jealousy and rage. But what if the two deaths were related in a different way? Maybe Terry simply knew more about David's death than she had revealed to me. And maybe the murderer had decided to kill her as a way to guarantee her silence.

I jotted down a list of secondary suspects in David's murder, people related to him by marriage, friendship, or innuendo:

Secondary Suspects
William Haas, Marion's father
Joey Pisano
D.J. Cruiser

<u>Motive</u>
Fury at treatment of his daughter?
Bad blood between old friends?
Drug deal gone sour?

With a grimace, I added Frederick Rodammer to the list. After all, he had provided Marion with a false alibi. I put an asterisk next to his name. What if Rodammer had something of his own to hide? His eagerness to close the case quickly, without regard to the facts, was uncharacteristic.

The next question that had to be answered was who had opportunity. I started a third column.

So far, I knew that Marion had means, motive, and opportunity for killing David. But her whereabouts the night of Terry's murder was still open to question. The same held true for the Hammer.

I stared at the next name. Sam Fasani. His alibis for both nights were unknown. Then there was Larry and Virginia. Jill, our part-time assistant, had agreed to check with the precinct about Larry's assignment on the day David was killed. As for the night of Terry's murder, they had left K.T.'s shortly before me, giving either or both of them plenty of time to get to Terry. With a chill, I noted that Virginia was the only one who I knew for certain had opportunity in both cases.

I leaned back in my chair. I had plenty of work ahead of me. For chrissakes, I wasn't even sure *how* David was killed. If not by a bullet, then what? What weapon could have created a head wound so analogous to a bullet's entry that it fooled not only the officers on the scene but even the medical examiner? And then there was the couple who supposedly visited David Ross shortly before his death. Were they the same people who accompanied David to Atlantic City?

I created a new column for unanswered questions. Referring to my notes, I jotted down the extraneous pieces of data I had collected so far. I began with David's alleged drug connection, his Atlantic City jaunts, and stopped with his comment about paying off someone named Cruiser. I shuffled through the rest of my notes, then picked up the pictures of Terry and David shot in Atlantic City. If David Ross was in fact involved in drugs, could Terry have been immersed in the drug culture as well? Maybe that's why she needed the red wig. I examined the moisture-damaged photos closer. Then it hit me.

The person in the photograph could just as easily be Joey Pisano. Could David have been having an affair with both Terry *and* Joey? If so, Vic may have had as strong a reason for murdering David as anyone else. And maybe Terry just knew too much to be allowed to live.

For a moment, I felt like the pieces were about to slip into place. And then the picture melted in a spontaneous combustion. In the end, my head was spinning and I felt as far from resolution as I had been when I first sat down.

I retreated to the kitchen and poured myself a cup of lukewarm cocoa. The house was still. From where I was sitting on the kitchen stool, I could see the cats spooning on the coach. For some strange reason, the sight brought back the memory of my night with Terry. I shook my head sadly. After all the passion between us, I had bolted from her bedroom like a spooked colt.

We never said good-bye.

I glanced at the Sierra Club calendar hanging next to the refrigerator. I didn't even know when her funeral was planned. I swallowed the last sip of cocoa and dialed information.

The phone rang unanswered at Joey Pisano's house. I got the number for the gym and dialed again, my stomach just starting to protest against breakfast.

A recorded message came on. "The Body Shop has been closed. At this point, we have not determined when and if the gym will reopen. If you are calling about a partial refund on your membership fees, please hold on and a representative will answer your questions. Thank you for your patronage."

My curiosity peaked, I hung on.

"Can I help you?"

I recognized the voice. The Incredible Mismatched Hulk. I put my cup into the sink and asked, "Is this Vic?"

"Yeah."

I explained who I was, then asked, "What happened to the gym?"

"None of your business."

"Terry told me you guys were having some financial problems—"

"Christ! She had no...look, we're doing just fine. Little Joe just has more heart than he has sense. I'm taking care of that now. Hiring us a good business manager—" He cut himself off. "Man, this conversation is *over*. I don't need to explain nothing to you."

I gritted my teeth and said, "Then let me talk to Joey."

"Joey can't talk right now." In the distance, I heard a muffled cry. It wasn't hard to imagine what Joey was doing.

"Look, all I want to know is the time and place for Terry's funeral." I could feel my own voice breaking up. "I'd like to pay my respects."

"Terry's funeral is none of your business." Vic's repertoire was unusually limited.

"I know you have no reason to trust me—"

"You're right, lady. So why don't you keep your nose where it belongs."

Another voice broke in. "Give me the phone, Vic." It was Joey. "Hi. Sorry. We're both under a lot of stress right now."

His voice was hoarse from crying. I felt my own throat knot up. "It's all right. I just wanted to know...would it be okay if I attended the funeral?"

After a few seconds, he said, "No. We want to keep it small. Just family."

I nodded to myself. I was going to have to find another way of saying good-bye. "Fine. I understand."

There was a moment of silence, then some muted conversation. When he came back on, he spoke in a tight whisper. "I know what happened between you and my sister." I felt my blood turn to ice. "Terry was really taken with you. I never heard her sound that way."

"I didn't seduce her." I felt like a defensive teenager.

"I know that. I just wanted to tell you she really cared. That's all. I thought you should know." My eyes filled. How could he take time from his own mourning to comfort me? Or was his concern an act?

I said thanks, then swallowed hard. "Look, I know this is a bad time, but I need to ask you some questions."

"Can't it wait?" he asked quietly.

"No." I took a deep breath. "Try to understand. I'm doing this for your sister." I plunged ahead. "I know you're gay, Joey. Don't ask how. What I need to know is…were you and David involved?"

He blurted, "Christ, that was years ago."

A burst of adrenaline flooded my system. "What about you and Vic?"

"Only in my dreams, honey, only in my dreams."

I couldn't tell if he was laughing or crying. "Joey?" I asked. He sounded close to hysteria. Guilt swept over me. "I'm sorry. You okay?"

He coughed. "Please. I can't do this now."

I decided not to press. "Is there anything I can do for you?"

His laugh was bitter. "Do you know how to put a world back together?"

I understood his pain all too well.

After the call with Joey, I needed a break. I picked up the magazine I had stolen from Marion Ross's garbage and started delving through the glossy pages. Just when I was starting to relax, the phone rang. As I reached for the receiver my eyes settled on a picture of a long-legged woman wearing a mint green miniskirt and sea foam high heels. Next to her lay a man's glistening bronze body. The sharp heel of one slim-ankled foot was angled right above his buttocks. The article was titled, "The New Submissive

Male." All at once, a new investigative line clicked into position. I was so electrified by the possibilities that I missed the caller's first words. Then they sank in like a fishhook.

I rubbed the burn above my ear nervously and asked, "Mrs. Emerson?"

She hadn't identified herself, but something in her voice told me my guess was on the mark. "Carla said you was trying to help my boy." She sounded like a child herself. Her whisper barely carried through the phone lines.

"Where are you?" Keep cool, Miller.

"You didn't answer me. You working with the cops, or what?"

"I want to work with you."

"Thomas is no killer."

"I believe you, Mrs. Emerson. And I think I have some information that will help prove his innocence."

Her voice dropped into the background. I heard Thomas's teenaged voice answer hers. The sound made my hands shake.

"Mrs. Emerson, you can't run from the police. It'll only make matters worse."

She ignored me. "As soon as I hear that second teacher got killed, I knew they was going to come for him. My boy ain't going to take the rap—"

"They have only one witness and—"

"That man ain't no witness."

"You're absolutely right. That's why we have to meet. I know I can help you."

There was a pause, then she laughed angrily. "Why you wanna help? We don't mean nothing to you." The suspicion in her voice was infuriating.

Surprising myself, I blurted, "Look…I accidentally killed my sister when I was just three years old." I could feel the coolness stretching from my stomach to my limbs. Struggling to hold myself together, I said, "I know Thomas was there when that stray bullet killed his younger brother. I also know that sometimes the hardest part of watching someone you love die is accepting that you're still alive." The words clattered inside my head like marbles tossed onto a glass table. Taking a shallow breath, I continued, "Thomas has suffered enough."

Another beat of silence, then a deep breath. "I'll call back."

Before I could say another word, the phone was buzzing in my ear.

Chapter 16

I put in a quick phone call to T.B., who was more receptive to my idea than I had even hoped.

With typical effusiveness, he promised to get back to me within twenty-four hours. I spent the rest of the morning waiting for the phone to ring. When it finally did, I dove for the receiver. The room did a quarter spin. Definitely an improvement over yesterday's full loops.

"Meet us in a half-hour at the corner of Flatbush and Seventh. You know the pizzeria there?"

I said yes.

"No cops. Just you. Thomas got something to say I don't want no one else to hear. Understand?" "I understand."

I was at the pizzeria in fifteen minutes flat. I ordered a slice and a Coke and sat down at a table in the rear. An hour later, I was still sitting there alone. I was contemplating leaving when a slender black woman wearing a green bolero and black fedora walked in. The newspaper photographs hadn't done her justice. Martha Emerson couldn't have been much older than me. She had the high cheekbones, slim carriage, and gracefulness that usually distinguish high-paid models. It wasn't till she was right in front of me that I could see the hard edges life had carved into her expression.

"Thomas is outside in the blue Chevy. Alone. That Reverend Whaley wanted to come along with us, but I don't trust him any more than I trust you."

She turned around and walked back out. I felt a grudging respect for her. Hiding Thomas from the cops may not be a smart move from a legal point of view, but I had to admire her commitment to protecting her son.

I found the car parked by a meter. I let myself in on the passenger's side. Thomas's eyes jumped from me to the phone booth on the corner. His mother pretended to be using the phone. I had the distinct impression she was on the lookout for cops.

"It's okay, Thomas, I didn't bring anyone with me."

"Why should I believe you?"

"Because I believe you."

Despite the scar on his cheek, despite the hardness in his eyes, he was a good-looking kid. He had an intelligent, stubborn face. He can survive this, I thought. With a little help, he can survive this.

"Hyung Kim's lying about seeing you," I said. Thomas stuck his chin up at me and shook his head. "No. He ain't."

My heart skipped a beat. Maybe I didn't want to hear this.

"You hear me, lady? Kim ain't lying. That's part of the problem."

"Maybe you better explain."

"What you think I'm here for?"

I nodded. He pulled a pack of cigarettes out from the glove compartment and smacked the bottom, knocking half the pack onto the floor. He glanced nervously toward his mother and swept the cigarettes back into the box.

"You smoke?" he asked, sounding like a kid forced to grow up so fast, the part didn't quite fit.

"No. To me, it's like sucking mud. Just don't like the taste."

He smiled. "Mr. Ross felt the same way. He used to say I smelled like a wet ashtray. Didn't stop me though." He put an unlit cigarette between his lips and replaced the pack back into the glove compartment. "You ain't afraid to be in here with me?"

"I figure your mother will take care of both of us."

"Damn straight," he laughed. He looked at me appraisingly. Finally he said, "I forgot my jacket in the classroom, so's I go back upstairs. I'm just around the corner, but I hear this shouting. Now, I know better than to mess in someone else's business so I stop. But I decide to dip, you know, listen in. Three or four voices. That's what I heard. Mr. Ross's voice was clear. He was joking. Or so I thought. Then a woman and a man start shouting shit at him. The guy says 'You can't play with someone like that.' He was real agro—"

"Agro?"

"Pissed off," he said impatiently. "He goes, 'You took advantage,'" and Mr. Ross laughed and said something low. Then I hear this 'pow.' Man, I knew something bad went down as soon as I heard that sound."

"A gunshot?"

"No gun made that sound. It was like you hear in the movies. Skin popping. I was gonna go back down the stairs, but I heard someone coming up. Must've been that son of a bitch Kim. So I pull my pipe. By now, it's all quiet, 'cept for the sound of them running down the hall. I wait till they gone, then check out the room. Mr. Ross is just lying there in a pool of blood. Weird. Like he was sleeping. Then I go over to him and see his wallet on the floor. Anyway, I picks it up. The wallet…" He paused, waiting for my reaction. I struggled to remain expressionless. "Then I hear Kim down the hall, so I pocket the wallet and tear out of there."

"Why didn't you tell the cops all this?"

"You stupid? I knew I was ass out."

I raised my eyebrows in a question.

"In trouble. Man, where you hang out? You think some black kid holding a pipe and a dead guy's wallet's gonna get a break? As it was I didn't get more than twenty blocks before Johnny comes screaming after me in a cruiser. As soon as they put them cuffs on me, I shut my mouth."

"What did you do with the wallet?"

"Tossed it. All this shit I been through, and it didn't even have any bank."

"Thomas, you have to tell the cops what you know. It'll help you get out of this."

"I thought that was what you were going to do." Right. "Is there anything else I should know?"

"Yeah. D.J. Cruiser saw the two people I told you about."

"D.J. Cruiser?" So the dealer really did exist.

He looked at me suspiciously. "He's a friend of mine, okay? No questions about him. Do what you gotta do, but don't get him involved."

"Cruiser saw the killers?"

"Promise me." His mouth turned petulant.

"I promise…but you have to tell me what he saw."

"Okay. Cruiser said he saw this couple go into the school. Dark-haired guy and a redhead. Through the back door. Mr. Ross took them inside."

A sharp rap on the window made me jump. "Enough. Get out." Mrs. Emerson swung open the door and grabbed me by the elbow.

"I need—"

"A patrol car has circled the block twice. We're pulling out now." She tugged me out of the seat and made Thomas shimmy over. "You get my boy off," she shouted over the top of the car. Two seconds later, I watched the Chevy roar down Flatbush.

It took two hours to track down Zack. I told him everything I knew, with one exception. Reluctantly, I kept my promise to

174

Thomas and left out Cruiser's story.

By six o'clock, I dragged myself home. Upstairs, the cats were mewing fiercely and the answering machine was doing its impersonation of Christmas lights. Somehow I knew the first message was going to be from Tony.

"If you're healthy enough to be shoving your nose where it don't belong, you're ready to be back at work."

I growled at the machine.

The next call was from K.T. I wasn't ready to deal with her yet. Still I replayed her message twice. Her voice was like a tonic. Slightly calmer, I reset the machine and started to sort through my mail.

As usual, everyone wanted my money. Con Edison. North Shore Animal League. The Wilderness Fund. I flipped through the envelopes, then froze. Without turning my head, I lowered the answering machine, then tore open the letter.

The small, precise handwriting transported me instantly back to San Francisco. Cathy Chapman.

Dearest Robin,

For months, I have thought of calling you. Our last days in New York have remained with me like a festering wound. Perhaps, this wound remains open because we have never talked about what happened between us.

In so many ways, you remind me of my father. Always demanding closeness, then retreating into your own world whenever I approached. Maybe I responded so strongly to you because I also recognized myself in you. Did you ever notice how my emotions vacillated in response to yours? We were on a seesaw—magical, exhilarating, maddening.

Please know that I will always remember my time with you as a time of discovery. The most important discovery, though, was that I had become strong enough to love wholly, continually, despite my fears and private demons.

If it weren't for you, I would not now be able to share my life with a wonderful—

I dropped the letter onto the kitchen counter, the remaining words blurring together. A woman named Sarah. Moving to Oregon. Maybe one day we'll be able to meet somewhere in the middle of our memories and heal the past. The door closed on a possibility I had somehow come to depend on. A place I could return to when I felt safe. When I was ready to love. When I was ready to risk the possibility of losing someone I loved. Again. I grabbed the keys to the Volvo and ran down the stairs. I drove fast, reckless, unthinking, the radio blasting songs whose words I couldn't listen to. What I wanted was the numbing beat, the bass pumped up and thrumming through my thighs. The sound of the motor, the wind whipping through the open window.

When the fire in my veins finally subsided, I was in Canadensis, Pennsylvania. I slowed down on the dark, winding country roads and breathed in the sweet, pine-scented air. I was minutes from Telham Village, a heavily wooded community where two of my closest friends lived. I drove up to their house. It was after eight o'clock and all the lights were out except those in the front bedroom. I sat in their driveway, just out of reach of the light sensors. As much as I wanted to ring their doorbell, I couldn't.

I put the car in reverse and headed home. Three hours later, I was home in bed. Anesthetized. Around four in the morning, I finally fell asleep.

The wall was back in place.

"Robin, you did it."

I tried to focus on the face of my alarm clock. "Zack?" It was eight o'clock.

"They dropped the charges against Thomas Emerson."

I rubbed my eyes and sat up. "Why?"

"Why? We talked to Hyung Kim again. Under a little strategic pressure, the guy folded like a wilted flower. Not a bad guy, really. Misplaced anger. He corroborated Emerson's story in full."

"That's great news, Zack," I said flatly.

"Gee, can you tone down the enthusiasm? You sound like a zombie. You on pain killers, or what?"

"Or what." I threw the blanket aside and shuffled into the bathroom.

He laughed. "Know what your problem is? You worry too much. Look, I'd love to get into a metaphysical discussion with you, but the Hammer is chewing on nails this morning. Wait till you see what the papers do with all this. I'm glad to see justice done, but I got to tell you the department's not real pleased."

"I'm not surprised. So who's on the firing line now?"

He paused. I had a feeling he was thinking about the Hammer's role in this whole mess. "Marion Ross is still a possible. But Sam Fasani's another strong link between the two murders. The problem is no one knows where he is. I'll let you know how it shakes down." He sounded eager to hang up.

Quickly, I asked, "Does Marion have an alibi for Terry's murder?"

"Yeah. Look. I gotta go." He hung up before I could ask another question.

Puzzled by Zack's behavior, I headed toward the bathroom. After showering, I decided to put in an appearance at the office just to prevent more maddening phone calls from Tony. I eased the front office door open.

"The coast is clear, Rob. The preacher's out in the field."

I smiled and walked inside. Jill, our part-time assistant, was watering a plant that had all but died during her honeymoon. Her long, thick, salt-and-pepper curls brushed her shoulder as she turned to me. Her piercing green eyes make me feel like there's no place to hide. With her, I don't mind.

"You and Tony sure don't have that nurturing touch," she said, pinching a leaf.

I winced.

"Oops. Touched a sore spot there. Sorry." Jill crossed the room and hugged me tight and long. "Hey! She's a married lady now."

I glanced over Jill's shoulder and saw her husband John exiting Tony's office.

"You rifling through the boss's office?"

"Just dropping off a present," John replied, quickly kissing my cheek. "A photograph of sailboats at sunset. A John Feyre original. I left yours on that mess you call a desk."

I headed into my office and picked up the elegantly wrapped package. Even before I opened the paper I could smell the fresh scent of developer. "When did you have time to do this?"

John didn't answer right away and I mentally kicked myself. Sometimes I forget he's hearing-impaired. I turned and repeated the question.

"Last night. Open it."

The photograph was magnificent. A vivid rainbow stretched from an ominous gray cloud in the far left corner to a clear stretch of sky on the right side, where the sun struck a resplendent green hill that plunged into a white sand beach.

I hugged him for the gift.

"Far better than words," he whispered into my ear. I watched him kiss Jill, the passion barely restrained, then exit quietly.

"If I weren't gay, I would have battled you for him."

"I would have won in any case." Her smile was unambiguous. The woman was so happy I almost expected to see her float.

"Marriage seems to agree with you."

"What could be wrong? This morning, we made coffee, we made love...life is good."

"Just don't go mush on me, okay?" I swept papers on my desk to one side and positioned the frame dead center. "So what do you have for me?"

"Not much. Tony's using me as backup on the Torstar case. Take a look in his office."

I crossed the central room and opened his door. My jaw dropped in astonishment.

"Is that a computer on the King Luddite's antique typing desk?"

"A gift from Torstar. So now the preacher expects me to become the resident data genie and link us to all these databases.

Tomorrow that thing is moving into my anthill of an office. The good news is that he finally agreed to have me work full time. The bad news is that I'm supposed to be a computer expert by the end of this week."

I told Jill to call Michael "The Roach" Flanagan. He'll tell you more than you'll ever want to know about computers."

"I'll do that. In the meantime, let me tell you what I've got so far," she said. I followed her out to her desk and watched her flip through a new set of carefully labeled index cards. Jill is probably the most organized person I know. She even makes lists of lists. I had a feeling she'd take to the computer in no time.

She picked up a color-indexed card and started reading. "Larry Savarin was off duty the day David Ross was killed. I canvassed a few of his Bay Ridge neighbors on my lunch hour. Boy, do they love to talk. The elderly woman next door saw Larry leave the house at noon. He didn't return till dinnertime. I decided to not interview him directly. Cops don't take lightly to interrogations from private operatives."

I chuckled. Siccing Jill on Larry would be about as fair as pitting a Chihuahua against a Doberman. But then again, Chihuahuas can be pretty damn tenacious.

"As far as Sam Fasani goes," she continued, "I called in a favor from an ex-boyfriend who works at the National Personnel Records Center in Overland. Fasani's service record is A-one. No offenses, no complaints. An exemplary soldier. I'm not sure if that's a mark in his favor or a strike against him."

"Neither for right now." I hadn't even considered referencing military records. In most cases, you need the veteran's written permission. Even then, it can take weeks to obtain the most innocuous information. "Can you conjure up another miracle? I need to know why a Bay Ridge gym called the Body Shop closed down this week. It's probably financial, but I'd like to know for sure."

In answer, she pulled out another index card and jotted down three numbers using some complex recording system I have yet to decipher. "Got it. I'll need at least two days for this, but I'll do my best."While she was talking, I made a photocopy of the case notes I had been working on at home, remarking with a certain degree of embarrassment how they paled next to Jill's pristine, cross-indexed cards. The first two pages of my notes had Yoo-Hoo stains. I shrugged and decided to consider it my own form of color keying.

"Take a look at these," I said, handing her a copy. "But keep it under wraps still. Tony's going to be madder than hell if he finds out I have you working on this case."

Jill took the papers wordlessly and sat down at her desk, already engrossed in the subject matter.

I put in calls to Marion Ross and T.B., neither of whom was in, then decided to work for my share of the company's take for a change. A little before noon, Tony called in. It took me a red-hot minute to realize I was lunch. He chewed me out for fifteen straight minutes. At some point, I simply put the phone on the desk and got myself a cup of coffee. Tony was quoting some Old Testament passage when I returned. I decided to hang up before he reached the part about brimstone.

Twenty minutes later, the phone rang again. I picked it up reluctantly, expecting another Tony Serra tirade. Instead, a warm voice rang into my ear.

"Did you forget about me?"

For a split instant, I felt heat spreading through my limbs. K.T.

"It's Maureen. From Atlantic City? Remember?" The disappointment stung. "Hi. What's happening?"

She laughed. "Now I get it. You were expecting someone else."

"Pretty good. But I'm glad to hear from you. What's up?"

"I've been playing Dick Tracy and loving it. I think you'll be pleased."

The news was what I had expected. David Ross was a high roller. He had won small fortunes and lost them every time. The dealers loved him. Nicknamed him the Teflon Man because his winnings wouldn't stick. The last time he was in Atlantic City, he won thirty grand in an hour. Five minutes later, he was down forty. That was when his friends dragged him away.

I checked the dates. Eleven days before he was killed.

The dealers didn't know anything about David's companions. Even the descriptions were sketchy. A dark-haired woman, slight. A fiery redhead with an infectious laugh. And a reticent male who spent most of his time at the juice bar. No names.

Pieces of the puzzle had finally begun to fall into place. The OTB stubs and racing forms in Marion's garbage. The magazine article on wives coping with the addictive behavior of husbands.

David Ross was a compulsive gambler. And he had sustained big losses shortly before his death. The next question was who were the people with him, and how much did they know about David's murder?

There was no way Tony was going to let me head back out to Atlantic City, so I settled for the paper trail. I started with the credit card statements Marion Ross had given me. No hotels or restaurants listed. Only one purchase made outside of New York. In Smithville, New Jersey. The name triggered a memory.

I checked the telephone bill. Sure enough, there were several calling-card calls made to Brooklyn from Smithville. I rummaged in my desk drawer and retrieved my tattered atlas. Smithville was just a few miles outside of Atlantic City. I leaned back and dialed the number.

"Agate Inn." From the voice, I gathered I was talking to an elderly woman.

"I'm hoping you can help me. I just got a phone bill indicating a number of calls to your place of business."

"Yes?" The woman on the other end already sounded suspicious. I had to think fast.

"You see," I said, suddenly choked up. "My husband passed away last week. I'm not sure whether this bill is correct or not. The telephone company is already on my back for late payments, but I'm not even sure that David made these calls…he traveled so much."

"I'm not really—"

"Oh, I wouldn't ask you to do anything wrong. Couldn't you just tell me if David stayed there? I don't want to take on the telephone company if I don't have to." I started to sound panicky. Funny thing, it felt real.

"Okay, honey, calm down. Give me the dates and your husband's name."

A few minutes later, the woman returned.

"Sorry. We don't have a David Ross registered on those dates."

"I can't believe they made a mistake that many times. Did you have anyone staying there from Brooklyn? Maybe he registered under his boss's name."

"We're a small hotel, honey. Let me check . . . no. We had a V. Sirroco, A. Lipson, V. Savarin—"

"Savarin?"

"Is that it?"

"Without question."

I hung up the phone feeling queasy.

Chapter 17

The pieces were falling together all right, but I wasn't crazy about the pattern.

I tried to picture Virginia running off to Atlantic City for weekend jaunts with David Ross. The image wouldn't come. I had only spent a short time with her, but she struck me as the kind of person who lived strictly by the book. And that book sure as hell wasn't *Peyton Place*.

But I had to face facts. If Virginia was involved with David, I had to consider her a possible suspect.

K.T.'s sister. And Tennessee's.

Which could explain the lost bullet, as well as why T.B. had been so enthusiastic about my off-the-wall theory.

I recalled the first time I saw Virginia, her long, delicate hands reaching out to David with a poignant tenderness. It just didn't seem possible that those hands killed the same man hours later.

Unless the murderer was her husband Larry. Could he have been one of the two people who visited David shortly before his death?

I sat back and tapped my pen against the desk. There was only one person who could shed more light on the mystery couple. I checked my notes and dialed. When the connection clicked in, I crossed my fingers. "Mrs. Emerson?"

"Who's asking?"

I had to smirk. The lady was made of steel. I gave her my name. Her thanks for my role in freeing Thomas was curt, but sincere.

"I need a favor."

"You white people always want something."

I laughed out loud. 'Tell me you don't." I won a reluctant snicker.

"As long as it don't cost me or my family…"

"I just want to make sure the people responsible for this murder are caught. For that, I need Thomas's help. I have to talk to his friend Cruiser. "Cruiser ain't no friend to my boy."

"Your son thinks differently."

Her voice dropped an octave. "He's a dealer. Do you understand? I spend half my waking hours trying to keep Thomas safe from his kind, and you want me to encourage—"

"All I want is for Thomas to arrange for a meeting between us. That's it."

"Why should I do this?"

"You mean what's in it for you?" I made sure the sarcasm was apparent. She didn't miss it. This time her laugh was fuller.

"Thomas is in the other room. Told him to take the day off from school. Right now, I'm cooking up a turkey to celebrate the end of this nightmare. I'll talk to him…but if this goes through, you owe me."

"By my calculations, we'll be even."

She made a clucking noise. "Your calculations don't count. I need a good lawyer. Someone who's got more on their mind than making the news or a hot buck."

I started flipping through my rolodex. "Let me guess. You

want to sue the pants off the entire NYPD." I pulled out a card for an ex-girlfriend who spends more time on pro bono cases than her pocketbook or banker-father likes.

"Don't forget the mayor, him sitting up there on his high horse forgetting what color's on his skin."

I read off the name, feeling a perverse twinge of pleasure at the trouble Martha Emerson was about to cause.

"I'll call back in ten minutes," she said. "Don't leave."

I didn't hear from her for almost an hour. But when I did, the news was good. Thomas was planning to meet me outside his school at two p.m. I had twenty-five minutes to get there.

The Volvo's engine clicked like a cicada.

Now I locked the car, praying the radio would still be there when I returned.

Thomas was pacing back and forth in front of the school as I turned the corner. The first thing he said was, "I can't believe I'm doing this. My mother tells me I can stay home today to celebrate, and now you got me standing here about to put my ass on the line."

I realized with a start the kid was scared. My confidence level down-shifted a notch. "What's wrong?"

He looked up, surprised at the question. "Cruiser's all right. Shit, I know he deals. My mother thinks that makes him bad. But it ain't that way. The man deals straight with me. One day these three dudes started messing with me. Cruiser stopped them. Bam, pow!" he said, sounding like the soundtrack to the old Batman television show. "I don't want to piss him off."

"There are no cops involved, Thomas. I promise. And so far, I've kept my promises to you." He nodded at my words. "Right now, I'm not interested in what Cruiser does. Only what he saw."

He didn't answer. Instead he headed in the direction of the abandoned building catty-corner from the school. Instantly I realized who Cruiser was. The tall black man I had watched from the window the day David was murdered. The guy built like a boxer. When I saw the Mazda RX-7 parked on the corner, I knew

I was right.

"Wait here," Thomas said, his shoulders straight now. He had shifted modes. Now he was my protector.

As he sauntered inside, I checked out the building. All the windows were bordered up, except one on the top floor. Planks had been removed from a corner and for a split second I caught a glimpse of someone watching me. My spine tingled. Maybe Dinah was right. I had lost my mind. Why else would I choose putting my life on the line over writing silly, sordid romances for romance-starved wives in middle America?

Thomas reappeared. "He says go on up. Third floor."

I waited for him to lead the way. He didn't move. My anxiety level jumped off the Richter scale. "I'm supposed to go in alone?" Suddenly, I felt like the teenager.

He pegged me instantly. "You a big girl now, detective lady."

I watched him walk away, each step shooting new fears through my body. Finally, I took a deep breath and headed inside.

The darkness was blinding. As soon as the poorly hung door swung behind me, I knew I was in never-never land. The air was acrid, a mixture of ammonia, fire and plain old musk. Something else too. Sweat. The kind of sweat that hits your nose like a firecracker, exploding in your nostrils with its message of fear, sickness, and despair.

I stood still, breathing through my mouth, waiting for my heart rate to level out, my vision to clear. Slowly my eyes adjusted. Urine-stained mattresses lined the far side of the room. Under one of the boarded-up windows was a makeshift barbecue pit composed of bricks from the outside of the building. The plywood-planked floor was blanketed in litter and human detritus.

In the corner, something scuttled across the floor, its body as thick as a cat's.

I headed up the stairs.

The rotten steps threatened to give way under my weight. I put my hand on the banister for support. Instantly a splinter pierced my skin. I didn't dare pause.

Near the top, the light suddenly intensified. I braced myself and exited onto the landing. No voices or movement other than my own. I stopped breathing. I was in a long, dimly lit hallway with four doors. All closed. A nightmare version of "Let's Make a Deal." I didn't want to play, but I had no choice. Hesitantly, I edged toward the right-hand door in front of me. As I touched the door knob I kicked myself for not turning this task over to Zack. The door jerked open and a hand slammed over my mouth. I started kicking and wailing like a banshee. Another pair of hands grabbed my ankles, locking me in place as securely as a vise. A third man stepped behind me and locked my arms back. They moved so quickly I couldn't even make out their faces. A hand probed my back, another plunged under my shirt. Terror and fury rushed through me. I bit an earlobe, stabbed my knee into a groin. The air was crackling with moans and screams. All mine. Then suddenly, the whirlwind died. One of the men hurled me onto a mattress like a sack of potatoes. My only thought was if these bastards tried to rape me, I'd kill them with my bare hands. Kill them or—

"Sorry for the reception."

My attention shot across the room to where an incongruous gray leather armchair sat next to an elegantly arranged bookcase. The man's boxer-thick body filled the chair. I glanced back at my attackers. A short, squat white guy that looked like my uncle Seymour was zealously cleaning his teeth with a toothpick. The other two, an Hispanic and an Asian, were propped up on the window sill, the gleam in their bloodshot eyes telling me just how much they enjoyed their jobs.

Great, I thought, I've stumbled into the United Nations of crack dens.

"I'm glad to see that you're not wearing a wire," Cruiser announced from across the room. "That would have been extraordinarily foolish." He stood up and approached me. Quickly, I lifted myself up off the mattress.

187

My legs slightly akimbo, I said, "Nice reception committee you got." My voice was steady. Thank God for small favors.

"I have a business to protect. I'm sure you understand." He articulated his words carefully. The man was educated, wily. A dangerous opponent. I watched him closely as he circled me, his eyes darting to my sneakers, back up to my hip, then my eyes. His hand hovered instinctively over the bulge under his navy pullover. Something about his manner seemed familiar. Then it hit me like a dart in the behind.

"You're a cop!" I exclaimed spontaneously, then bit my lip.

He stopped, his eyes digging into mine. Unblinking. Probing. "*I used to be* an officer of the law. The system," he said, stretching the word till it hissed, "the system failed me. You risk your life for shit. No money. No respect. The next thing you know, the punk that almost sliced your throat two days ago is out on the street, thumbing his finger at you. I found a better way."

I tried to wipe the surprise off my face.

"But I try to conduct my business like a gentleman." I could tell he was waiting for me to react. I did my best to disappoint him.

He smiled. "Good." A firm hand the size of a ping pong paddle landed on my back and propelled me to the wall. "If you don't mind…" He kicked my feet apart and pushed me forward so that I couldn't move my hands from the blistered plaster without falling on my face. He frisked me from head to toe.

A real professional.

He patted down my ankles and said, "One thing I learned from my days on the force, you can't be too careful."

When he was finally done, I straightened up and turned around. His hands dropped to his sides, his posture more relaxed. "Now, why don't you tell me why you've ventured into my space?"

I wanted to look formidable. I had a feeling I looked like I was going to throw up. Which I was. "You're the only one who can describe the two people who visited David Ross the day of his murder."

He snorted and pulled out a small vial from his back pocket. I watched as he poured drops into his eyes. "Who says?"

"Thomas Emerson."

A rivulet glistened along his cheek like a streak of tears. The effect was jarring. "Pooley's just a kid," he said.

"He hasn't been a kid for a long time."

We stared at each other for a long, hard minute. Then, without taking his eyes off me, he gestured at his cohorts. They left the room soundlessly. Strangely, I felt even more vulnerable than before.

"There's no way I'm going to make an official statement." He pulled out a pack of cigarettes and lit one. "Besides, a dealer's testimony is worth shit. Believe me, I know."

I recognized the bitterness in his voice. For the hundredth time I wondered at how cops like Zack can remain sane and honest despite the pressures they face every day.

"Just tell me what you know," I said. "I'll take it from there."

He smiled and tapped the cigarette into a gold-plated ashtray. "Take it where?"

"Did you recognize either person?"

"What are you planning to do? Track down these perps by yourself? You got a Cagney complex, dickie girl?"

It took me a second before I realized what he was talking about. "I'm not playing cops and robbers. A second teacher has been killed...this one was my friend. So why don't we stop jerking around—"

Before I could finish my sentence, a pocketknife flashed in his hand. The three-inch blade whizzed by my ear and plunged deep into the wall behind me. My knees threatened to buckle. Instead, I spun around and whipped the knife out, praying to God he wouldn't make me use it. "What the hell was that about?" I asked, my voice edgy.

He thundered toward me. "This is my world. I run it. Like a king," he hissed into my ear. "You want a favor from me, you better change your damn attitude fast. Before my benevolence wears thin."

With a flick of his thick fingers, he twisted the knife from my hand.

"Fine." The sarcasm was so sharp, it almost made my mouth pucker. "What did your majesty see—"

He sunk his fingers into my hair and twisted till the pain was almost unbearable. "You think 'cause I used to be a cop, I'm not going to burn your hide, but you're wrong. I left my ethics in the back pocket of that fucking blue uniform. So there's nothing stopping me now. Nothing."

I swallowed hard, the pain rippling through my nerves. "I'm sorry."

He let go and nodded. "You got money on you?"

"Fifty, sixty bucks."

I reached for my pocket, but he got there first. "Just so you remember, you never get something for nothing. Sit down."

I did exactly as I was told.

"The day Ross got bucked, I noticed this chick going into the school. Red hair, great legs. She looked familiar, but I didn't know the guy. He was real macho. Dressed down. Sweats, T-shirt. So I say to myself, that's an odd couple. I mean, the woman was dressed to the nines, tight dress, spike heels."

My adrenaline surged.

"Guess my training still holds. I see what other people miss. Small variations in patterns," he continued. "You wouldn't expect someone like that to be walking into some East New York school. The guy was medium-frame, six-one tops. Dark hair. Didn't see his face."

So far, I hadn't learned much. I bit the inside of my cheek and tried a different tack. "Did Ross ever buy from you?"

He looked puzzled. "Buy? As in coke?"

I nodded.

The suspicion slid back into his eyes. "Thought you wanted to know about this couple?"

"I want to know who killed Ross and why. If Ross was doing

drugs…"

He strode over to a glass table studded with crack vials and a dozen or so white anthills. Dipping a finger into the snow, he muttered, "You think I got something to do with his death?"

I stood up and said, "Right now, your business means nothing to me. I don't care if you sold Ross a kilo of dope, all I care about is the murder. That's it."

"Ross was no user," he said, licking his finger like a cat. "And I don't deal to no teachers or school kids." He smiled at me. "Bad for business. You start messing with kids, the cops take greater interest in you. A bust like that makes better headlines. Me, they leave alone."

"What about Ross?"

"The man was an addict, no question, but not to the white knight. He was a gambler. Big time. I used to see him all the time at the OTB on Court Street. That's how we knew each other. One time, I saw him go up to the window and lay down ten G's like it was nothing. On a long shot. Fifty to one. I go up to him and say, man, you got balls. And he laughs. Says that was why he bet on the horse. Great Balls of Fire. That was the horse's name."

Cruiser had a straight-edge razor in his hand now. The sight of its cool steel made the hair on the back of my neck stand straight up. Time was running out for me, I realized with a start. If I didn't get out of here soon…"

One last question, I warned myself. Make it a good one. "Did Ross owe you money?"

His head snapped up. "What did Emerson tell you?"

I didn't like his tone. Somehow I had just become more threatening to him. "Nothing. The kid's played straight with you. I'm just taking a stab in the dark—"

"Watch where you stab, sweetheart." He waved the razor at me and approached. Slowly. I backed up to the door. The blade was under my nose, then my neck. He was so close I could smell his breath. Cigarettes and Chinese food. Black bean sauce.

"Ross borrowed fifty-three grand from me over a month ago.

Imagine borrowing that kind of bank off a guy like me, and not paying off."

I did.

Ross would be dead.

It suddenly struck me that Emerson and Cruiser could be working together to create an alibi. The mysterious couple may just be a figment of their joint imaginations.

"Predictable, very predictable." Cruiser was talking more to himself than to me. I had the feeling he had seen something in my eyes that amused him. "He paid me off the day before he got killed. Every dollar." He paused, then said, "Here's your choice. Either I'm lying, or I'm telling the truth. If I'm lying, you're going to be dead in about thirteen seconds." He lightly drew the razor across my neck. I could feel the beads of blood begin to drip. I tried hard not to swallow. "But if I'm telling the truth, Ross got that fifty-three grand from somewhere else."

He stepped back.

I didn't ask any questions. I ran out of that building as if my life depended on it.

I have a feeling it did.

Chapter 18

Cruiser's words replayed in my head as I slipped into the driver's seat and cleaned my neck with a Wash-n-Dry. If Ross did pay him back, where the hell had he found the money? According to Maureen, Ross had lost forty thousand dollars in Atlantic City just eleven days before his death. I doubted he would have asked his wife for the money. So either he had been pretty damn lucky at OTB that week, or he had borrowed the money from someone else. Or stole it. Or blackmailed someone. Or...

The Volvo had just turned over when I saw Virginia rushing toward her car. A sky blue Ford Taurus. I glanced at the dashboard clock. Three-ten.

She looked agitated as she rammed the key into the door lock. But then again, I was no pretty sight myself. After my encounter with Cruiser, my hair was damp with perspiration and my lungs just remembering how to function.

More than anything, I wanted to scamper home and plunge into a steaming bath. But this case was plaguing me. I pulled out behind Virginia's car.

Following a car in New York City is like trying to pin the tail on a donkey while everyone around you is intent on playing dodge ball. The only good part is that your chances of being detected amid the chaos is practically nil.

Virginia was a competent, careful driver. Signaling turns, slowing at stop signs, yielding for school buses. The longer I tailed her, the more convinced I became that she wasn't exactly the type to commit crimes of passion.

We drove over the Brooklyn Bridge into Manhattan. There my job became almost impossible. Cabs cut me off, people lurched into the street unexpectedly. Twice I had to run red lights to catch up to her. When she began circling around Twelfth and Thirteenth streets, I nodded to myself. The hawk was searching for a place to land.

I squeezed in front of a fire hydrant, and watched her maneuver into a spot that rightly belonged to a Volkswagon. Then she slammed the car door and started trotting up Thirteenth Street. Halfway up the block, she stopped at a brownstone. She bobbed up the steps and rang the doorbell, glancing furtively at her watch. A buzzer let her in. A minute later I was on the stoop checking out the name plate. B. Marcelescu.

An hour passed before Virginia reappeared, her arm entwined with that of an older woman. She seemed calmer. Even serene.

The woman with her was tall and thin, her gray hair pulled back into a tight bun. They talked on the stoop for a few minutes, then Virginia practically floated down the stairs.

"See you at Our Daily Bread at seex," the older woman shouted after her in a heavily accented voice. She watched Virginia walk away, her arms folded across her bony chest. I crossed the street for a closer look. She wore a black double-breasted jacket with wide flat cuffs over a black ankle-length dress. Her thick-heeled pumps were ink black.

A vision from the eighteenth century.

I cleared my throat. "Ms. Marcelescu?"

She turned her gaze on me, totally disinterested. "Yes." She drew the word out till it sounded almost musical.

I climbed the stairs and handed her a business card. "Just a few minutes of your time…"

"Time eez not a geeft I geeve freely."

Her tone was dismissive. I didn't let that stop me. After D.J. Cruiser, this woman was a piece of cake. "Of course, you don't have to talk with me. But I am investigating a murder. If you decline, I will have to provide your name to the police—"

"Mees," she said impatiently. "I have survived much in my life. Communeest Romania. Nicolae Ceausescu. Do not threaten me." Unexpectedly, she extended a small, square hand distinguished only by the length of her thumbs. "Come. I vill answer your questions, but only because that eez what I choose."

I followed her up a brightly lit staircase. A dark walnut door swung open at the top and I found myself in an unbearably warm loft-like space. My eyes darted to the windows automatically. They were all closed tight and shielded by heavy drapery the color of garnets.

For the second time that day my lungs struggled for air. "Can you open a window?" I practically gasped.

"No," she answered simply. She sat down on a cherry wood Windsor chair positioned next to the most magnificent harp I had ever seen. Come to think of it, the only harps I had ever seen were the ones in Daffy Duck cartoons.

She gestured to a matching chair on the other side of the harp. I sat down and stared at her through the silky strings.

"So…" she prompted me.

For an instant, words failed me. Who the hell was this woman? "What is your connection to Virginia Savarin?" I ventured.

"Virgeenia?" she asked bemused. "You ask me about Virgeenia."

The woman made me feel young and foolish. I decided to wait her out.

"So," she said after an interminable minute. Sweat was dripping off my chin. "Virgeenia eez an angel." She punctured her words by flaring her thumbs in opposite directions. "Do you know anyteeng about zee harp? No, I would guess not. You are of today."

The words were clearly a condemnation.

"Let me tell you, if I wanted to do zee rap muzique, I could play eet and make the beeg bucks. But I don't. I play the harp." She lifted her chin imperiously. "I play it not for money, but for love. Virgeenia understands thees."

She stopped with an air of finality. I felt my eyebrows press together in puzzlement. Was that supposed to explain everything?

"I'm sorry. I still don't understand your relationship."

She pursed her lips, amused at my confusion. "She eez my student. We share zee same lover." I perked up.

"Zee harp," she said dramatically, drawing one of her amazingly long thumbs backwards along the strings.

The loft vibrated with the sound. Magical. I closed my eyes. I was drifting on a cool stream of sound. The notes bubbled inside me like champagne. Suddenly, I slammed into silence. When I opened my eyes, B. Marcelescu was assessing me from under her heavy gray brows.

"Perhaps you do have soul. Your response eez good," she said, nodding with satisfaction.

Surprisingly, I felt myself beam. "You're Virginia's teacher."

"No. I am her beacon, and she a sheep saileeng toward zee light. You understand?"

Sheep saileeng. Right.

"How much do you know about her?"

"Everytheeng there eez to know. She eez a musician." She stabbed her hyperactive thumbs against her chest. "She has heart. If you theenk she can keel—"

"I'm not accusing her of anything, Ms. Marcelescu."

"Beatrice."

"Beatrice. I'm also sailing toward the light. Searching for answers."

Absent-mindedly, she began strumming the harp. The honeyed notes made it hard to concentrate on details.

"Do you know if Virginia is happy in her marriage?"

She laughed. The sound seemed odd coming from her gaunt frame. "What woman eez happy? Marriage eez a seelly concept, no? One man, one lifetime. But Virgeenia, she is a woman of character. Her husband eez a deeficult man. But she loves heem, yes." Her coal black eyes widened as if she had just reached that conclusion. "One time, she tells me she eez tempted to stray from her vows. I guide her to zee harp. She plays teell she weeps like a child. Then I hold her and she says, 'I dream of being free, free to do zee wrong theeng.' I theenk she never gave in."

"Love," she said, her fingers darting along the strings like bumblebees among a bed of flowers.

"Love eez crazy, no? Such chances you take to geeve your heart. And always, such hurt hidden in the joy."

She gave herself to the music fully, till the notes exploded through me, till she plucked emotions from me that I hadn't recognized till then. My eyes filled, my breathing thinned.

Over the euphony her voice carried like brass accompaniment. "But the risk of not loving at all is so much graver than the risk of losing love."

I left her at the harp, her black-clad body a beacon of light that stung my eyes.

Outside I gulped air greedily. Marcelescu's words had penetrated deep, tearing open the part of me that had responded so intensely to K.T. Bellflower. I thought again of K.T.'s eyes, the electric charge that they shot through me. When I was near her, I could feel the air between us vibrate just like the strings of the harp. More potent even than my initial response to Mary.

The only woman I had really loved.

And here I was investigating K.T.'s sister.

I trudged back to the car. The ticket on the windshield made me wince. Maybe it was time to start looking for a new car of my own.

But then I paused.

Since I already had a ticket, there was no need to rush. I decided to make a couple of calls before pulling out. The first one went to T.B. No answer. Next I called the office. Tony answered on the second ring. Surprisingly, he was in a good mood. I was so taken aback that I made the mistake of telling him where I was. He didn't ask questions, all he said was, "Good. Take care of the O'Donnell business while you're there. She's getting impatient." I made a face at the receiver and agreed.

All in all, the day was rapidly becoming a contender for one of the year's worst.

It took me twenty minutes to find a legitimate parking spot, then walk over to St. Vincent's. I scurried past the security desk with purpose and headed toward the elevator bank. There was a small mob trying to squeeze into one small, peroxide-scented elevator. I intended to wait for the next car when a shock of gray hair seized my attention. An elderly man edged in, giving me a clear view of a man with thick eyebrows. I barreled through the crowd, ignoring the woman who pronounced me a pig at the top of her lungs.

William J. Haas. Marion Ross's father. With a commanding voice, he instructed a red-eyed teenager carrying a wilted bouquet to press the button for the fifth floor, the same as Weaver's room.

When the doors creaked open, Haas shouldered his way to the front of the elevator. I followed closely. He stamped down the hall authoritatively. Without question, the man had been here before. He disappeared through an unmarked door. Definitely not a patient's room. I hovered nearby, pretending first to tie my shoelaces, then to search my wallet. Finally another man headed toward the door. A quick glance over his shoulder revealed a circle of chairs. A twelve-step meeting?

I made a mental note to check up on Haas, then went in search of Mike Weaver. The search was fast. As I turned around, he rolled himself right into my hip. "Sorry," he said in a hoarse whisper. He didn't move his hands from the sides of the wheelchair. "Mike Weber?"

He looked up at me, then to the door behind me. A puzzled look passed over his features. "The name's Weaver. Now if you'll excuse me, I have a meeting—"

"I'm a private investigator. Christine O'Donnell hired me to find you."

The words fell on him like a slow-moving avalanche. At first, his expression hardly changed. I realized with a pang of disgust that he didn't recognize the name right away. Then it sank in. Without a word, he backed up and started wheeling down the hall.

The lights were off in his room, the only illumination coming in through the filmy window. I pulled a straight-back chair next to him. Up close, he looked like a concentration camp survivor. Sunken cheeks, skin the color of gray pottery clay.

He slumped forward and asked, "What does she want from me?" His voice was so weak I was astonished that he had been able to move the wheelchair up and down the hall.

"Do you even remember her?" The words unleashed the anger within me. I shook my head. Stay even.

"Yes. A silly woman. Mistook passion for romance."

The anger exploded. "She's sick." When he didn't respond, I snapped, "She's dying."

His laugh was like the sound of rocks rattling in a glass bowl. "Aren't we all? Even you."

I met his eyes. Despite the frailty of his body, there was a fire in his gaze. Denial. Fury.

"Why did you do it?"

"Do it?" he repeated sarcastically. "You mean, fuck her? Look, we all take our chances. Sex today is a goddamn game of Russian roulette. For me, the bullet went off one night in Las Vegas. A highclass prostitute who grabbed my balls under the blackjack table. She was good, but not worth the price I've paid." He gestured at the wheelchair, then broke into a coughing fit. I could feel my lips curl with disgust as I fetched him a glass of water.

Poor guy. I recalled a dozen friends who died of AIDS with dignity and love. The memory made me want to spill the water over the guy's head.

His cough dwindled into a steady wheeze. "Look at me now. You know I used to change Mercedes like other men change socks. When they first told me I had AIDS, I wouldn't believe it. Then I tried to buy my way out of it. But after a while, I just said fuck it. I'm just going to keep living my life the way I, want to and to hell with anyone who gets in my way."

"Including Christine?"

"What happened between us was as much her fault as mine. Christine never asked me squat about my background. She was so taken with my charm, she couldn't wait to get into bed. Neither could I."

"Would you have told her if she had asked?"

He narrowed his eyes at me and smirked. "Probably not. Back then I thought I could beat this thing. Just a matter of will." His face darkened. "I'm still trying. I don't let anyone wheel me around. And I still piss by myself."

Despite the sour taste his words left in my mouth, his pride touched me. Still, I fired point-blank. "She plans to sue you."

Color flashed into his cheeks. "She can't!" There was more force behind his words than he could afford to expend. Resting his head against the metal back of the chair, he explained that as far as his wife was concerned he had contracted AIDS from a fabricated blood transfusion. Worse, until three months ago, she didn't even know he had AIDS. I listened to him drone on about her and his children. Inexplicably, this callous, bitter man was fiercely protective of his family.

"It'll kill Theodora. She believes in me—" His voice broke. "And my kids. Christ. Don't do this to me."

I stood up and crossed to the window. The view was of a brick wall. It seemed appropriate. I must have stared at that wall for a good five minutes, my options swimming inside me like a school of drunk guppies.

I recalled my last conversation with O'Donnell. What the woman really wanted was money. And I'd be just as happy not to see this case end up in court. I sighed and turned around. "She needs money for proper medication. Write her a check and I'll convince her to forget the legal action." I didn't add that neither one of them had time for the slow gears of justice.

I could almost feel him weighing his choices.

Finally he said, "Come here." I approached him. He backed up to his night table and pulled out a checkbook. "How much?" The question was flat. A simple business transaction. The man must be even wealthier than I suspected.

I stated a number. He gazed at me openmouthed. "How do I explain that kind of money to my wife?"

"I don't really give a shit."

We stared at each other till he realized I wasn't compromising. Then he practically spat at me, "This is. fucking blackmail. But it figures. Some hot-shot jackass like Haas can live a double life and get away with it—" Goose bumps erupted on my flesh. "But not me, I got to have you trailing my ass all the way from Atlantic City. Shit. How'd you even find me?"

I wasn't about to answer his questions. I had too many of my own. "William Haas has AIDS?"

He cocked his head at me like a curious puppy. "Yeah," he said smiling. The guy loved to spread misery. "Haas is a closet case. His damn marriage has been a matter of convenience for the last fifteen years. He's in the support group for us discreet, executive types. The one down the hall."

I took the check and ran.

The group was still in session. I checked my watch and figured they wouldn't break for another ten, twenty minutes. I found a phone and called Tony back.

"The bastard!" he shouted into my ear as I recounted Weaver's conversation. "I've been so damn careful since my diagnosis..." He cut himself off. Tony never talks about how AIDS has affected his social life. Apparently, he wasn't about to start now. I let his fury run its course, then I filled him in about Haas. His silence confused me.

"Why you telling me this, Miller?"

"C'mon, Tone, you know I'm still investigating the Ross murder. David Ross paid a fifty-three-thousand-dollar debt back the day before he died. He got that money from somewhere. What if he blackmailed Haas? No games now. I need your help."

He cleared his throat. A stalling tactic. Then I rolled my eyes and smacked my palm against the wall. Tony knew something he wasn't telling me. "Give it to me, Tony."

"Haas and I go back a number of years. He was my first client when I went private."

I searched my pocket for loose change. I had a feeling this was going to be a long story.

"The first job was a simple background check on a high-level employee. Then he came to me with another name. Turned out the guy was gay. And about as far out of the closet as you could get. When I gave Haas the news, he was obviously broken-hearted. At first I thought maybe this guy was a relative. Then I got it. See, Haas was real careful. Anyone he dated had to be as discreet as he was. This guy didn't fit the bill so he cut him out." He paused. "When he got sick, he came to me again. He knew about me and thought maybe I'd know some good, quiet doctors. I did. He's been seeing Dr. Kleinau for over a year now."

The operator interrupted and I pumped in another coin. "What's this have to do with now?"

"When Marion came to us, I gave him a call." He cut off my protest. "I know that's not ethical, but Haas has been good to me. A lot of the business we got today, including Torstar, stems from his recommendations. So I figured I owed him. When Ross kicked the can, he called back and asked me to pull you off the case."

I twisted the telephone wire around my hand, pretending it was Tony's neck. "For God's sake, why?"

He took a deep breath. "Promise me you'll keep this quiet."

I muttered agreement. This partnership was stretching mighty thin.

"Ross was blackmailing him."

"So what did Haas do?"

Now Tony laughed. "First, he told him to hump a horse. A direct quote. But then he realized that Ross was serious. At this point, he's not as concerned with bad publicity as he once was. But he agreed anyway. Gave him twenty-five big ones a week but then he got tired of the game and told Ross to take a hike. He wasn't going to be blackmailed anymore." He coughed. "Haas was afraid if the news got out, the cops would start investigating him."

Through clenched teeth I asked, "Tony, did you ever stop to think that Haas could be the murderer?"

"Sure. But he's not. Twenty years as a cop tells me that."

With those words, he hung up on me.

I rested my forehead on the wall. This case was a pain in the ass.

I reviewed the facts. Maybe Tony was right. After all, Haas didn't match the description of the man who visited David Ross the day of his murder. And I couldn't imagine what motive he'd have for killing Terry Fasani. Or me. Unless Terry knew something incriminating.

Then there was another factor. According to Tony, Haas forked over twenty-five thousand dollars. But David Ross owed Cruiser fifty-three thousand dollars. So where did the remaining twenty eight thousand dollars come from?

There were two strong candidates for the loan. And I knew just where to find one of them.

Chapter 19

The restaurant was bustling. I sized up the clientele in a glance. Disenfranchised yuppies. They occupied almost every table and had even formed a line that trailed out the front door. I slipped inside, the smell of ginger and stewed vegetables from a nearby table enveloping me. I took another whiff and scanned the room. Virginia saw me first.

I waved like an old friend. "Do you mind?" I pulled out a chair next to her and sat down.

From across the table Beatrice Marcelescu gave me the evil eye. "Can't we even eat in peace?" They had just started on their entrees. Schnitzel for Beatrice and a Mexican salad for Virginia. My mouth started to water.

Virginia patted Beatrice's hand soothingly. "Maybe you should give us a few moments alone."

With a snort, Beatrice scraped her chair backwards. I watched her walk into the kitchen with a haughtiness that made me smile.

"She's a wonderful woman," Virginia said. She had angled her seat so that she could look me in the eye. She wasn't entirely surprised by my presence. I had a feeling she knew every last word that had transpired between me and her harp instructor.

"Let's cut to the chase. Right now, you're pretty damn high on my list of suspects."

Her tiger eyes glared at me. "I'm not amused."

"Look Virginia, I'm not just shooting in the dark, pardon the expression." Her countenance didn't change. She must be damn good at poker. "There's evidence pointing in your direction." I decided to stretch the truth a little. "And witnesses."

She cocked her head and smirked, an expression that seemed to say, "Show me."

Time for a jab to the jaw. "How did David Ross get the fifty-three grand he owed Cruiser?"

Her eyes widened, mouth dropped, cheeks flushed. Knockdown. Round one goes to Miller.

"How do you know…" She reached for a glass of water and drank deeply.

Merciless, I took another poke. "It sure wasn't from his last jaunt to Atlantic City."

Water splattered from her mouth. A few droplets landed on my knee. Detecting could be a mighty messy business.

"Should I go on, or do you need a breather?"

I was feeling pretty damn pleased with myself until I realized how hard she was struggling just to breathe. I felt worse when, from behind me, one hand landed on my shoulder and another lightly brushed the side of my hair. The hands smelled like butter. K.T.

"Just when I was beginning to think the mountain might have to go to Mohammed." She leaned over and kissed my cheek. Soft. Melting.

"How cozy," Virginia cooed, suddenly levelheaded. "Do you know why your friend is here?"

Score a knockout for Virginia. I wanted to crawl from my

seat.

K.T. squeezed my shoulder. "For my company and my good food. Why else?" There was an edge to her voice. I looked up. She knew why I was there, and she still didn't move her hand away. Shock sizzled through me.

The two sisters stared at each other. The battle was silent, but unmistakable. Then Virginia nodded. "Okay," she said weakly. "Can we use your office?"

"Sure. I'll tell Beatrice she can return to her seat. By now, she's probably fired half of my kitchen staff."

The two of us rose and crossed through the swinging doors. The noise was familiar, but exaggerated. Pots rattled, knives stuttered over cutting boards, oil sizzled in three different frying pans. With everything that was going on, I couldn't believe the hunger pains my stomach was shooting through me. Surreptitiously, I grabbed a freshly baked dill roll as I followed Virginia into the office.

The space had none of the playfulness of K.T.'s den or the country charm of her dining room. Just four walls encompassing a basic desk, two filing cabinets and a computer table. Clean, organized and businesslike. The only personality in the room was a larger-than-life framed poster of Katherine Hepburn in one of her best tough-guy stances.

Virginia sat behind the desk, leaving me the folding chair on the other side. I opted for the desk. I hopped on top and folded my legs beneath me. The closeness unnerved her and I liked it that way.

She tilted the chair backwards and asked, "You believe that I was having an affair with David, don't you?"

I nodded.

She rubbed a finger under her right eye, looking suddenly weary. "You seem good at your job. But just because you can gather clues like some squirrel hoarding acorns for a cold winter doesn't mean you know what to do with them."

Her Southern accent had become as thick as molasses. I took

another bite from my roll and leaned closer.

"Your assumptions are all wrong," she added, as if I hadn't picked up on the barb. I had, it was just that the delivery was so sweet, it hadn't stung.

"Correct me," I said, wondering whether I could steal another roll on the way out.

"You're right about Terry and David. Their affair started practically the day after her husband left for the Gulf. She was distraught, and David adored a distraught woman. I should know."

I had put half of my roll on the desk. Now she reached for it. I almost slapped her hand.

"Last spring, Larry and I hit...a nadir in our relationship." She tore off a piece of bread purposely. The woman knew how to cause pain. "Marriage to a police officer isn't easy, but he was being considered for a promotion and it became simply unbearable. Days would pass and the only time I'd see him is when he'd drag himself home to sleep. David and I became... close. So close, I was tempted to, uh, consummate our—"

"Closeness," I prompted her.

The fire in her eyes quickened. Damn, the Bellflowers are an attractive bunch. Even if some of them might be killers.

"The point is, I refrained. I promised myself to Larry years ago, and he warned me about what our life together would be like. So I was under no delusions when we said our vows. When push came to shove, I didn't stray."

Her pride was touched with ache. If she was lying, she was a damn good actress.

"Your name was on the registry at the Agate Inn."

Looking spent, she finished the roll and nodded. "But I wasn't there. I had the misfortune of being close friends to both Terry and David. That made me the perfect cover story. According to the tales they both told their respective spouses, I was the most social woman in all of New York City. I told them they could register under my name, but sometimes they charged phone calls to my number. It got so bad, Larry started accusing me of having affairs. And what could I say? When I finally told him the truth, he thought it was another lie."

I bit my lip. Good story. But was it concocted for my benefit? "Do you know who accompanied them?"

She looked puzzled. "Excuse me?"

"Witnesses in Atlantic City said they were often accompanied by another couple. A man and a woman."

"I don't have the faintest idea. Joey may have gone with them once or twice. I even joined them one time," she grimaced. "So I could lie more effectively. The whole scene made me ill."

"What about the money?"

"I knew about that too. The day you saw me with David in his classroom, he told me he had paid Cruiser off. Every dime. But he was miserable. Apparently, he had done some things he wasn't proud of—and before you leap down my throat again, no, I don't know what they were."

"Did you loan him money?"

"On my salary?" she laughed. "Good heavens, no. He asked, though. A few times. Then he left me alone. Said he knew where he could get it."

"His wife?"

She shook her head and began lightly tapping a stapler on the far side of the desk. "Marion kept her purse strings tied tightly. David knew better than to ask her for money."

My legs were starting to cramp. I shifted my weight from one cheek to the other, then asked, "So where'd he get that kind of money? Joey Pisano?"

"Not from what I've heard. Joey's business is on its last leg. He could barely afford to fix his Toyota, never mind shell out a few grand."

"How about Terry? Did she have access to that kind of money?"

"I have absolutely no idea," she said, her face knotting with impatience.

I was getting nowhere fast. "Were you angry with Terry for sleeping with David?"

"No." She smacked the stapler, then splayed her hands in exasperation. "David was a dear man and a terrific manipulator. If anything, I felt bad for Terry. Her marriage was loveless, and she was desperate for attention. To David, she was little more than a good lay. Still, it was enough for him to consider divorcing Marion."

"Did he tell her that?"

"No. He was afraid of his wife. She's rich, powerful and vindictive. Not a woman you'd want to cross."

"What about Sam Fasani?"

"Sam's not bad, not in my eyes anyway. Just preoccupied. Before the war, it was football. Before football, it was hunting. Before that, it was bowling. Watching him and Terry talk was like watching a U.N. session without translators."

I paused for a moment, digesting what she told me, then I asked, "Why should I believe anything you've told me?"

She stared into my eyes and rose slowly, "Because it's the truth. And because you have no choice."

"How come it took you and Larry so long to get home the night Terry was killed?"

Fire erupted in her eyes. She stormed out.

I didn't move till the door closed behind me. Then I slumped into a chair. A few minutes later, the door opened. K.T. stood there, shaking her head. "And here I thought you were interested in pursuing me, when it was my sister you were after."

Despite myself, I smiled. "Sorry."

"I can't stay in here long," she said, her tone turning serious. "My chef's out with a cold and the kitchen crew is still raw. But I want you to know my feelings haven't changed. You have your business, and I'm not holding that against you. I also know Virginia well enough to know she's innocent of any charge you may dream up, except maybe a touch too much of Southern pride."

She stepped so close to me all I had to do was lift my arms and she would be there, against me, her sweet skin brushing mine. I fought the impulse, tore my eyes away from hers, from the pull I felt from her.

"Do what you have to," she said, touching my chin with her fingertips, bringing me back to her gaze. Just above me her breast rose with a sigh. "When you're done running, come to me and I'll find a place for us both to rest."

Without another word, she left the room.

I darted out of the restaurant, leaving K.T. and the dill rolls behind.

Another sleepless night. I paced back and forth till the cats started to complain. Then I lay on the couch, a fireball billowing through me. Too much all at once, I thought. I punched a throw pillow across the room in exasperation.

Maybe my feelings for K.T. were clouding my brain, but I was starting to believe that Virginia and Larry were innocent.

I was running out of suspects fast. According to Zack, Marion Ross had an alibi for Terry's murder. Haas and D.J. Cruiser also seemed clean. And with the information I had gleaned over the past two days, Joey and Vic no longer qualified for the jealous-lover scenario. So who was left?

I ran over the list in my head. One name stood out in relief.

Without hesitating, I got up, gathered some tools and quietly exited the brownstone. I knew where I was going, but wouldn't let the words from inside my head. Not till I pulled into a spot just a few doors down from Terry's house, dear brother Ronald's picks in my back pocket.

I had to walk three blocks before I found a pay phone. The phone rang twelve times without answer. I just hoped that meant Sam Fasani was still "missing." I retraced my footsteps and walked up to the front door. A polite intruder, I rang the doorbell first. The silence within the house reverberated through me. The memory of Saturday night was still too vivid.

I shook it off and went to work. The door sprung open in less than a minute. I slipped inside, sending a telepathic thank-you to Ronald. Then I froze. The apartment's emptiness was palpable. Each step sounded to my ears like thunder. The living room and kitchen were almost exactly as I had found them the other day. Even the burnt teakettle remained on the stove. The only noticeable difference was the coating of fingerprint powder that lingered like Vesuvian ash.

I checked the guest bedroom next. The room must have doubled as their workspace. A black metal filing cabinet was positioned to the right of a small, curtained window. In the opposite corner, next to the high-riser bed, was an old-fashioned writing desk. I searched through everything, looking in and under the drawers. Nothing but bills, mortgage records, student papers and insurance forms. I took down some key numbers, then stalked toward the master bedroom.

Where Terry and I had slept together. Where she had been killed.

The room looked different. Then I realized why. It was the first time I had seen it in daylight. In the harsh light, the walnut furniture looked worn, the edges nicked and the polish thinning. The bed was stripped bare, leaving the stained mattress stranded in the center of the room. I could feel breakfast gurgling in my stomach. Air. Without thinking, I lifted the window and gasped.

The carpet near the bed had been cut away by the forensics team. But the plywood base beneath revealed brown stains that could have passed for blotches of dried Coke or wine. I lowered myself and examined the remaining carpet, then searched under the bed.

I spent a good half-hour combing the room, hoping I'd find something the police hadn't. I even recreated my attack, trying to pinpoint the direction of the blow to my head. I threw myself across the bed, feeling again the force of the metal butt against my head. Then I sat up. Impossible. The way I remembered it, the blow would have had to come from the closet.

Unless the door had been open.

211

I slid the panel to the right and stared inside. A rolled up venetian blind was angled in the corner. With the tip of my foot, I brushed the metal base. A dull rattle drifted toward me.

The sound I had heard the night of Terry's murder.

I plunged into the closet and searched every inch. A pale orange wrapper was wedged behind the blinds. I tugged and held it up to the light.

A candy wrapper. Gray's toffee.

With a shudder, I realized who must have killed Terry.

Chapter 20

Zack didn't call back until after three o'clock. By that time, I had consumed about twenty Oreos, one tuna fish sandwich, and three Yoo-Hoos. If his call had come much later, I would probably have been attached to a stomach pump in Methodist Hospital.

"Where the hell have you been?"

"I got a real job here, Miller. Remember?"

I had no patience for small talk. "Marion Ross killed Terry. I was in Terry's apartment, Zack." He tried to interrupt, but I barreled on. "Can the lecture. You want to arrest me, be my guest. In the meantime, listen. I found a candy wrapper from Gray's toffees. Twice I've seen Marion shoving those things into her mouth.

He laughed out loud. "You're a case. You confess to breaking into someone's home, then expect me to arrest some lady 'cause you found a damn candy wrapper. Are you on drugs these days?

I can get my ass hauled in front of IAD just for listening to you."

"Stop being so damn paranoid about Internal Affairs and hear me out. The wrapper was right in the spot my attacker stood. We both know Marion Ross has carried a gun before, and witnesses have heard her threaten to kill anyone who slept with her husband. Tell me it doesn't add up."

"I'll tell you what it adds up to. Circumstantial evidence. Flimsy as a used tissue. Christ, my wife would probably threaten to kill any woman who so much as touched me. Besides, Marion Ross has an alibi for the night of Terry's murder." He suddenly sounded less confident.

"What's the alibi, Zack?"

He hesitated, then said, "At the time of the attack, your 'murderer' was at the movies with my boss."

The room spun. "The Hammer."

"Right."

I like Zack, but right then I wanted to shove a banana up his right nostril. "How can you trust him?" I shouted into the phone. "Dammit, Zack, he's already lied once to protect Marion. Don't you think it's mighty odd that he can provide Marion with alibis for *both* murders?"

"I would if it were anyone but the Hammer. I hate the guy, but he's cleaner than my dishes. Trust me. I did some checking, and the Hammer's telling it straight."

For the first time ever, I hung up on him.

I sat back down with the box of Oreos and my case notes, but a fever was still running through me. I had to move. I changed into sweats, dragged my bike out of the basement and rode over to the park. Two loops did nothing to clear my pounding head. As a matter of fact, the rest of my body wasn't too happy about my level of activity either. I ignored it and zipped out of the park.

There's something almost daredevilish about bicycling on Brooklyn streets. Cars aim at you. Pedestrians glare at you with suspicion or assess whether they can steal the bike from under your butt. I weaved through traffic with an ease that made my adrenaline pump. I picked up speed. The next thing I knew I was on the promenade outside Marion Ross's apartment.

I smiled to myself. Predictable, Miller. I locked the bike, released the front wheel and walked over to the building. Marion's voice squawked out of the intercom. I gave my name. She didn't greet me with a great deal of warmth.

"What do you want?"

"Manners, manners," I tsked. "We have to talk about your case. If you want, we can do it right here over the intercom. That way, the neighbors can listen in."

The buzzer rang out.

Marion was waiting outside her door. She had curlers in her hair and a man's robe wrapped around her. I almost laughed out loud. I had obviously caught the elegant Mrs. Ross at one of her low points. Then I remembered the blow to my head and pictured her arm swinging toward me with the butt of a twenty-two caliber. The laugh died on my lips. I dropped the wheel in front of her door and followed her in.

The place was more magnificently gaudy than I had expected. We walked through a long foyer and entered the dining room. I wasn't quite sure what rococo looked like, but I had a feeling this was it. There was more ornamentation in that one room than in all of New York City during Christmas. And about as much good will.

"If you're here about money—"

"Aren't you even going to invite me to sit?"

Marion's eyes were dull. I had a feeling she hadn't even noticed the bandage above my ear. Unless she had expected to find it. The possibility made me more alert.

She pointed to one of the chairs. I waited for her to sit first, then picked one just opposite her. If she was going to attack me again, I wanted to have plenty of time to react.

"Ms. Miller, I pay my debts promptly," she said, her voice a stuffy monotone. She explained that I had fulfilled the job requirements and could expect a check within one week. As her

215

words dwindled into silence, 1 examined the room more closely. A fine layer of dust coated the room. In the corner, next to a massive marble-topped sideboard, lay a shattered wine decanter. From the way the wine had soaked into the wood, I guessed that the breakage had occurred much earlier. I looked back at Marion, who was listlessly tearing at her cuticles.

The pendulum had swung. Clearly, she was in a depressive cycle.

Ignoring a pang of conscience, I decided to press my advantage. "Ms. Ross, where were you on Saturday night?"

She raised her head and stared at me as if surprised by my presence. Then she pursed her lips and said, "I don't quite remember." Her features had shifted slightly. Suspicion now laid just under her glazed stare. Obviously, the depression wasn't so deep that my question hadn't penetrated. She sat up straighter and wet her lips with her tongue. "Why are you asking?"

I weighed my options. Her response time was off. The risk of her acting quickly was small. I took the chance. "You dropped a candy wrapper when you slid into Terry's closet. The cops have it now."

Without question, something flashed in her eyes. "Yes."

"Yes?" I asked surprised. After all this, was it really going to be this simple?

She gathered the robe around her, pinching the collar around her neck, then she dug into a pocket and pulled out a pack of Carltons. Rodammer's brand. The robe looked like it could be about his size. A shudder ran through me.

I steadied myself and asked, "Were you at Terry Fasani's house on Saturday night?"

She was having a hard time lighting the match. I didn't offer to help. Finally, it caught and she jerked backwards. I waited until she took a deep puff, then repeated my question.

"I was with Detective Sergeant Frederick Rodammer. At the movies."

The answer was rehearsed. Poorly rehearsed. "What movie,

Marion?" I approached her, all fear gone. Marion was about to hang herself.

She stared at the smoke billowing from her mouth. "I stopped smoking, you know. For years. Then all this…" The ash dropped into her lap. "It was Switch, I believe."

"What's it about?"

When she looked at me this time, she almost seemed amused. "I have no idea, and you know that, don't you?"

"Yes."

She stood up and paced in her Betty Davis fashion. I made sure to keep out of arm's distance. All of a sudden, she swiveled toward me and nodded. "The only reason I struck you was to protect myself. You were carrying that butcher knife, for heaven's sake."

The image of Terry's body drifted in front of me. I closed my eyes. I had led Marion right to Terry's doorstep. My spirit dissipated like steam. "Why'd you kill her?"

Her silence made me open my eyes. We were standing toe to toe. Up close, her face looked like a road map. I read the lines and the direction was clear. Marion was puzzled. "I didn't kill her." She was whispering now. "After you called, I was furious. That witch had stolen David from me. Now he's dead…she had to die, too. Do you understand? I was his *wife*."

Sure. And Norman Bates was just a devoted son. I took a step backwards.

"I drove to her house Saturday night and sat there. I had just put my handgun into my skirt pocket when I saw him leave…"

An alarm went off in my head. This wasn't a rehearsed story any more. My gut told me Marion was telling the truth.

"Sam Fasani?" I tried to keep my tone even.

She shook her head irritatedly. "I don't know who it was, for chrissakes. I wasn't there to spy."

Of course not, you had murder on your mind.

"He left the door open. That's all I cared about. So I went in. No one noticed. I was so confused, I didn't even pull the

217

gun out. Then I went into the bedroom. How appropriate, I thought. Kill her where she sleeps. But she was already dead." The disappointment in her voice made me queasy. "You came in just a few moments later. The closet door was open, so I slipped in and hid. When I saw the knife in your hand, I didn't know what to do. I knew you weren't the killer, but I couldn't let you see me. So I took out the gun—"

I knew the rest of the story.

"What's Rodammer's connection?"

She lit another cigarette, stalked over to the sideboard and rummaged through the drawers till she found a gold-plated flask. By now, I had picked up on her rhythm. I waited for her to answer.

A long sip and then she spoke calmly again. "We were lovers long before I married David. We were great friends, but the passion was...thin. David was the only man that ever made me..." She stopped herself. "Frederick married a woman from his neighborhood just a year later. For both of us, the marriages were a disaster."

From what I knew about Rodammer's ex-wife, I had to agree. The woman was a well-known director of a city program for the homeless. How she ever got together with a man who shelters a pet pig in his garage but sneers at homeless women on winter nights is a mystery Zack and I have spent hours discussing.

Marion capped the flask and turned to me. "Frederick was with me when we heard the news about David," she said after another long pause. "It was like a switch had turned on. For the first time in over a decade, we were both free. This time, we're not looking for sparks."

"Just murder victims."

The sarcasm sliced deep. "I've told you everything. Now, you'll have to leave."

"You understand I'm obligated to report all this to the police."

She shrugged. "Frederick is very powerful."

"Not this powerful. You're withholding evidence."

"What evidence? Oh, you mean the man I saw? I'm afraid that won't help anyone very much. All I saw was his back. The man walked like a cop. Very masculine." She was on an even keel now, sharper than before. "I'm not sure what color his hair was."

"What about his jacket?"

"Very nondescript. A pea jacket, I think it's called. Now, if you'll excuse me."

I watched her float into the library. Before I could get there, the door locked. Classical music filtered out from under the door. No sounds of glass, no screams.

I took a shot from the flask and left.

Dinner was waiting for me when I got home. Beth had left a note on my door inviting me to indulge in her magical, intestine-cleansing chile con carne. I didn't even bother opening my door.

"I knew the only way we'd see you is if we offered you food," Beth said as she spooned the thick, spicy mess into my plate. I seized the bowl of shredded cheddar cheese and dumped half of it onto my plate.

"Ah jeez, you didn't have to invite her, did you?" Dinah had just joined us in the dining room.

"She just wandered in, honey, honest."

The two of them smooched over the stove. I used the opportunity to steal the chopped onions, chips and sour cream. Then I took a swig of an ice-cold Corona. Heaven. Slowly, I began to feel human.

A few hours later I left their home, full, belching, and ready to sleep. But one careless touch on the answering machine's play button, and the mood was shattered.

"Bella, bella! My beautiful friend, you have saved my career. My life. Your guess was right. Bless your sweet, intuitive, feminine soul."

Get on with it, T.B.

"I reexamined the specimens I had taken from the wound. On one I found a microscopic, barely perceptible fragment. A piece of leather! I pored through my forensics texts, and there it was. A case in L.A. that baffled even the experts. But not you and me, my *bellissimo* compadre."

Damn him! I was jumping out of my skin.

"The suspected weapon: a twenty-two caliber handgun. The actual weapon: a single, simple spike high heel. Swung in rage, with incredible force. In other words, my dear Sherlock, the person behind the blow had to be mighty strong. Given those circumstances, the markings for both types of wounds can be astoundingly similar. As I promised you, I will keep mum on this for twenty-four hours. Tops. After that, all bets are off."

The phone call had come in seven hours ago.

Chapter 21

I stayed up all night with my notes. It was like playing a perverse version of the game Clue. The killer is Colonel Mustard in the living room with a high heel shoe. But in this case, knowing how the murder was committed still left me far from knowing who.

While I now had a better idea of how those bloodstains at the scene of David's death had formed, I still couldn't figure out who had actually swung the heel.

Worse, as far as I knew, Virginia and Marion were the only female suspects. And from what T.B. had said, neither one of them seemed strong enough to have dealt the killing blow.

Assuming they were innocent, who was the woman who had visited David Ross? Could it have been Terry? I remembered her finely muscled arms. She definitely would have had the strength. If she had killed Ross and her companion knew it .. .

Wrong, wrong. In a flash, it came to me. Terry knew about

the murder all right, but she wasn't the one who swung the shoe. Someone else did. And Terry knew who. That's why he killed her. And tried to kill me. Twice.

Jackpot. Flashing lights. Sirens.

I showered and headed into the office. Four cups of coffee later, Jill arrived.

"Are you on banker's hours now?" I asked testily.

"Whew. Pleasant mood this morning. Guess the insomnia's kicked in."

I backed off. But only slightly. "Have you found out why the Body Shop went bust?"

"Not yet, my dear Mussolini. But I'm working on it."

I grunted and stalked into my office. Time to take the bull by the horns, Miller.

Joey Pisano answered on the second ring. I was ready to spar, but he would have made one hell of a lousy partner. He sounded half asleep.

"The funeral was yesterday," he mumbled as an excuse. "I just can't believe that Terry's gone."

The mention of her name made me antsier. "Can you answer a few questions?"

"I'm on way out to the gym."

"This will take just a minute." He didn't protest.

"Did you ever accompany David Ross to Atlantic City?"

"Yeah, sure." An edge slipped into his voice. "How'd you find out?"

I ignored his question. "Did you know he was in financial trouble."

"Shit." I heard him slam a drawer. "Everyone knew that. Dave was a gambler. So what?"

"Did you lend him money?"

He emitted a sound that was a cross between a snicker and a groan. "Sure. So did Virginia and Terry. That's what friends do. Or maybe that's alien to you ."

"Twenty-eight grand requires a lot of friendship."

"Twenty…you think…damn." I had him spinning. "I run a small gym, for chrissakes. Damn. You're reading this all wrong. And I'm just making things worse. Come to the gym and I'll explain."

He didn't have to ask twice.

The front door was unlocked when I arrived. The reception area lights were out, but I could see a dim glow inside the equipment room. I yelled out Joey's name.

"In here."

He sounded so much like Terry I froze for an instant.

Without the normal bustle and clang of weights, the room was eerie. Joey was on one of the Nautilus machines designed to trim and strengthen the thighs. I couldn't figure out why. His legs were gorgeous.

"I'll be done in a second."

Joey finished his routine, then wiped his face with a towel and crossed to where I was sitting on a bench press. "Do you exercise?" he asked, now mopping his firm, slender arms.

"Not regularly."

"You look in pretty good shape."

"Thanks for the compliment, but looks can be deceiving." I started fiddling with the weights. I used to be pretty damn good at this stuff, I thought nervously. He smiled, but his red-rimmed eyes looked unbelievably sad.

"I heard that the kid got off," he asked softly. "The one who killed Dave. Was that your handiwork?"

"Joey, the police wouldn't have let Emerson go free if the evidence hadn't been overwhelming." I tensed my muscles. "Look, you said you needed to set the record straight. So what did you want to tell me?"

He edged backwards, slapping the towel against his lean thigh. Guilt crept into his eyes. I stood up and moved closer to him, till I could almost feel the steam of his sweat-covered limbs. Doubt flickered in his eyes. Suddenly, he turned on his heels and darted into the locker room. I started in after him, then stopped.

The office was just to my left. I retraced my steps and tiptoed inside. Quietly, I closed the door behind me and turned on the desk light. Maybe the files would tell me what Joey wouldn't. The pool of light zeroed in on a framed photograph. Terry. Her wounded gaze pinned me. I dropped the picture face down on the desk and continued my search. What I wanted was the gym's ledger. I found it in the third drawer.

"Trespassing is a crime, you know."

It was Vic, the body builder from hell. I straightened up so fast my back cracked.

"Maybe I can help you." In the dim light, the guy looked seven feet tall.

I put my hands up. No lie was going to get me out of this one. "It's an occupational hazard," I said, making a stupid attempt at levity. "Something about dark, empty offices just gets to me."

"Why don't we step outside?" It was one of those invitations you couldn't refuse.

He led me back to the bench press. With a tap on my shoulder that felt like the punch of a mallet, he lowered me onto the bench. Then he just stood there, his bulging biceps crossed over his thick chest. Ugh. Cornered by Arnold Schwarzenegger. Hasta la' vista, baby.

"I guess I should explain…"

Make it good, Miller.

"Terry meant a lot to me. We didn't know each other long, but…her death really stung. You understand?" I looked up, tears easily filling my eyes. Appeal to his tender side. The guy grunted.

Right.

"So?" He wiped one hand under his nose. Slowly. Chills crept up my spine.

"I'm investigating her death. I hoped Joey would be able to help."

"So you break into the office?"

"No, no." Yes. That's right. Arrest me, your bulgingness.

"In two minutes, I call the police. Your license is going to be history."

Ah hell, Miller. Think. "Okay, okay. One of the other suspects in the case told me Joey used to accompany David Ross to Atlantic City. She said they were lovers and that Joey killed him because Ross wanted to break off the affair. I'm looking for evidence to clear Joey."

The iceberg started to melt.

"Who told these freaking lies? Was it that Southern bitch Ginny?"

My cheeks flushed. "No. Someone else. The point is, I wasn't trying to hurt Joey. I was just trying to help out. Terry would have wanted that." Surprising myself, I really started to choke up.

"Don't worry about it. I understand," he said. "Wait here. I'm going to stop this thing right in its tracks."

I believed him. The guy could probably stop a locomotive.

He stormed into the locker room. After a minute, I could hear his voice booming behind the metal door, shouting something about how the lies have to stop. I had a feeling if anyone could get Joey to tell the truth, it was the Hulk.

I slipped back under the bench press while the screaming match continued. Four lifts later, Vic thundered into the room. As I went to replace the weights, he loomed behind me. "You a weight lifter?"

"Not really. Can you spot me?"

"Sure." He slapped another weight on the left side. My elbow buckled.

"I meant help me up!"

"I know." A second weight clanged onto the right side. My arm folded instantly. The bar was now just a scant inch from my Adam's apple. There was no way I was going to be able to lift the damn thing.

"Consider this a gift." He pounded out of the room.

Sweat poured off my forehead. In a second, my arms would give out and this damn barbell would crack my neck. Desperately, I fought to raise it high enough to inch my head out of the way.

Impossible.

Closing my eyes, I pushed against the weight, my arms trembling, the blood pounding in my ears. My head was about to explode.

Hold on, I urged myself. Then my arms dropped lower. The rod started to choke me. I tried to swallow, but couldn't. Burning. My lungs, throat.

Adrenaline racing, I heaved again. My biceps burned. Just then, the barbell swung off me and clanged against the floor.

I gulped for air, my vision reduced to a pinpoint of fuzzy green light circled by gray mist.

"Slow, slow." An arm lifted me up, rubbed the center of my back. Almost tenderly. I turned my head.

Joey.

"What?" My voice was a low rasp. Words wouldn't form.

"He's out of control," he sobbed. "The first time was an accident, but then Terry...how could he think I'd ever forgive him?"

The room spun and I steadied myself against him. "Terry and Vic." I shuddered. Her words crept over me like a swarm of spiders: *There's this incredible high that comes with making it with a man. Sometimes, I pretend I'm riding a bronco.*

Shaking the words off, I stood up.

"You don't get it, do you?" Joey was rapidly approaching hysteria.

"Tell me." I massaged my arm. The pain was excruciating.

"Vic killed them both. And now he's after Ginny."

Chapter 22

I ran behind the juice bar and picked up the phone. I called 911, then glanced down at my feet and groaned. Sawdust coated the floor.

"Joey, get over here now." I thrust the phone into his hand, shouted instructions, then blasted out of the gym and jumped into the car.

My left arm was practically useless. I slung my wrist onto the bottom of the steering wheel and pulled out. The pain was nothing compared to the fear.

Once again, I had pointed a killer in the direction of someone I instinctively liked. I would not have another death on my head.

Especially not K.T.'s sister.

I put my foot on the gas and screeched down Fourth Avenue. Red lights didn't stop me. Neither did three near-misses. I made it to the school in record time. It was just after noon. I barreled past the school guard, shouting at her to call the police.

Virginia's office was empty.

Two nights without sleep were taking their toll. I stood there, unable to think. Then I saw her purse. Damn!

I ran next door to Webster Bainbridge's office. He was brewing coffee and chatting on the phone. I grabbed the wire and tugged the receiver out of his hand.

"Have you seen Virginia?"

He looked appalled.

"Answer me."

"For heaven's sake…yes. Just a minute ago. She was going out to lunch with a friend."

I shot out of the school, my left hand tucked into my the waist of my pants. Every step jolted me. I reached the curb and stopped.

Now what? Where the hell would he take her?

I scanned both sides of the street. Then my eyes fixed on the remnants of a building that had been demolished just two weeks ago.

I raced across the street and entered the ruins. The sun was relentlessly beating down on my back. Would he kill her in the broad daylight? The answer came to me with a pang. In East New York, people are trained to see nothing. Especially another person's death. I stumbled over cracked bricks and rubbish, creeping around the edge of the building's razed facade.

A rat brushed past me. I stifled a scream. But Virginia didn't.

The sound came from behind a wall of crumbling plaster. I lifted a brick with my right hand and shifted forward. The bottom half of a window clung to the top of the wall. I stood on the back of a smashed television set and gazed through to the other side.

Vic was standing over Virginia, a twenty-two aimed between her eyes.

No time to think. I shouted like my ass was on fire. He spun around. I threw myself against the wall, the plaster cracking under my weigh. I sailed over and crashed onto my chin.

As the blood dribbled into my mouth, I heard him take a step in my direction. I lay still as stone, willing my breath to stop. Let him think I'm dead.

"Get up!" he shouted.

He's not sure. Good. I focused on the blinding pain and held my breath.

A body slammed into the rubble. Virginia. "Stay there, bitch."

I could feel his body rumbling toward me like a tidal wave. At the same time, my lungs were caving in. I gasped. He started to run toward me. I bounded up. The brick was still in my hand.

"Run, Ginny!"

I launched the brick with all my remaining strength. It bounced off his arm like a moth. Still, the impact was enough to send the gun sailing into the rubbish. I turned on my heel and started running in the opposite direction of Virginia. From the thuds behind me, Vic had opted for me. At least, Virginia was safe for now.

In the distance, I heard the wail of a police car. I didn't have time for hosannas. I leapt over the ragged edge of a rusted bed frame. A spring caught the laces of my sneaker. I fell forward.

Vic lifted me by my underarms, then tossed me like a volleyball. A concrete slab smashed against my cheek. I stopped moving. No act this time.

"Freeze!"

No problem.

I was steadily losing consciousness.

But not before I heard Zack read Vic his rights. Only then did I give in to the blackness with a welcome relief.

I spent the next eight days in bed, the left side of my face a dead ringer for Beth's chile and my arm in a sling. The only visitors Beth allowed into my inner sanctum were Dinah, K.T. and Zack.

The story unfolded slowly. David Ross knew there was one person who could not refuse him. Joey Pisano.

A few days before his death, David hit on Joey for the money

229

he owed Cruiser. Without Vic's knowledge, Joey withdrew the funds from the gym's accounts. Apparently, David had repeatedly assured him that the money would be fully repaid within one month.

The day of the murder, Joey was trying on a new outfit for drag night at Scarlet's when Vic showed up at his house. He had just come from the bank and demanded to know why Joey had withdrawn twenty-eight thousand dollars without his approval. When Joey told him the reason, Vic insisted that they find David immediately and demand repayment.

They drove to the school, Joey still wearing his red wig and cocktail dress, and confronted David Ross. Vic demanded that he return the money. That's when Ross made his first mistake. He laughed. With a cavalier tone, he told them just where the money had gone. Joey threw himself at Ross, who knocked him to the floor. When Vic leaned over to help Joey up, Ross made his last mistake. "Christ. The two of you are such fags," he snickered. "Just admit it."

Vic had whirled around with Joey's high heel in his hand and pounded it deep into David Ross's scalp.

The next day, Joey confessed to Terry. She had decided to tell me the whole story, but Vic stopped her with the beating on Friday. When she kept on insisting that they turn themselves in, Vic went to the apartment and shot her. He threatened to do the same to Joey if he talked.

So much for lifelong friendship.

As I drifted in and out of consciousness, every now and then sipping Yoo-Hoo from a crazy straw, the other loose ends came together. Vic and Joey frequently accompanied David and Terry on their trips to Atlantic City. David used to joke that Joey was his good luck charm, especially when he was wearing his femme fatale regalia. As I later discovered, Joanie was the name Joey used when he was dressed in drag.

The most surprising thing was that Vic had not tried to blow me up or break into my apartment. That honor went to one of

Dinah's patients. The one that had always given me the creeps. The one that used to circle our block at all hours just to see if Dinah's lights were on. One night he drove by and saw me and Terry grinding on her doorstep.

Just another homophobe.

"You're sounding a lot perkier this morning." It was K.T.

"No one has ever accused me of being perky." I balanced myself on the end of the couch, surprised at how pleased I was to hear her voice. "Sorry I haven't returned your calls. I just needed some alone time."

"Robin Miller." She said my name so quietly and yet with such force, it struck me like a bolt of sunlight piercing a sky heavy with storm clouds.

"Yes?"

"For now, there is no case. There is no past. Okay? For now, there is only this phone call."

I smiled. Her voice was hypnotic. "What's so special about this phone call?"

"I just rented a car. Right now, I'm on the way over. Wait for me downstairs. The day is luscious."

Before I could decline her invitation, she hung up. By the time I re-dialed her number, she was gone. I stormed through the house, annoyed that she assumed I was ready to leave the house. My arm was just starting to move freely again, and I still felt like Quasimodo.

I ran downstairs and let myself into Beth and Dinah's back door. In their bathroom I found some makeup that I inexpertly applied. I still looked like I was suffering from hepatitis, botulism and other assorted diseases. I washed off the makeup and headed outside.

K.T. was right. After ten days locked up in my apartment, the day seemed especially magnificent. The sky was as blue as a glacial lake and the air was crisp, with just a hint of warmth. The tree outside our brownstone had bright green leaves, the color so vivid I could almost see it vibrating.

I sat down, closed my eyes, and breathed deeply. The air carried the scent of early summer. Flowers. I felt my muscles loosen.

"My lord, you are one beautiful woman."

I opened my eyes to find K.T. staring at me from the driver's side of an open-air red jeep. She jumped down and beckoned to me. I rose slowly. K.T. was wearing a dungaree shirt and a pair of well-worn jeans that accentuated the curve of her hips. The soft wind blew her hair back from her face. As I walked over, I could feel something breaking inside me. For an instant, I wanted to run back inside. Instead, impulsively, my hand brushed the side of her head.

"Your hair is like a wood fire. An ember." I cringed at the sound of my voice.

K.T. just lowered her eyes, a smile starting at one corner of her mouth. "Honey, you better hop in right now or I won't be held accountable for my actions."

I scrambled into the passenger's seat.

For a few minutes neither of us spoke. Then I suddenly realized that we were on the Brooklyn-Queens Expressway heading east. "Where are we going?"

"Some place we can breathe easier."

She stretched out her hand and covered my knee. My flesh burned under her touch. From the corner of my eye, I saw her glance at me.

"You feel it, don't you?"

I turned on the radio. Loud. It was a country station. I reached for the dial, but her hand stopped me.

"Listen," she said simply.

The song was vaguely familiar. A woman's voice. "Patsy Cline. Don't tell me you don't know her." I shook my head. "I'm not a fan of country music."

Another sideways glance. "Listen to the words. The emotion. It's so raw. Unflinching."

I let the words sink in. Unexpectedly, my eyes filled.

"That's 'Crazy.'"

For a split second I thought she was referring to my tears, then I realized she was telling me the name of the song.

"When Patsy Cline was just a kid, she developed some kind of throat infection. If I remember correctly, it got so bad her heart stopped beating at one point. When she came back to life, her voice had changed. My mom told me that story when I was just seven years old. I still think about it whenever I hear her songs. Tragedy sometimes comes with gifts.

My cynicism kicked in. "Tragedy is not romantic." The bitterness in my voice carried over the wind.

"That's not what I said."

We fell into an uneasy silence.

"Patsy Cline died when she was just thirty. That's how old my dad was when his truck turned over…" Her voice was brittle. "Believe me, I know tragedy is not romantic."

There was something behind her words, a weight heavier than her father's early death. I wanted to ask her, but the set of her chin warned me off.

"I'm sorry."

She squeezed my knee. "Do me a favor. Let me keep the station on. The music may surprise you. Country music is a lot more than just twangy, beer-hall songs."

I agreed reluctantly. I leaned back in the seat and waited for the Johnny Cash barrage. Instead, another woman's voice surrounded me. Silky, sexy tones. The words zeroing in on chinks in my emotional armor. The wind whipped the tears off my face. K.T. didn't say another word till we pulled off the highway.

I checked the exit sign and felt myself sink. "We're heading toward the Cherry Grove ferry, aren't we?"

K.T. responded instantly to my tone. "Bad memories?"

I shook my head. "No. Wonderful ones. I spent one summer here with the only woman I've ever really loved."

"Oh…" K.T. put both hands on the steering wheel. My knee immediately longed for her touch again. "A recent breakup?"

"Five years ago," I said with a tight laugh. "When it's real, the hurt never stops. Too bad we usually don't know it till it's too late."

"Have you ever told her?" The question was tentative. I got the feeling K.T. was afraid of my answer.

"I didn't get the chance. And now... She's gone."

She's gone.K.T.'s hand fluttered back to my leg, like a fallen leaf. "I bet she knew." Her palm traveled over my thigh lightly, awakening a response so deep in me it had no counterpart in spoken language.

Memory flooded me—Mary standing at the shore's edge, the waves breaking fiercely behind her. "Take a chance," she had taunted me, knowing how terrified I was of the undertow. "Trust me," she had yelled against the wind. "I can't lose you." And I had run into her arms without hesitation and held on as I watched the water swell against us. She plunged us through the curling wave, her powerful arms tight around my waist, and when the whitecaps shattered beyond us and we held still against the undertow, she had kissed me passionately and whispered, "See. Nothing can touch us. Nothing."

We pulled up by the ferry. K.T. shut the jeep off, then stared into my eyes. She touched my cheek with the back of her hand. "C'mon. Let's create some memories of our own."

The ferry was almost empty. I walked straight up to the top.

"It may be cold once we get out on the water," K.T. said. The sky had darkened and the air had a new chill.

"Good." I took her hand and led her to the front. When the engine rumbled in the belly of the ferry, I could feel the tension in me begin to shake loose. K.T. moved behind me and slipped her hands under my vest. As we sailed into the bay the wind picked up, stinging my cheeks with cold, saltwater. Suddenly, I smiled. K.T. nestled closer to me.

By the time we docked on the other side, a quiet joy had settled in. Wordlessly, K.T. led me across the boardwalks to the beach side. Still early in the season, the Grove was quiet. At this time of the year, Fire Island reminded me of a place from an earlier time. The trees hugged the boardwalk tightly and birds zipped over our heads. Early summer was powerful here, the scents of new flowers heady and rich. As we neared the other side, the excitement became unbearable. I walked ahead of K.T. to one of the staircases leading to the beach. The boardwalk rose slightly over a dune and then suddenly, magically, the ocean appeared.

Raw. Unashamed. Irrefutable.

I dropped my hands onto the railing and started to weep.

K.T. stood next to me. I folded myself into her arms and sought her mouth greedily.

**Publications from
Bella Books, Inc.
*The best in contemporary lesbian fiction***

**P.O. Box 10543, Tallahassee, FL 32302
Phone: 800-729-4992
www.bellabooks.com**

TWO WEEKS IN AUGUST by Nat Burns. Her return to Chincoteague Island is a delight to Nina Christie until she gets her dose of Hazy Duncan's renown ill-humor. She's not going to let it bother her, though...
978-1-59493-173-4 $14.95

MILES TO GO by Amy Dawson Robertson. Rennie Vogel has finally earned a spot at CT3. All too soon she finds herself abandoned behind enemy lines, miles from safety and forced to do the one thing she never has before: trust another woman.
978-1-59493-174-1 $14.95

PHOTOGRAPHS OF CLAUDIA by KG MacGregor. To photographer Leo Westcott models are light and shadow realized on film. Until Claudia.
978-1-59493-168-0 $14.95

STEPPING STONE by Karin Kallmaker. Selena Ryan's heart was shredded by an actress, and she swears she will never, ever be involved with one again.
978-1-59493-160-4 $14.95

SONGS WITHOUT WORDS by Robbi McCoy. Harper Sheridan's runaway niece turns up in the one place least expected and Harper confronts the woman from the summer that has shaped her entire life since.
978-1-59493-166-6 $14.95

FAINT PRAISE by Ellen Hart. When a famous TV personality leaps to his death, Jane Lawless agrees to help a friend with inquiries, drawing the attention of a ruthless killer. No. 6 in this award-winning series.
978-1-59493-164-2 $14.95

YOURS FOR THE ASKING by Kenna White. Lauren Roberts is tired of being the steady, reliable one. When Gaylin Hart blows into her life, she decides to act, only to find once again that her younger sister wants the same woman.
978-1-59493-163-5 $14.95

THE SCORPION by Gerri Hill. Cold cases are what make reporter Marty Edwards tick. When her latest proves to be far from cold, she still doesn't want Detective Kristen Bailey babysitting her, not even when she has to run for her life.
978-1-59493-162-8 $14.95

A SMALL SACRIFICE by Ellen Hart. A harmless reunion of friends is anything but, and Cordelia Thorn calls friend Jane Lawless with a desperate plea for help. Lammy winner for Best Mystery. No. 5 in this award-winning series.
978-1-59493-165-9 $14.95

NO RULES OF ENGAGEMENT by Tracey Richardson. A war zone attraction is of no use to Major Logan Sharp. She can't wait for Jillian Knight to go back to the other side of the world.
978-1-59493-159-8 $14.95

TOASTED by Josie Gordon. Mayhem erupts when a culinary road show stops in tiny Middelburg, and for some reason everyone thinks Lonnie Squires ought to fix it. Follow-up to Lammy mystery winner Whacked.
978-1-59493-157-4 $14.95

SEA LEGS by KG MacGregor. Kelly is happy to help Natalie make Didi jealous, sure, it's all pretend. Maybe. Even the captain doesn't know where this comic cruise will end.
978-1-59493-158-1 $14.95

KEILE'S CHANCE by Dillon Watson. A routine day in the park turns into the chance of a lifetime, if Keile Griffen can find the courage to risk it all for a pair of big brown eyes.
978-1-59493-156-7 $14.95

ROOT OF PASSION by Ann Roberts. Grace Owens knows a fake when she sees it, and the potion her best friend promises will fix her love life is a fake. But what if she wishes it weren't?
978-1-59493-155-0 $14.95

COMFORTABLE DISTANCE by Kenna White. Summer on Puget Sound ought to be relaxing for Dana Robbins, but Dr. Jamie Hughes is far too close for comfort.
978-1-59493-152-9 $14.95

DELUSIONAL by Terri Breneman. In her search for a killer, Toni Barston discovers that sometimes everything is exactly the way it seems, and then it gets worse.
978-1-59493-151-2 $14.95

FAMILY AFFAIR by Saxon Bennett. An oops at the gynecologist has Chase Banter finally trying to grow up. She has nine whole months to pull it off.
978-1-59493-150-5 $14.95

SMALL PACKAGES by KG MacGregor. With Lily away from home, Anna Kaklis is alone with her worst nightmare: a toddler. Book Three of the Shaken Series.
978-1-59493-149-9 $14.95

WRONG TURNS by Jackie Calhoun. Callie Callahan's latest wrong turn turns out well. She meets Vicki Brownwell. Sparks would fly if only Meg Klein would leave them alone!
978-1-59493-148-2 $14.95

WARMING TREND by Karin Kallmaker. Everybody was convinced she had committed a shocking academic theft, so Anidyr Bycall ran a long, long way. Going back to her beloved Alaskan home, and the coldness in Eve Cambra's eyes isn't going to be easy.
978-1-59493-146-8 $14.95